DATE DUE

ILL: SSOS OCT 0 4 2018			
GAYLORD			PRINTED IN U.S.A.

The Return of Señorita Scorpion

OTHER SAGEBRUSH LARGE PRINT WESTERNS BY
LES SAVAGE JR.

Copper Bluffs

The Legend of Señorita Scorpion
A Circle Ⓥ Western

The Return of Señorita Scorpion

LES SAVAGE, JR.

A Circle Ⓥ Western

Sagebrush
Large Print Westerns

Library of Congress Cataloging in Publication Data

Savage, Les.
    The return of Señorita Scorpion : a western trio/ Les Savage, Jr.
      p.   cm. -- (Circle V western)
    ISBN 1-57490-089-7 (hc, alk. paper)
    1. Large type books. I. Title. II. Series.
[PS3569.A826R45 1997]
813'.54--dc21   97-24403
                                                      CIP

Cataloguing in Publication Data is available from
the British Library and the National Library of Australia.

First Edition

Sagebrush Large Print Westerns are published in the United States
and Canada by Thomas T. Beeler, Publisher, Box 659, Hampton Falls,
New Hampshire 03844-0659. ISBN 1-57490-089-7

Published in the United Kingdom, Eire, and the Republic of South
Africa by Isis Publishing Ltd, 7 Centremead, Osney Mead, Oxford
OX2 0ES England. ISBN 0-7531-5589-0

Published in Australia and New Zealand by Australian Large Print
Audio & Video Pty Ltd, 17 Mohr Street, Tullamarine, Victoria, 3043,
Australia. ISBN 1-86340-733-2

Manufactured in the United States of America

ACKNOWLEDGMENTS

"The Beast in Cañada Diablo" first appeared in somewhat different form under the title "The Ghost of Gun-Runners' Rancho" in *Lariat Story Magazine* (5/46). Copyright © 1946 by Real Adventures Publishing Company, Inc. Copyright © renewed 1974 by Marian R. Savage. Copyright © 1995 for restored material by Marian R. Savage.

"Sundown Trail" first appeared in *Frontier Stories* (Spring, 1949). Copyright © 1949 by Fiction House, Inc.. Copyright © renewed 1977 by Marian R. Savage. Copyright © 1997 by Marian R. Savage for restored material.

"The Curse of Montezuma: A *Senorita* Scorpion Story" first appeared in *Action Stories* (Spring, 1945). Copyright © 1945 by Fiction House, Inc. Copyright © renewed 1973 by Marian R. Savage. Copyright © 1997 by Marian R. Savage for restored material.

TABLE OF CONTENTS

The Beast in *Cañada Diablo*   1

Sundown Trail   101

The Curse of Montezuma
A *Señorita* Scorpion Story   154

THE BEAST IN
CAÑADA DIABLO

The so-called brasada, or big thicket, region of southwestern Texas in the Big Bend area fascinated Les Savage, Jr. He used it as a setting as early as 1944 in the first short novels about Señorita Scorpion, now collected in **The Legend of Señorita Scorpion** *(Circle Ⓥ Westerns, 1996), and would return to it in later novels like* **Treasure of the Brasada** *(Simon & Schuster, 1947) and* **Outlaw Thickets** *(Doubleday, 1951). However, his first extended use of this region after the first two Señorita Scorpion short novels occurred in the short novel that follows. Malcolm Reiss, editor of Lariat Story Magazine, retitled this short novel "The Ghost of Gun-Runners' Rancho" when it was first published in the May, 1946 issue. It was subsequently published—restored to the text of author's original manuscript version and under the author's own title—in the story collection,* **Shadow of the Lariat** *(Carroll & Graf, 1995). That restored version is also available in a paperback audio edition from Durkin Hayes, and has been included here.*

I

IT WAS THE FIRST APPREHENSION EDDIE CARDIGAN HAD felt since this started. His saddle emitted a mournful squeak as he turned to stare behind him. There was nothing but the gaunt pattern of brush the border Mexicans called *brazada* and the dim shapes of running, bawling cattle, half hidden in a curtain of acrid, yellow dust. Navasato came back, wiping his sweating brown face, a burly man in buckskin *chivarras* and vest, bare shoulders and arms patterned by brush scars, fresh and old.

"Why did you stop them here?" Cardigan asked.

"We come to *Cañada Diablo*."

"All right," said Cardigan, shifting his long body irritably. "All right, so we come to *Cañada Diablo*. You just gonna sit here and let them catch up to us?"

"We got to go back till we hit the Comanche Trail," said Navasato. "I didn't realize we'd crossed it. We can't go through *Cañada Diablo*."

Cardigan leaned toward Navasato, his dark eyes narrowing. There was a lean intensity to his face that might have indicated a certain violence in him, and deep grooves from his prominent, aquiline nose to his thin mouth that might have indicated a rigid control of his natural tendencies. The wool vest he wore over his red, checked flannel shirt had not been designed for brush country, and it was ripped in several places, and covered with burrs and dirt.

"You know we'd walk right into them if we turned around now. Why can't we go through here?"

"Nobody ever goes through this part of the *monte*."

"*¿Nagualismo?*" said Cardigan.

"The *nagual*, the *nagual*," said Navasato, waving a square, callused hand half impatiently, half fearfully. "*La onza*."

Pinto Parker had milled the cattle from the point by now, stopping them, and came trotting his spotted broncho back through the settling dust, sitting his seat with the same broad swagger that marked his walk, white Stetson shoved back on blond hair that took on a tight curl when it got wet with sweat this way.

2

"What's our tallow-packing pard babbling about now?" he asked.

"*Nagualismo*, or something," said Cardigan.

"*Sí, sí*," muttered Navasato. "*La onza, la onza.*"

Pinto Parker threw back his head to laugh, and Cardigan wiped his hand irritably on his shirt. "What is it?"

"Some crazy Mex story," grinned Pinto, his teeth flashing a white line against his sun-darkened face. "You get it all the time down here. Started with the Indians farther south, I think. Has to do with their religion or something. It spread up here and got the *brazaderos* in a big lather."

Cardigan pulled his reins in and felt the jaded dun draw a weary breath and stiffen to go. "Forget your ghost stories, Navasato. We're going through."

"No, Cardigan, no. *En el nombre de Dios....*" With an abrupt decision, Navasato pulled his big Choppo horse around. "I ain't going."

The dun was ready for reaction when Cardigan put his reins against the neck, and it stepped broadside of Navasato's Choppo, putting Cardigan face to face with the man, their animals standing rump to head. "They'll get you if you go back, Navasato," he said through his teeth. "You ever seen a bunch of rustlers hanging from a tree? That's what you'll get, Navasato. No less."

The Mexican turned pale but tried to urge his Choppo on past Cardigan's dun. "I don't care. Let me go, Cardigan. You can find your way to the border from here if you want. Not me. I won't go through *Cañada Diablo.*"

Cardigan realized what a primitive fear must hold the man if he would risk hanging rather than go on, and he understood there was only one thing now, and he did it.

"You're coming with us. Go up and help Pinto on the point."

Navasato stared at the big .46 in Cardigan's hand. The little muscles around his mouth twitched. His eyes met Cardigan's for a moment, and Cardigan didn't know whether the fear there was of him, or of something else. With a small, strangled sound, Navasato jerked on his reins. The Choppo jumped with the big Spanish bit biting his mouth, turning sharply after the cattle Pinto had started up again. Once the Mexican turned back to look at Cardigan; then he disappeared in the haze of rising dust.

There were maybe a hundred head of the animals, and it would not have been a big job for three men in the open, but through this brush it was hell. Cardigan had ridden brushland before, but nothing like this. The *brasada* was really a dry jungle, and for hours he had fought it as he fought no other country; the black chaparral clubbing at him constantly with a human malignancy, the *granjeno* clawing his bare hands and face, alkali settling in each fresh cut to sting and burn. Yet, this was the first time they had stopped since running into it that morning, and the utter primal force of the land had not clutched at Cardigan till he had pulled his dun to a stop there a few minutes ago and stared back. Well, they had told him how it would be, hadn't they? Or had tried to tell him. No man could describe in words the sensation that came when he stopped like that, for the first time, with the dust settling back into the stark ground from which it had risen, and the dull, cattle sounds dying out in the emptiness of the brush, and the inimical *mogotes* of chaparral closing in on all sides, black with a hostility that was almost human, suffocating, waiting.

4

"*Hyah!*" shouted Cardigan, trying to dissipate the oppression in him by yelling at a thirst-crazed *orejano* that had tried to break into the thickets away from the main herd. "Get on back, you bug-eyed cousin to a...."

It was the sound that cut him off. At first he thought it was a woman screaming. It rose to a shrill, haunting crescendo, somewhere out in the brush, and, stiffened in his saddle by the utter terror of it, Cardigan sensed more felinity in the cry than humanity. It ended abruptly, and the silence following beat at Cardigan's eardrums. As if snapping out of a trance, he put spurs into his dun with a jerk, leaping it ahead to meet Pinto Parker as the man appeared in the dust ahead.

"Did you hear it?" shouted Pinto.

"Sounded like a cat," said Cardigan.

"I never heard no bobcat squall like that," said Pinto. "Where's Navasato?"

"He's supposed to be riding point."

"Cardigan!" It was the Mexican, his voice carrying a cracked horror in its tone, coming from the brush somewhere ahead. "Cardigan, I told you, *la onza, la onza.* Come and help me. *Dios*, Cardigan, *madre de Dios*, come and get me...!"

The crash of brush around him drowned the cries as Cardigan raced through a prickly pear thicket. His own animal whinnied with the pain of tearing at the thorned plants, and Cardigan's sleeve was ripped off as he threw his arm across his face to shield his eyes.

He pulled the horse up and swung down, hauling the reins over its head and whipping them around a branch. As he whirled to dive through the thicket on foot, he saw Pinto erupt from the prickly pear behind. Then Cardigan was struggling through the beating madness of black chaparral, tearing at the branches with one hand,

5

his gun in the other. He could hear no sound but his own labored breathing as he finally ran into the next clearing, and saw Navasato. He stood there a moment, staring at the spectacle. Pinto crashed through behind Cardigan. Cardigan was the first to move over toward Navasato.

"Dead?" said Pinto, in a hollow voice.

Cardigan nodded, squatting down beside the mutilated body. "No brush clawed him up like that."

Parker was stooped over, looking at something on the ground, beyond Navasato. "What did he say about the *onza*?" he asked.

"Perhaps you had better ask Florida that, *compadres*," said a man's voice from behind them, and Cardigan started to raise his Remington as he turned, and then let it drop again.

The man standing there possessed a strange affinity with the brush. His face was lean and saturnine, and dark secrets stirred smokily in his strange, oblique eyes. He had thick, buckskin gloves on his hands, holding a gun in a casual, indifferent way, as if he wouldn't have needed it anyhow.

Pinto Parker's equanimity had never ceased to amaze Cardigan. Parker spoke to the man now without apparent surprise, a grin crossing his face easily. "You Florida?"

"No, Lieutenant Dixon," said the man. "I am not Florida. I am Comal Garza."

"Lieutenant Dixon?" asked Pinto.

"Yes." Garza's murky eyes passed over the animal lying beyond Navasato's torn, bloody body. "I see you brought the Krags. Where are the rest of them?"

At first, Cardigan had thought it was Navasato's Choppo horse, the dead animal over there, but now he saw it was a mule, with an army pack-saddle on its

6

back. Its throat had been ripped, and steaming tripe was rolling out of a great, gaping hole torn in its belly, and Cardigan did not look long. Pinto had taken his rifle from the saddle scabbard on his horse, and he glanced at it involuntarily.

"Yeah, I got a Krag. What cows does that rope?"

Comal allowed a faint puzzlement to cross his face, studying Pinto. "I refer to the Krags on the mule. Where are the other mules? Stampeded?"

"This is the only mule I seen," said Parker.

Garza's gun had raised enough to cover them again. "What are you trying to do, Lieutenant Dixon? It is unfortunate your guide had to die this way, of course, but you certainly can't blame me. It's rather obvious what caused it. We all knew you were coming today, but we didn't expect you to appear driving a herd of cattle. Did you have to use the beef as a blind?"

"The beef is all we had," said Pinto. "You must have us mixed up with someone else."

"No one else would have come this far south of the Comanche Trail, *señor*," said Garza sibilantly, and he drew himself up perceptibly as if reaching a decision. "I did not expect you to act this way, Lieutenant. But of course, if you would betray others, it's not inconceivable that you wouldn't be honest with us. Did you think we weren't prepared for that contingency?"

"You're riding an awful muddy crick," said Pinto.

"I will make it clearer. I will ask you to relieve yourself of the implements."

Garza inclined his head toward the Krag .30 Parker had. Pinto grinned, dropping the rifle, fishing his Colt out and letting it go. Cardigan did the same.

"Kamaska," called Garza.

Cardigan could not help growing taut with surprise

at the man's appearance. He made no sound coming from the thicket behind Garza. He was short and stubby and walked like an ape with his thick shoulders thrusting forward from side to side with each step. Kamaska's broad, black belt was pulled in so tight it would have dug deeply into a normal man with a belly as big as that, yet it made no visible impression on his enormous, square paunch. His eyes passed over Pinto and Cardigan with opaque indifference in a wooden face, and Cardigan was expecting him to grunt when he bent over to pick up the guns, and was disappointed. Pinto Parker looked at Navasato in an automatic way, and Garza's voice came with a nebulous, hissing intonation.

"We'll leave him there."

"¿*Nagualismo?*" said Cardigan.

Garza's head raised, and a thin smile caught at his flat lips. "Perhaps, *señor*. Perhaps. And now?"

His thin, black head was inclined toward the prickly pear, and he let them precede him. Pinto swaggered ahead of Cardigan, grinning back at him once, not caring much what this was about or trying to figure it out, because he was that kind. There were two other saddle animals with their horses. There was no room between Kamaska's belly and that belt, cinched up as it was, for the revolvers, so he dropped them in a fiber *morral* hung on the saddle horn of the hairy, black mule he had, and swung aboard with surprising alacrity for such a bulk, still holding the Krag in one hand.

Garza did not mount till Cardigan and Parker were in their saddles. Kamaska led through the brush, moving so steadily and surely that Cardigan finally realized they were following some sort of trail. Mystery was in Garza's vague smile, and his eyes were smoky and secretive.

8

"We will be there presently."

"I don't suppose it would do to ask you who you are?"

"I am Comal Garza."

Up ahead, Pinto laughed. Kamaska turned for an instant, staring opaquely at Parker as he would stare at an animal he did not understand.

Cardigan had no measure of the distance they rode through that weird brushland before they reached the house. It was hidden by chaparral until they were almost there; then the clearing thrust itself upon them, with several *ocotillo* corrals on the near side and an adobe structure across the intervening flat that might have been a bunkhouse. Some two hundred yards past that was the main building. It was typical of the dwellings in the Southwest, though larger, its rafters formed by *viga* poles thrusting out the top of the wall a foot or so to cast a shadowed pattern across the yellow mud, shutters closed against the heat of the summer sun. A man rose from where he had been hunkered against one of the uprights forming the *portales* that supported the porch roof that ran the length of the front. He wore the usual *chivarras* and a tattered, red Chimayo blanket, poncho style, its four corners dangling to his knees. His eyes were small and bucolic, and his mouth was thick-lipped and brutal. Garza tossed his reins to the man.

"Did Florida get back, Innocencio?"

"No," said the man. Garza pointed toward the house, and Cardigan took it they were to go in. The living room was dim and musty.

"All right, Lieutenant Dixon," Garza told Pinto.

Parker's mouth opened slightly. "Lieutenant Dixon?"

9

"You were the one with the Krag," said Garza.

"Krag? It's my rifle."

"I'm glad you admit it," said Garza. "Now, if you'll tell us where you've got the other Krags...?"

"Oh, the Krags," said Parker, as if something had dawned on him abruptly. Grinning, he turned to Cardigan. "Now just where *did* we put those Krags, Cuhnel Cahdigan?"

There were times when Parker's irresponsible sense of humor galled Cardigan. "Shut up, Pinto," he said. "Can't you see they mean business?"

"Yes, Lieutenant Dixon," said Garza. "We mean business."

"Now, Cuhnel Cahdigan, suh," said Parker with mock gravity, "you-all know Ahm serious as all hell. Ah jes' can't seem to recall where we put those Krags. By Gad, muh name ain't Lieutenant Dixon if Ah can...."

Garza had taken his forward step before Cardigan realized what he meant to do, moving without perceptible effort, and his hand made a dull, slapping sound across Parker's face. Garza had put no apparent force in the blow, yet it sent Pinto reeling back against the wall so hard, a hand-carved *santo* fell from its niche. Pinto stood there with his hand up to his face. Finally he grinned again, without mirth.

"You shouldn't have done that, Garza."

"I don't appreciate your broad humor, Lieutenant. Or were you being humorous? When Zamora came from contacting you in Brownsville, he said we might have some trouble. If you think of holding out for a higher price, don't. We already made the arrangements, and you are here. Now, tell us where the Krags are and you'll get your money."

"You made a mistake," said Cardigan. "This isn't

10

Lieutenant Dixon. It's Pinto Parker. We were just running some cattle through."

"Your cattle, I take it."

A trace of Pinto's humor had returned. "Now, you don't suppose we'd be herding somebody else's beef, do you?"

"You have a bill of sale for a hundred Big Skillet steers?" said Garza.

"Is that what they were?" Pinto asked.

A thin impatience entered Garza's voice. "Let's quit this sparring. If you chose to use a bunch of rustled Big Skillet cattle as a blind, it is no concern of mine. You know what I'm interested in."

"Oh, is there a woman in the *brasada*?" said Pinto.

Garza drew a sharp breath; then he inclined his head toward a hand-carved Mendoza chair that sat in high-backed austerity against the wall. "We'll put him in there, Kamaska."

"Wait a minute."

"I would advise you to keep quiet, *señor*," said Garza, turning the gun on Cardigan. "Innocencio will be watching you, and his characteristics are hardly those his name would imply."

Innocencio had taken a singularly evil looking *belduque* from beneath his Chimayo blanket, and he moved toward Cardigan, running a thick, callused finger down the bright blade. Garza was forced to snap the gun bolt before he could persuade Pinto into the chair. Cardigan stood by the wall, bent forward tensely, his breath fluttering white nostrils in a hoarse audibility. Kamaska got a rawhide dally from a wooden stob in the wall. Parker started to jump from the chair as he realized what it meant, then sat back down slowly for the cocked hogleg was aimed at his belly. Kamaska pulled the rope

11

so tight it dug into Pinto through his fancy-stitched shirt. Garza shoved Pinto's white Stetson off, and it rolled to the floor.

"Now, Lieutenant Dixon, are you going to tell us where the Krags are? You have one more chance."

Cardigan never ceased to marvel at Pinto's reckless nonchalance; even now the man's grin held nothing forced. "You got us wrong. Parker's my name. We're just a couple of 'punchers."

"Very well," said Garza softly. Kamaska had gotten an ancient Spanish nutcracker of beaten silver from the oak table. Pinto's arms were lashed along the arms of the chair with his fingers protruding over the edge. Garza watched Kamaska slip Pinto's right index finger into the jaws of the nutcracker. "It was made to crack Brazil nuts, Lieutenant. It executes a remarkable pressure."

Pinto could not help the gasp, and his grin turned to a grimace of spasmodic pain. His eyes remained closed while Kamaska opened the nutcracker from his finger. The beaded sweat stood out on his face. Finally he opened his eyes and looked at the mashed nail.

"Hell," he said, and grinned.

"*Muy bien,*" said Garza. "Very well."

Kamaska slipped the nutcracker on Pinto's middle finger. Cardigan knew his first anger; it had only been irritation before. He had not comprehended fully what it was all about, and it had only been irritation, and a remnant of the revulsion at what had happened to Navasato; but now it was anger. He had seen how Pinto's first gasp drew Innocencio's attention for that moment, and he watched Kamaska begin to squeeze the nutcracker. Innocencio stood facing Cardigan with that *belduque* in his thick fingers. Pinto's face contorted

12

again, and once more he could not stifle a deep moan. This time Innocencio's reaction was less marked. Cardigan barely caught the flicker of his eyes toward the sound, and moved when he did.

Innocencio tried to jump backward and throw the knife at the same time, but Cardigan's foot lashed up and caught his hand before the blade had left it. The knife flew upward to strike the low roof with the impetus of Innocencio's toss.

"I told you to watch him," shouted Garza, whirling with the rifle. Cardigan's jump had carried him to Innocencio, and he caught the man about the waist, whirling him toward Garza before the man could fire. Innocencio struck Garza like a sack of sand, carrying him back across Pinto and knocking chair and all over onto the floor. Cardigan heard Parker shout with the pain of their weight smashing down onto him. Cardigan had tried to set himself, but his legs would not hold the terrible force of Kamaska's charge. He felt himself stumbling backward across the hard, earthen floor, and the wall struck his head and sent a roar of pain through his whole body like a cannon going off.

He tried to roll over and drive an elbow between them as a wedge to keep Kamaska from grabbing him, but the man caught his elbow and jammed it aside, and then one of those thick arms was about Cardigan's neck, and he thought he had never felt such incredible strength in a human being before. He heard the snap of bones and his own scream of pain. Then Kamaska's fist exploded in his face, and the room spun, and then he couldn't even see the room. Somewhere, far away, he felt his own body make a feeble effort at struggling, and one of his arms moved dimly. Then Kamaska's fetid, sweating bulk shifted against him, and he knew that fist was

13

coming again, and he knew that would finish it.

"Kamaska!"

At first Cardigan thought he had said it. Then he realized it had come from across the room. Kamaska's arm slipped from around Cardigan's neck, and the man stood up, breathing heavily. Cardigan had trouble focusing his eyes. At first all he could see was the Burgess-Colt repeater held in the small, brown hands of a dim figure across the room, light from the open door glinting on the rifle's silver-plated receiver. Then he heard Pinto's voice.

"I guess it was no joke. There *is* a woman in the *brasada*!"

II

HIS NAME WAS ESPERANZA, AND HE SHUFFLED AROUND the bunkshack like a ringy, old mossyhorn, growling through drooping, white *mustachios* so long their tips were dirty from brushing against the chest of his white, cotton shirt. After the fight in the house, Innocencio had brought Cardigan and Parker out here to the bunkhouse, a structure even more ancient and odorous than the main building, its roof so low Pinto had to remove his Stetson before entering. Cardigan sat at one end of the long, plank table, still too sick from Kamaska's brutal blows to eat anything of what was before him. Innocencio stood by the door, glowering at Cardigan, nursing his hand.

"*El mano*," he kept repeating.

"You must have broke his hand with that boot of yours," said Pinto, the pain of his mashed fingers having little effect on his appetite. He forked up a huge mouthful from the tin plate grimacing as he spoke

14

around it. "This is the foulest concoction of hogtripe I ever wrapped my lips around."

The deafening crash of guns drowned him out, and he jumped up, knocking over his chair and spewing the food all over the table. Cardigan was bent forward, both hands gripping the planks, staring at Esperanza. The old man held a smoking, stag-butted .45 in each hand, his red jowls quivering.

"You don't like my food," he shouted apoplectically.

"Don't get me wrong, *amigo*," laughed Pinto shakily, staring at the smoking guns with the surprise still on his face. "Your *alimento* is marvelous. I wouldn't eat anywhere else. It's just an old Texas custom. Like throwing salt over your left shoulder. You say it out loud, see. You say this is the foulest concoction of hogtripe I ever ate, and then...*Diablo*, he don't come up to get it. An old Texas custom."

"*¿El Diablo?*" said the old man, squinting at Parker, still suspicious. They were literal-minded in many respects, these *brazaderos*, with the superstition of peasantry, to whom the devil was as real as the coma trees in front of their *jacales*.

"All right," growled Esperanza finally, waving one of his .45s. "Sit down and eat it then. I make the best *chiles rellenos* in all *Méjico*. Why do you think they call them the children's dream, ah? I take the greenest of peppers and stuff them with the tenderest of chicken and the yellowest of cheese and dip them in a batter *El Dios* Himself would be proud to be dipped in, and I cook them in the purest of hog fat till they come out as golden brown as my very own skin. For twenty years I cook them for General Díaz. Porfirio Díaz Santa Anna Estevan Esperanza. That's me. Why do you think they call me that, ah?"

"Esperanza," said Florida Zamora from the door. "Haven't our guests already been shown enough bad hospitality?"

The grin that spread Pinto's face as he looked toward her held an infinite appreciation. "It's about time you come out," he chuckled. "I wasn't going to wait much longer."

Cardigan had seen women in Brownsville react to Pinto's animal magnetism. Florida took in his great height, and the breadth of his muscular shoulders beneath his fancy-stitched shirt, and his blond hair, and her smile answered his. It drew a resentment from Cardigan he could not understand; and, angered at himself for feeling it, he did not smile when the woman's eyes passed to him. He met her gaze almost sullenly, and her smile faded. Her rich underlip dropped faintly, as if she were about to speak; then she closed it again, and moved to the table. There was nothing masculine about the way her buckskin *chivarras* fitted across the hips, or about what she did to the white, silk shirt just beneath its soft collar; and Pinto was taking that all in as she placed the Krag she had brought on the table, and then pulled their revolvers from her waistband and put them down.

"You must forgive us, gentlemen," she said. "Esperanza is an irascible, old reprobate. I'm sure you'll overlook his peculiarities. As for Garza, he made a very grave mistake. We were expecting someone else. He mistook you for him."

Cardigan tried to keep his eyes off her, and could not. There was something gypsy in the way she wore a red bandeau drawn tightly about her head, hair with the sheen of a blue roan falling soft and black from beneath that to caress the shoulders of her white shirt. There was

16

undeniable aristocracy to the arch of her thin, black brows, the proud line of her nose.

"I'm glad to see Esperanza fixed up your fingers," she said, and Cardigan sensed her mind was not on the words.

Pinto glanced at his bandaged fingers. "I never knew prickly pear poultice...."

"Will cure anything from *dolor de las tripas* to a fifty caliber hole through your head," smiled Florida faintly. "Or almost."

Pinto let his eyes cross her features. "You've got some white blood?"

"My father was Mexican," she said. "He married an American woman from Brownsville. This is *Hacienda del Diablo*. It's not really as forbidding as Estate of the Devil would suggest. The country south of the Comanche Trail has always been known as *Cañada Diablo*. I could never see why."

"*¿Nagualismo?*" asked Cardigan.

Her turn toward him was sharp, as if she had forgotten he was there. "The land was named long ago," she said finally.

"And this *nagualismo* only started lately?" said Cardigan.

"You seem to know," she said.

"Garza seemed to think you were the one to know," said Cardigan. "Just what is *nagualismo?*"

She hesitated, her eyes dropping from his face, then she spoke abruptly. "*Nagualismo* really originates farther south, in the Mexican peninsula. It's a belief among the Indian tribes down there. The Caribs subscribe to it, I think. In Yucatán, a *nagual* is an Indian dedicated at birth to some animal by his parents. The rapport between child and animal finally becomes so

17

strong the *nagual* can change himself at will into the animal."

"A cat, maybe?" asked Pinto.

She nodded. "They have jaguars down there."

Cardigan remembered, then, how Pinto had been bent over beside Navasato, looking at something on the ground, when Garza came. "That's what you found?" he said.

"By Navasato?" asked Pinto, and nodded. "Big ones. Just like cat tracks. Only they couldn't have been cat tracks. Cats don't grow that big in Texas. Or anywhere."

There was something frightening in the silence that fell. Florida stared at Pinto for a moment, then gave a rueful little laugh.

"We're letting our imaginations carry us away. Why even dignify such an absurd superstition by considering it in that light? I've lived in the *brasada* all my life, and admit having seen some strange things. I've never seen any evidence of a man having the capacity to change himself into an animal at will, however. If Garza came on you right after you found your dead friend, you undoubtedly did not get a chance to study the tracks closely. We have large bobcats around here, and a few jaguars come up from Mexico. Even a mountain lion or two from the Sierras. I'm sure you'd find one big enough to account for the tracks."

"I've seen the biggest mountain lions they got," said Pinto. "I never seen one with feet that big. And the way it took Navasato. He didn't even have his gun out."

She sat tapping the table with a long finger, finally shrugged it off. "Garza said you were running a cut of Big Skillet steers. Have you got a bill of sale?"

The abruptness of it took Cardigan off guard, but Parker's grin was easy. "Garza picked us up so fast we didn't have a chance to bring our duffel along. The bill was in my sougan."

"I thought so," said Florida.

Parker's look of growing indignation was almost genuine enough to convince Cardigan. "You don't mean to insinuate...?"

Florida Zamora stopped him with an upraised hand. "Never mind. Whether those cattle were wet or dry doesn't concern me. I just wanted to know. Men who run wet cattle wouldn't be as particular about the kind of jobs they do as men who run dry cattle, shall we say."

"Their discrimination between the legal and illegal aspects of an occupation might not be as keen as a man who never ran wet cattle, true," said Pinto.

"Would you like a job here?"

Pinto picked up his Colt, spun the cylinder. "What's going on?"

"Nothing particularly. We just run *mestenos*," said Florida.

"You just run mustangs," mused Pinto, slipping his gun back into its holster, "yet you'd rather hire a man who might overlook a legal technicality than one who wouldn't."

"If these weren't your cattle," said Florida, "you couldn't get to the north without running into a posse. Sheriff Sid Masset's a hard man to shake if he happens to be riding your trail. On the other hand, no lawman has come into *Cañada Diablo* in a long time."

"*¿Nagualismo?*" said Cardigan.

The woman turned sharply toward him again, a faint flush of anger rising into her cheeks. With an audible, indrawn breath, she turned back to Pinto. He had begun to eat again, and spoke around a mouthful of beans.

19

"The advantages of your little *estancia* sound pleasing. Tell me more."

"The financial arrangements might interest you. For a hundred steers on the wet market you couldn't get more than three *pesos* a head. I could see that you draw down more than that in a month here."

"A man would have to work pretty hard for that kind of chips."

"It all depends on what you do," she said. At Pinto's inquiring look, she smiled, tapping his Krag. "You're not unknown down here. We've heard what you can do with an iron."

Pinto nodded, forking in more *frijoles*. "Then you're not hiring us to run mustangs?"

"I'm hiring you to run mustangs," she said. "But if something comes up that necessitates the use of that hardware you pack, I hope I'm right in thinking a man who runs wet cattle would be less reluctant about using it than a man who runs dry cattle, and more skillfully."

Pinto wiped the gravy out of the plate with the last piece of tortilla, leaned back, smacking his lips. "Doesn't sound bad to me."

Florida turned to Cardigan. "How about you?"

"What if we don't take the job?" asked Cardigan.

She hesitated a moment, then spoke with a certain control tightening her voice. "It seems to me you would be better off accepting it."

"You say no lawman has been here for a long time," said Cardigan. "Maybe this *nagualismo* business has scared everybody else out, too. Maybe we're the first outsiders you've entertained in quite a spell. Maybe you'd rather not have us reach the outside again, knowing you were expecting a Lieutenant Dixon."

"You take an unfortunate attitude." Anger was

slipping through that control in her voice.

"I just wanted things clear," he said. "Does Garza still think Pinto is Lieutenant Dixon?"

"I don't," she said.

"Does Garza?"

She pulled her lips in impatiently, then shrugged. "All right, so he does. What difference does that make?"

"It might make a big difference."

"What does it matter, Card?" asked Pinto. "She's right about us not being able to get out of the *brasada* by the north now. This is as good a place to camp as any till the Big Skillet ruckus blows over, and we get paid to boot."

"I'm glad you will stay," she said, moving toward the door. She took a last glance at Cardigan, then spoke as she turned away. "We're riding this afternoon. You might like to come along."

Pinto got up and went to the door to watch her walk across the sunlit compound toward the house, making various appreciative noises. He leaned against the door, tucking his good hand into his gun belt, turning to grin at Cardigan.

"She really must have wanted hands bad."

"Why?"

Pinto laughed softly. "She didn't even ask us if we knew how to run mustangs."

III

THE WIND WHISPERED THROUGH MESQUITE WITH A haunting sibilance and the black chaparral was so thickly matted and so low in some places that a man trained in the brush could see a buck's antlers rising above it half a mile away, and so tall in other places a

21

horsebacker could ride for miles without ever seeing more than twenty feet ahead or behind. Riding through it, behind Florida Zamora, Cardigan was filled with a nebulous oppression he could not shake off. They had left *Hacienda del Diablo* earlier that afternoon, riding past the huge cedar-post corrals filled with half-tamed mustangs. They went at a fast trot that kept Cardigan dodging post-oak limbs and ducking outstretched branches of chaparral, his face and hands continually clawed by mesquite. He marveled at the ease with which Florida seemed to drift through the brush, her movements to avoid the growth hardly perceptible. Finally they crossed a clearing, and she allowed her pony to drop back, smiling faintly at Cardigan as he dabbed irritably at a scratch on his face.

"Riding the brush is a little different than open country, isn't it? You don't learn it in a day, Cardigan. I've been running the *brasada* most of my life, and I still get knocked off now and then."

"Garza seems adept enough," said Cardigan. "I got the impression somehow that he wasn't native to the brush."

"He's only been with me about six months," she said. "He came from Yucatán, I think."

"Funny he would give me the idea you were the authority on this *nagualismo*," Cardigan told her. "If it originated in the Mexican peninsula, I should think a man from Yucatán would know more about it."

"Maybe he does," she said. "How about you, Cardigan? Where are you from?"

"I've been a lot of places," he answered.

"How long have you been with Pinto?" she asked him.

"I met him in Brownsville."

"You're so specific." Then she was looking at his hands. "They don't look like Pinto's."

"They've got ten fingers."

She drew her lips in that way, with irritation. "The rope burns on them are fresh."

"We were working cattle when you found us."

"But all the rope burns on your hands are fresh. Pinto's got some old ones."

"Maybe I got tired being a bank clerk," said Cardigan.

"You don't get legs like horse collars sitting on a stool."

"Maybe I used to tuck my feet in the rungs."

"Then you admit you haven't been in the wet cattle business long?"

"How long have you been in the mustang business?" he asked.

"That's irrelevant," she said hotly. Then she quieted, something pensive entering her eyes. "Who are you, Cardigan?"

"I'm the hand you hired to run mustangs," he said, and saw the impatient anger that drew from her before he had to swoop beneath a hackberry limb. He rose in the saddle again. "I never heard of an outfit this size spending all its time chasing mustangs. What happened to your cattle?"

"Mustanging is a profitable business," she said evasively. "We're coming to the watering hole for a herd we've been after for some time now. We haven't staked out here for a week or so now, and our scent should be gone, and the wind's toward us, so they shouldn't smell us. Tighten the noseband on your animal. When they show, try to keep the *manada* from breaking into thick brush."

23

"¿*Manada?*"

She glanced at him. "They run in *manadas*, herds of twenty or thirty mares with a stallion. Get the stallion, and the mares are all disorganized."

"¡*Caballos!*"

It was Kamaska's voice, and it settled an immediate silence over all of them. Garza stood beside his *pelicano*, a stiff, arrogant figure in the gloom. Parker was beside him, taller, his broad shoulders carried back in a sway-backed stance. He felt his spotted broncho's throat swell with a nicker, and he caught at the noseband. Then Cardigan saw them, drifting into the open as silently as a file of thunderheads climbing from behind a peak. The leader was a huge, white stallion, prodigiously muscled for a brush horse, his chest and shoulders moving with the striated sinuosity of thick snakes beneath his pale, silken hide. He was wildness incarnate, moving with a delicate, ferine prance that barely touched his sharp, clean hoofs to the ground, the proud arch of his neck never still as he moved his head ceaselessly from side to side. Rather than marring his appearance, the brush scars patterning his body only lent it a bizarre beauty. Cardigan watched, fascinated, his breath catching in him as he saw the animal stop and raise its head, and thought it had scented them. Then it went on, switching its long, white tail, and the mares followed. When they were almost by, Cardigan saw Garza turn and lift his foot into the stirrup, and knew it was the sign. Without a word, all of them mounted, the faint stir of movement they made rising above the other sounds at dusk and then breaking into a shocking, thundering noise, as Garza laid the guthooks into his *pelicano* and jumped it through the brush with a pounding crash into the open. Cardigan lost his hat

24

bursting through that first *mogote*, and after that all he could see was the white stallion. It was reared up at the brink of the water hole, noble head twisted toward them. With a piercing scream it whirled, plunging directly into the mucky water and floundering across. Cardigan drove his horse directly after Garza, hearing someone's wild shouting and not realizing it was his own till he was in the water himself.

The spray shooting around him was sticky with mud. He came out on the other bank, pawing at his eyes and cursing. He saw Kamaska make a throw at a mare and forefoot her, and the ground shook as she went down. Then Florida passed Cardigan, bent over her pony. She hit the first growth hard on Garza's tail, and passed through its massed brush with a swift ease. Then Cardigan met it. He saw a branch of chaparral dead ahead and dropped off to one side to go under, and put his face right into a growth of prickly pear. Howling with the pain of torn flesh, he brought his head upward to escape that and was caught by the branch he had tried to dodge in the first place. The blow on his head knocked him backward, and he barely caught himself from going over the dun's rump. Blinded, cursing, he was still in that position when some mesquite caught one of his outflung feet, tearing it from the stirrup, and he slid over the other side of his horse.

He managed to catch the fall on his other heel, bouncing it off on his buttocks and rolling over to smash into a low spread of mesquite. He got to his hands and knees, shaking his head, spitting out grama grass and dirt. Finally he got to his feet and looked after his horse. It had disappeared in the brush, along with Florida and Garza. Then the thud of hoofs from the other direction turned him that way, and he saw Kamaska riding in from the sink on his black mule.

"It takes a lifetime to ride the *brasada* with such skill as the *señorita* possesses," he said enigmatically.

"Hell with the *brasada*," snarled Cardigan, wiping dirt and blood off his cheek. "I thought you were taking care of the mares."

"I have two tied to mesquite trees," said Kamaska. "The *señorita* told me to keep an eye on you."

"I thought, maybe," said Cardigan. "And who keeps an eye on Parker?"

"He knows the *brasada*," said Kamaska.

"That isn't why she wanted you to watch me," said Cardigan.

Then his head raised slightly. He had never seen Kamaska evince any emotion before. Perhaps it was the man's eyes. The opacity had left them, and they were filled with a luminous, startled light, that changed in a moment to the animal fear Cardigan had seen in a dog's eyes when it sensed something beyond the pale of human perception. Kamaska's dark hands tightened around the reins of his mule till the knuckles shone white, and his voice shook on the word.

"*Nagual*," he said hoarsely, and gave a jerk on the reins that pulled the mule completely around, sending it crashing into the brush, Kamaska's voice echoing back as he said it again, in what this time was almost a cry: "*¡Nagual!*"

The wind had ceased and, after the sound of Kamaska's passing had died, the utter silence pressed in on Cardigan with a physical, suffocating weight. The ashen *cenzio* across the clearing was still trembling from the passage of the man who had appeared through it an instant before, only

26

accentuating the complete quiescence of the man himself, as he stood there, and of his two shaggy hounds, moveless, on either side of him. A pair of greasy *chivarras* were his only covering. His black torso was bare, a scabrous covering of fresh scars and scar tissue peeling from old scars giving him a leprous, revolting appearance. His black head was covered with hair like a thick mat of curly grama grass. The whites of his eyes gleamed in his dark face as he spoke, and his voice held a hollow, bell-like intonation.

"I am Africano," he said.

"Cardigan's mine."

It was almost as startling as watching a statue come to life when the man named Africano moved, coming toward Cardigan with a smooth, flowing, soundless walk. "You came to help *Señorita* Zamora?"

"I didn't know she needed help," said Cardigan, stifling with some effort the desire to put his hand on his gun.

"You must know," said Africano. "You came to help her."

"There are a lot of things I don't know," said Cardigan.

"But would like to."

"I would," said Cardigan. "And a lot of other folks, too."

"But you, especially," murmured the man, his eyes white and shining on Cardigan.

Cardigan studied the Negroid features, trying to reconcile the luminous intelligence in those eyes with the primal brutality of the low, heavy brow, the coarse line of lips and nose. "What do you mean, me, especially?"

"Comal Garza thought your *compadre* was Lieutenant Dixon."

"Are we going through that again?" asked Cardigan wearily.

"Comal Garza did not consider you." Cardigan could not help the way the lines deepened about his mouth. It was the only sign, but he realized Africano had noted it. The man took something from inside his *chivarras*. It was a flat leather case about a foot long and five inches wide. The light was fading, but Cardigan could still make out the lettering on the case as he took it. **Tío Balacar**. This time Cardigan tried to keep it from showing, but something must have passed through his face, for there was a satisfaction in Africano's hollow voice. "I thought it might mean something to you."

"He's here, then," said Cardigan, through set teeth.

"What else?" said Africano. "I found it down near *Mogotes Oros*. Camp had been made there."

"Anything else?"

"Rumors," said Africano.

"Why show this to me?"

"There was a man named George Weaver," said Africano.

Cardigan's brows raised as his head raised, wrinkling his forehead when he finally stared into Africano's eyes. "What's happened to him?"

"About a month ago." Africano waved a repulsive hand. "Also down near *Mogotes Oros*."

"What happened to George?" The grim insistence in Cardigan's voice drew Africano up.

"*La onza.*"

"Don't give me that!" Cardigan dropped the case in a sudden burst of anger, grabbing the man by his thick shoulders, voice rising to a hoarse shout.

28

"Everybody I asked says it that way. I'm damn tired of it. *Nagualismo. La onza. Nagual.* Give it to me straight, damn you. What happened to Weaver? The same thing that happened to Navasato? You know! What the hell made tracks that big around Navasato? And Kamaska. He called you *nagual?* I never thought I'd see him scared like that at anything. Tell me, damn you."

It was the sound that stopped Cardigan, before the actual pain. Africano had stood moveless in his grasp, and Cardigan did not realize why until the guttural eruption from his feet. Then he gasped, releasing his hold on Africano, jumping backward to lash out with his leg. Both dogs were at him now, the one that had bitten his leg leaping away and then darting back in savagely to catch at his swinging arm. Cardigan had been reaching instinctively for his gun, but the slashing pain of teeth, ripping his hand, caused him to pull it up again with a howl. His backward momentum carried him off balance, and he went down beneath them, kicking violently with his legs and throwing his arms over his face.

"Tuahantapec," called Africano, without much vehemence, "Bautista," and then it was gone. One instant Cardigan had been the center of a whirling, snarling mass of fangs and fur and claws; the next he was lying there on an empty clearing, the hoarse rasping of his own breath the only sound. He sat up, nursing the slashed hand, blood soaking down his Levi's from the long rip there. Perhaps it was the riders that had frightened Africano away. They came into the open with a crackling of brush, and Pinto Parker was the first to dismount from his steaming horse. Getting to his feet, Cardigan could see Kamaska behind Garza, his eyes still wide and luminous with that fear.

"I told you," Kamaska said. "Look at him, look at him. *Nagual. La onza.*"

Garza swung down, a strange, baffled look in his eyes as he stared at the slashes on Cardigan's hand. "What was it?"

"A Negro and a couple of big dogs," said Cardigan sullenly.

Cardigan saw relief cross Garza's face, and the man let his breath out, and seemed to force a small laugh. "You must mean Africano. He's not *negro*. He's *mestizo*. Part Aztec, he claims."

Parker had picked up the brown case from the ground, staring at the gilt letters on its flap with a frown that held more than puzzlement. "Who's Tío Balacar?" he said.

IV

THEY WERE CALLED *MOGOTES OROS*, WHICH MEANT the Gold Thickets, because of the *huisache* that grew through them in such profusion and turned yellow in the spring. Almost every Saturday the *vaqueros* held a bull-tailing there, providing almost their only form of entertainment, gathering to eat and drink and gamble. It was two days after the dogs had attacked Cardigan, but he was still feeling mean, his hand swollen and painful as he swung down off the dun and stood there a moment looking at the group of *jacales* to one side of the clearing, the inevitable house of brush and adobe in which the *brazaderos* and their families lived.

A pair of squat, ugly women in shapeless skirts of tattered wool and dirty, white *camisas* for blouses had begun building the fire and driving cottonwood stakes into the ground for the spit. Behind a *jacal* was a large

30

corral containing a dozen ringy bulls, the nervous lather about their jaws and their raucous bawls and incessant stamping showing how recently they had been brought in from the brush. And back of the corral, again, was the somber *brasada*, its depths stirring restlessly when a faint breeze fanned the summer heat momentarily. A saddle creaked beside Cardigan, and Comal Garza's voice was soft in his ear, mocking somehow.

"It is a strange land to a newcomer, no? Perhaps you are beginning to realize how impossible it would be for you to find your way out alone. Many men have been lost here, *señor*. The *brasada* is more deadly than the desert...to those who do not know it intimately."

A mirthless smile crossing his dark face, he moved toward the group of *vaqueros* lounging in the shade of a coma tree. Pinto had dismounted now, hitching the reins of his spotted pony to the mesquite, a narrow speculation in his eyes as he studied Cardigan.

"What's going on, Cardigan?"

"I thought it didn't bother you."

Pinto made an impatient gesture with his hand. "First the girl. Then this Garza *hombre*. What's between you and them? The way Florida watches you."

"Getting jealous?"

"More than that," said Pinto, easing his girth more onto one leg. "I wouldn't mind if it was your native charm attracting the girl. But it's something more." He studied Cardigan's intense face. "I really don't know much about you, do I?"

Cardigan shrugged. "I don't know much about you, either. We've got along that way."

"You know what I am, Cardigan."

"You know what I am, Pinto."

31

"I thought I did," said Parker. "Who is Lieutenant Dixon?"

Cardigan met Parker's eyes. "I don't know any more than you do, Pinto. Evidently this Dixon was bringing a bunch of Krags to Garza, and they expected him the same day we passed through, the same spot."

"Why should Garza want a load of guns?"

"Maybe he has other interests besides mustangs."

"Gun running? Who to?"

"How should I know?" Impatience had leaked into Cardigan's tone. "The revolutionists in Coahilla. The *Federales*. There's always a market down there."

Pinto shook his head, not satisfied. "More than that, Cardigan. Just a simple little smuggling wouldn't upset the whole *brasada* like this. I can feel it. See it. This *nagualismo* business is mixed up in it, too, somehow."

He trailed off as the sound of a fiddle rose from across the clearing. A blind *brazadero* was sawing on his ancient instrument and tapping a foot against the hard ground, and one of the younger Mexican girls had already glided into the Varsoviana, the high heels of her red shoes tapping the hard-packed earth like the click of castanets. Cardigan drifted that way, and Pinto cut out in front of him with a laugh.

"Not this time, *compadre*. I'm claiming this first dance with the prettiest gal here."

Florida had been talking to one of the women at the fire, and Pinto caught her with a whoop, swung her out toward the others.

Innocencio had brought his guitar, and as his playing joined in with the fiddle's, the excitement caught at Florida. Cardigan could see the flush climb up her neck into her cheeks, and her eyes widen and flash. She was laughing as Pinto whirled her into the cradle dance they

32

called a *cuna*, and more couples wheeled out until all Cardigan could see was Florida's shining black hair spinning through the brown faces and whirling bodies. He knew a twinge of envy at Pinto Parker's facility with women, and then smiled at himself for that. Garza was drinking *pulque* from a big Guadalajara jar with Kamaska and three other *vaqueros*, and Cardigan felt them glancing toward him once. Then he saw Parker and the girl had stopped dancing and were coming through the crowd toward him, a puzzled frown on Parker's face. Kamaska left the group of *vaqueros* and moved over toward the horses in his shuffling, anthropoid walk.

"I can't figure what you got on this gal," said Parker as he came up to Cardigan.

"What do you mean?"

Parker wiped his sweating face with a fancy bandanna, and his grin looked forced. "She wants to dance with you."

"I don't dance," said Cardigan.

"Then it's time to learn," Florida told him, and the soft touch of her hand against his back caused him to stiffen. She felt it, and looked into his eyes, and then laughed. It angered him, and he swung her out almost roughly. Why should he let her touch do that to him? Enough other women had touched him. She was still laughing as she tried to teach him the steps. As they swung in the *cuna*, she let herself come up against him with a bold smile, and he thought she was coquetting, and his lips spread back from his teeth in a disgusted way. Then he realized it wasn't for that she'd come near. Her breath was hot against the side of his face as she spoke.

"It's the only chance I'll get to tell you. They're up to

33

something. Watch yourself, and don't get off alone. I don't know what it is, but they're up to something."

The desperate intensity of her voice caught at him. "Who's up to something?"

"*Señores y señoritas*," called Garza from where the fiddler stood, "if you have had enough dancing, we shall turn out the first *toro* so we can get started with the feasting."

A cheer went up from the *vaqueros* around Cardigan, and they left their partners on the spot, running across the compound toward their horses. With excited squeals, the women scattered toward the *jacales*. Innocencio and another man had driven a bull from the corral; it was a wild-looking bay with brown points, switching its rump from side to side and pawing at the ground.

"*Muy valiente*," shouted Kamaska, leaping on his hairy mule, and the others mounted to follow him at a gallop into the open after the bull.

Garza led his *pelicano* from under the comas. "You have tailed the bull, *Señor* Cardigan?"

"I've tailed a few," said Cardigan.

"It is a practice more common near the border," said Garza. "If you watch, you will see how we do it, down here."

Cardigan couldn't help letting it goad him, though he knew that was Garza's intent. He stood by his dun, watching the riders haze down the bull. Kamaska was in the lead, and, as the bull broke for the brush, Kamaska ran his mule off to one side of the running animal and came in from there, leaning far out of the saddle to catch at the switching tail. The riders behind were whooping wildly and slapping at their *chivarras* with quirts, and the dust boiled up around the whole group as Kamaska caught the bull's tail and dallied the end around his

34

saddle horn as he would a rope. With his free hand he jerked the reins against the mule's neck and the mule veered sharply away. Cardigan saw the bull's tail stretch taut, swinging the animal's hind feet from beneath it. At that moment, Kamaska released the tail and galloped free, and the bull shook the ground with its falling.

"A good man can break its neck that way," Garza told Cardigan. "Perhaps you would like to ride the next one. Whoever throws him gets the honor of eating his brains."

Kamaska must have broken the bull's neck, for it lay inert as a *vaquero* roped its horns with his rawhide dally and hauled it off toward the fire. Innocencio was goading another bull out of the corral, a big *sabina* beast, hide mottled with red and white speckles, one of its horns growing in a broken, twisted way down across its eye. It's heavy, scarred head was tossing wickedly from side to side as it danced from the corral.

"Ah"—there was a certain satisfaction in Garza's tone—"this one I will ride myself. It is Gotch, *señor*. It will take a real man."

Cardigan swung an angry leg over his dun, knowing the men had little respect for him after the sorry spectacle he had made in the ride after the mustangs. Maybe he didn't know the *brasada*, he thought, but if he couldn't tail a bull he might as well sack his saddle right here. As he trotted the dun out after Garza, he thought he heard someone call from behind him.

"Cardigan, not that one, not Gotch...."

It was lost in the whoops that rose from the riders as they wheeled their horses out in the rising dust. Innocencio gave the bull a last jab with his prod pole. The *sabina* bellowed in rage, evil little eyes darting from side to side as it shied around the fire; then it

35

spotted the free brush ahead, and the scarred head lowered, and it made its first rush.

"*Viva*, Gotch," yelled Kamaska, his quirt popping against his *chivarras* like a gunshot, and Garza jabbed his *pelicano* with silver-plated spurs the size of cartwheels, and the animal leaped forward with a shrill whinny. A bitter satisfaction swept Cardigan as he jumped his own horse into a run and saw how quickly it closed the space between him and Garza's prized *pelicano*; then the excitement of reckless speed and wild sounds beat at him, and he didn't know whether the drumming beat inside him was the blood pounding through his ears or the thud of hoofs beneath him.

The yells of the *vaqueros* came to Cardigan through a din of galloping horses, and the dust rose up yellow and choking and blotted out the brush around him and the screaming women by the *jacales*, and all he could see was a glimpse here and there of a rider through the haze, and the snorting, running bull in front of him. His big dun was long-coupled and set low to the ground the way a good roper should be, and Cardigan could feel the steady, vicious pump of its driving hocks behind his saddle. He passed Kamaska, and the main group dropped behind him, and then Garza was on his flank, beating his *pelicano* desperately with a plaited quirt. *Give him a little slack on those ribbons and he might go faster*, was Cardigan's momentary thought, and then his long dun had stretched past Garza. In that last instant, his face was turned toward the coma trees where they had hitched their horses, and, through a hole in the choking dust, he caught a glimpse of Florida and Pinto Parker. The girl had hold of Parker's shirt, shouting something at him; his broad face turned toward Cardigan, then he whirled toward his pinto. As the dust

36

dropped back between them, Cardigan saw Florida leaping on her own horse.

Then the bull formed its heaving, running silhouette between them and Cardigan, and he was leaning from the saddle to grab that switching tail. He caught the hairy end and yanked upward, snubbing it around his horn. There was just enough room between his running horse and the bull to stretch the long tail tight, and as Cardigan saw it go taut, he laid his reins hard against the inside of the dun's thick neck. The horse responded with all the incredible alacrity of a roper, turning aside the very instant the reins made contact.

Cardigan saw the bull's hind legs slide from beneath the animal, and heard the shriek of his rigging as the weight was thrown against it. He let go his hold on the tail, instinctively stiffening for the sudden release of weight as the tail snapped loose from around the horn, throwing the bull. There was a loud pop, and the saddle jerked beneath him, and in that last instant he saw that the tail was still dallied onto the horn, and had time to wonder what had happened, and then to know, before the empty air beneath him turned to the hardest ground he had ever hit. His saddle had left the dun completely, and he hit still astride the rig, kicking free of the stirrups as his boots struck the earth. He rolled backward out of the saddle, his head striking the ground with a stunning impact, the bull's tail still snubbed on the horn, dragging the saddle across the ground behind it.

Through a haze of pain, Cardigan felt himself roll to a stop. He lay there a moment with noise droning around him. Then the sounds began separating themselves into something discernible.

"Don't turn him that way," someone was shouting, "you'll drive him right back at Cardigan. That saddle's

37

got him crazy, and he'll go right back. Let him go, let him go...!"

It was Florida's voice. Sight reeled back to Cardigan. He saw the *vaqueros* had cut the bull off from the open brush; the *sabina* had reversed.

"Let him stop, you fools." That was Pinto's voice, from somewhere behind Cardigan. "Give him a chance to slow down and his tail will slack up and let go that saddle. It's the saddle driving him loco."

It *was* the saddle. Crazed by the bobbing, rattling rig that followed its every movement no matter which way it turned, the gotched bull had reached the point of frenzy where it quit seeking escape, and wanted only to reach its tormentors and vent its wild rage. It whirled toward Florida as she came in from the quarter, tossing her rope at its frothed muzzle. The bull made a wily jump aside, and the dally spun on past and dropped on the ground. The *sabina* lunged at Florida's horse, and she missed getting gored by inches as she jabbed her can openers into her animal, jumping it past the running bull. With its head down that way, the *sabina* thundered on past the rump of Florida's horse, its momentum carrying the beast straight toward Cardigan. He had been trying to move, in a feeble, stunned way, and it must have been this that caught the bull's attention.

The shaking ground beneath Cardigan told him how close the bull was before he looked. Then his gaze swung up and caught that frothed muzzle and those wicked, little eyes and that great pair of speckled shoulders.

There was no time for fear in that last instant. Only a shocking comprehension of how it stood. He made one last effort to rise, and failed, and knew it would not have helped anyway. Then, from somewhere back of the

38

running bull, he heard a wild shout; dust rose in a great cloud about the animal, hiding movement for an instant, sweeping across Cardigan where he was crouching. The steady shake of the ground from the running hoofs of the bull changed to a great, roaring shudder beneath Cardigan. A dim shape pounded through the dust to his right. He thought it was the bull, and wondered why the beast had swerved. Then the dust began to settle, and he saw it had not been the bull.

The *sabina* lay in a heap not two feet from Cardigan's hand, the hot, fetid odor of its great body sweeping nauseatingly across him, its hind legs twitching in a last, spasmodic way before it lay completely still. The shape that had passed Cardigan was coming back now. Pinto Parker swung off his spotted horse and caught Cardigan's arm, sweat streaking the dust on his face, the inevitable grin revealing his white teeth.

"Guess that will show them how we tail a bull north of the Nueces," he said cheerfully. "You're all right, now, aren't you?"

Cardigan was staring stupidly at the *sabina*, and the full realization of how close death had come to him was bringing its reaction. He got to his feet as quickly as possible, pulling his arm free of Pinto's grasp, not wanting the man to feel him trembling.

"Yeah. Yeah. All right." Then Cardigan turned to meet Pinto's gaze. "Thanks, Pinto," he said simply, and saw the understanding in Pinto's eyes, and knew he needed to say no more.

Florida had brought her horse up, swinging off, with a wide relief in her big, dark eyes, and Garza pranced his *pelicano* in, glancing at the bull first. "I haven't seen a bull tailed like that in years, *Señor* Parker. You should have been born a *Méjicano*."

"Where are you going?" Florida asked.

Cardigan did not bother to answer. He stumbled in a grim deliberateness to where his saddle lay behind the *sabina*; the bull's tail was still snubbed tight about the slick roping horn, and he had to jerk it off and unwind the rigging from around it before he could turn the saddle over. He had to lift the skirt up off the front girth before he could find it, and now he understood why Garza had held his reins in so tight when he was quirting his horse, and why the dun had passed the *pelicano* so easily, and the others.

"That where the cinch broke?" asked Pinto, leading his pinto over.

"No," said Cardigan. "That's where it was cut."

V

EVENING FELL ACROSS THE *BRASADA* INSIDIOUSLY, darkening the lanes through the outer thickets first, then creeping into the clearing of *Mogotes Oros* till the firelight blazed redly in the velvet gloom. And new sounds came with the night. A coyote began its dismal howl somewhere far out in the brush. A hooty owl mourned closer in. Standing there at the edge of the clearing, Cardigan found it ineffably sinister. It was an hour after Pinto had saved his life; the *vaqueros* and their women were beginning to eat the meat of the dead bulls. Parker came across the clearing from the fire.

"Got your rig fixed?"

"I cut off a piece of my latigo and tied it to the cinch ring," said Cardigan. "It'll last till we get back."

"I still think you're loco, not having it out with them. If they cut your cinch."

"How would that improve our position?" said

40

Cardigan. "It wouldn't bring us any closer to finding out which one of them cut it, or why. It would only antagonize the whole bunch of them. We're hardly in a spot to do that right now. At least we keep them wondering this way. They don't know for sure I found the cut in the cinch."

Parker was studying him. "Why do you want to stay here?"

Cardigan's eyes opened a little. "How do you mean?"

"When a man finds out somebody's after his guts this way, his natural reaction should be wanting to get away."

"Should it?"

Parker studied him a moment longer, then a slow grin crossed his broad face. "No," he said, and chuckled. "No. I guess not. Not a man like you, Card. You'd want to stay and find out. You'd want to stay and nail the buzzard who tried to spill your guts on a gotch's horn that way."

"Wouldn't you?" said Cardigan.

"Let's go over and get some of that meat," said Parker. "I'm plumb ravenous."

Esperanza had come in a *carreta* drawn by a yoke of longhorn oxen, and he was officiating at the spit. "Ah, *señores*," he called, seeing Cardigan and Parker approaching, "you are just in time to see us unearth the head. We have a handful of oregano stuffed in its mouth for flavor, *sí?* All wrapped up in grass and tied with the leaves of the Spanish dagger, lightly roasted in ashes to make the fiber pliable. You have never tasted such a delicacy. And to you, *Señor* Parker, for tailing this *toro* goes the honor of the brains. Would you like the eggs, *Señor* Cardigan?"

"Eggs?" said Cardigan.

41

"Eyes," Parker muttered, beside him. "Take them. They're ribbing you."

Cardigan let his glance circle the men. He saw the speculation in Kamaska's face, and thought: *Yes, you big ape, I know my cinch was sliced. Do you?* The others were watching him, too. Garza had mockery in his smile.

"Sure," said Cardigan. "Back home I always get the eggs." Then he realized they were not watching him any more. Garza's glance was turned past Cardigan, and the mockery had been replaced by surprise. Kamaska made a sudden abortive shift, across the fire, and then stopped. Parker turned around before Eddie Cardigan did.

There were at least a score of men, and they must have come in on foot that way so as not to make any noise, and Cardigan had seen enough posses before to recognize one. The noise about the fire had dropped so low that Cardigan heard Garza's hissing, indrawn breath before the man spoke.

"Sheriff Masset," said Garza.

Sheriff Sid Masset moved with a graceful ease, surprising in such a prodigiously paunched man.

"Don't anybody do anything foolish," he said, and the lack of vehemence in his tone only lent to its potency. He moved on forward, the .45-90 he held across his hip swinging slightly with the side-to-side motion of his walk. "I'm taking you in this time, Garza. I've caught you outside your damn *Cañada Diablo*, and I'm taking you in, and you better not object the slightest because I've got twenty boys here just itching to push that fresh-roasted beef out the back of your belly with some law-abiding lead."

"I don't understand," said Garza. "You have no charge."

42

"I've got two or three charges. A hundred Big Skillet steers was run off their home range a week back, and we got a pretty good description of the operators, two of which I see among you now. It's the last bunch of cattle you'll take into that *Cañada Diablo*, Garza."

"They aren't my...."

"Then we got a number of dead men to account for," said Masset, his boots making their last sibilant creak as he stopped in a bunch of short grass. "Deputy Smithers was found dead last month just this side of the Comanche Trail, all clawed up. There was a government marshal named George Weaver found the same way near these *mogotes*. It wasn't no ordinary cat done that, Garza. In fact, there's some think it wasn't no cat at all. The Mexicans say this is some of that *nagualismo* bunk. Whatever it is, your crowd is mixed up in it. Now, I want you to step out in front of me here, one by one, and drop all your hardware."

The irony of it was what struck Cardigan first. To be taken in for those cattle, to have the whole thing spoiled like this for a mangy bunch of Big Skillet stuff, when it wasn't that at all. The fire made its soft crackle behind him, and he had already thought of it. They were standing in a bunch of short grass turned sere by the summer heat; there was a general shift through the crowd of *vaqueros* as Garza moved sullenly forward, and it gave Cardigan a chance to step back without being noticed.

Cardigan toed a coal from the edge of the fire; the heat of it had penetrated the leather of the boot before he had it shoved into the grass. Pinto Parker was unbuckling his Colt when Masset's head raised.

"Stamp it out," he yelled abruptly. "Behind you. Stamp it out!"

43

Cardigan jumped aside with the heat of the flame searing the back of his leg. The coal had caught in the brown grass, and the fire was leaping forward toward the posse beneath the fan of the wind. Yelling wildly, Cardigan began stamping at the ground on his side of the growing fire. Pinto Parker turned with an immediate understanding, stooping to grab a handful of grass at his feet and pull it up by the roots.

"Throw dirt on it," he yelled.

"Don't be a fool," shouted Masset. "You're just throwing more grass. You'll have the whole *brasada* afire."

"*Sí,*" shouted Garza, taking that chance for movement and jumping toward the fire, which brought him nearer the spot where his six-gun lay on the ground. "Stamp it out. You want all of the *Mogotes Oros* to burn up?"

The whole crowd of *vaqueros* was yelling and shifting now, and Cardigan saw Florida kicking more of the coals into the grass. Indecision spread through the milling crowd of possemen, some of them jumping forward toward the blaze, the ones in front of them backing up. The coals Florida had kicked out were catching, and the flames were rapidly forming a blazing wall between the posse and the *vaqueros*. Already Kamaska was turning toward the *vaqueros'* horses, hitched behind the coma trees. Cardigan was still kicking wildly at the fire and shouting, when the full realization struck Masset.

"I'll shoot the first man that moves," he bellowed.

"It's blowing right into us," yelled one of the possemen.

"Do what I say," shouted Masset. "Can't you see they did this on purpose? I'll shoot the first one that moves. Garza...."

44

Masset's rifle drowned him out, but Garza had already dived through a hole in the blaze, and the roaring flames made his running body a deceptive target. While Masset was still turned that way, pulling down his lever to put in another shell, Cardigan caught Pinto by the back of his shirt, yanking him straight into the blaze. They ran through the flames, choking, gasping. Cardigan heard another gunshot from behind them, and his flat-topped Stetson was jerked off. Then they were on the other side of the fire; Parker's shirt was ablaze, and Cardigan threw himself on the man, beating at the smoking flannel till it was out. He realized someone else was also beating at him, and, when Pinto pushed him away, he saw Florida had a saddle blanket half wrapped around him.

"Let's go," shouted Parker, laughing recklessly.

The *vaqueros* were running back and forth all about them now. Garza galloped past on his *pelicano*, followed by Kamaska. The second man wheeled his hairy, black mule toward Florida, jerking his foot from the stirrup. "*Señorita*," he shouted, "climb on with me."

Florida cast a wild glance at Cardigan. "Go on, Kamaska. Everyone for himself now. I'll get my own horse. We'll be safe as soon as we get into *Cañada Diablo*."

The fire had swept into the possemen, scattering them, and was rapidly filling the grassed-over section of the clearing and breaking into the thickets surrounding it. A great *mogote* of *huisache* went up in crackling glory and, beyond that, a growth of chaparral began to blaze, lighting the thickets about it weirdly. Three possemen who had run around one end of the blaze burst from the thickets near the *jacales* and began to fire. With a wild yell, Pinto turned on them and threw down with his Colt. Cardigan saw one of the men drop. Then he had reached the horses, tearing loose the reins of his frenzied dun, and the girl's rearing black. The bulls, maddened by the fire, had burst loose of the shaky *ocotillo* corral and were running wild through the clearing. Cardigan had all he could do to get on his frightened dun.

Parker was the first to break into the brush, the girl after him, a wild, swaying shape, her long hair flying, and again Cardigan knew amazement at her incredible ability at riding the thickets. She drove her animal straight at a growth of black chaparral covered thick with *huisache*. There must have been a hole, though Cardigan could not see it, for she crashed through the chaparral, trailing the *huisache* from her head and shoulders, leaving a big aperture for him to follow through. He leaped a low spread of *granjeno* and, while his eyes were fixed on an upflung spear of Spanish dagger and he was dodging aside to miss being impaled, a post-oak branch appeared out of nowhere. Shutting his eyes instinctively, he ducked abruptly.

He felt the mesquite rake across his arm, and he knew he had avoided it, and just as he opened his eyes, another outreaching oak branch caught his head.

Pain made a great roar in back of his eyes, and blackness swept over him, and that was the way he hit the ground, no comprehension in between the striking branch and the hard blow of the earth. He lay there spinning in a sick wave of nausea, trying to rise, and was dimly aware of a rattling crash somewhere above him. It was Florida, coming back; she drew her horse up onto its hocks and swung down.

"You've got to keep your eyes open," she called to him. "No matter what happens, you've got to keep your eyes open. You'll never be able to ride the brush unless you do that."

"Go on," he tried to wave her away, blood dribbling into his eyes as he shook his head. "If the fire don't catch up with you, Masset will. I'm not worth waiting for. I'll never make a brush rider. I don't want to. The hell with it."

Frenzied by the fire, Florida's horse was plunging and rearing against her hold on the reins. "Don't be a fool, Cardigan. Get on, will you? I can't hold him much longer. Cardigan...Cardigan, get on...!"

Cardigan was still too dazed to do more than make a wild, vague grab at the flying reins as the horse plunged forward, taking Florida off-balance, and tearing loose from her grasp. The hoofs made their shuddering pound past him, and the brush crashed, and then the animal was gone. Florida stood there, above Cardigan, her face flushed, her bosom heaving. She looked down at him, and her lips peeled flatly away from her teeth in whatever she was going to say, before, with a disgusted exhalation, she bent to help him up. He was on his feet when they both heard the crackle of brush from the direction of the clearing. For a moment, hope shone in Florida's face.

"No," said Cardigan. "That isn't a horse. I told you if the fire didn't catch up with us, Masset would."

VI

THE THICKETS ROSE IN SINISTER DESOLATION ON EVERY side, standing in impenetrable mystery beneath the pale light of the moon that cast the shadow of each twisted bush across the ground in a weird, tortured pattern. This pattern slid constantly across the back of Florida's white, silk shirt like some live thing, as she moved beneath the brush ahead of Cardigan. They had traveled on foot southward. The fire and its sounds were lost behind them, and nothing but the haunted silence of the night reached their ears, broken infrequently by the dim howl of a coyote, or the lonely call of an owl.

"We're in now," she whispered. "Masset won't follow us here."

"He doesn't look like the kind of man who'd be scared out by some Indian superstition."

"Masset's brave enough," she said. "So are a lot of other men. You don't see them in here, do you? You don't see any sheriffs or any marshals or any Texas Rangers, do you? The whole *brasada*'s always been a hotbed of border hoppers and rustlers and killers, and a lawman was taking his life in his hands to enter any part of it after a man, and *Cañada Diablo* is the worst spot of all. Even so, there were always men who'd pack a badge in here. They knew what was waiting for them, and they knew how to fight it. Until this last year, that is. They can't fight this, Cardigan. It's always the same. They send their men in, and a few weeks, or a few months later, some *brazadero* finds him in the brush that way.

"You heard Masset. That marshal, George Weaver. Deputy Smithers. They're only two, and they were the last ones, and that was months ago. And so they've stopped coming. There's no use just sending a man to his death. Especially when there aren't any men left who'll come in. Would you? If you were a ranger, or a deputy, would you come in, knowing what fate all the others had met? Even when they have something definite to follow, like those cattle?"

"You didn't talk that way back in the bunkshack," he
48

said. "You weren't going to dignify any Indian ghost story."

She looked up at him in a strained, pale way, then turned her face to the side. "I don't know, Cardigan, I don't know. I've tried to tell myself such a thing couldn't be. All along, I've tried. But it's all around. Just waiting out there."

"And yet you live right in the middle of *Cañada Diablo* as safe as a kitten up a tree," said Cardigan, and it brought her eyes around to him again. "If someone were doing something in *Cañada Diablo*, it would be very convenient for them to have this *nagualismo* business keeping the law away, wouldn't it?"

"What do you mean, doing something?"

"It still seems strange to me that a spread the size of yours would devote its whole time to running mustangs...or gathering Krags."

She started to answer him, but her mouth remained open without any words coming out, and her eyes were staring blankly into the thicket. It came to him finally, and he let his hand drop to the butt of his gun.

"Masset?" he whispered.

"I told you he wouldn't come in here after...."

It was the only way to stop her quickly enough. Cardigan felt her whole body stiffen against him as his arm snaked around her neck, and her lips mashed damply beneath his sweaty palm. The man rustled through the last chaparral and came into the open with his rifle held down at the hip, and Cardigan had met enough men that way to know what the expression on his face meant when he saw them, and to know what had to be done.

He already had his Remington out of leather, and he threw his weight against Florida as he fired. Masset's

49

.45-90 echoed Cardigan's gun, and the slug clattered through brush about the height of Cardigan's chest, if he had remained erect. Masset was already spinning around with the force of Cardigan's slug in him. It turned him in a half circle, and, by the time he took the stumbling step to keep from falling, it was carrying him in the opposite direction. He was bent almost double when he stopped, still on his feet, trying grimly to retain the rifle and snap its lever down again. From where he had thrown himself, lying half across the girl, Cardigan called to Masset.

"Don't, Masset. I don't want to kill you."

Still bent forward, Masset turned his head. His eyes, squinted with pain, took in the five-shot held at Cardigan's hip. Reluctantly, he dropped the rifle.

Cardigan got to his feet, lips drawn back against his teeth. "Go on back now," he said. "You were a fool to come this far."

Masset had one beefy hand gripped across his shoulder where the bullet had hit. His words came out gustily. "I'm tired of fooling around, Florida. I'm going to clean you out of here if it takes an army...."

"I told you to get out, damn you, before it's too late," snarled Cardigan. "You don't know what this is, Masset. You came in here just for a bunch of steers? You don't know what you're getting into. Now, get out!"

He almost shouted the last, in an anger he could not name himself, and Masset drew himself up, grunting a little with the pain movement caused him, his eyes narrowing even more. "What are you talking about, pard?"

"Just what I said," Cardigan told him.

"*Tío* Balacar?" said Masset.

"What about *Tío* Balacar?" Cardigan's voice held an edge.

"We heard he's been seen in here."

Cardigan was surprised to hear Florida's voice behind him. "Heard from whom?"

"That nigger. Africano. How do you think I knew you'd be outside *Cañada Diablo* tonight?" Masset was looking at Florida now. "What's going on, girl? What's Balacar doing in the brush?"

"Masset, if you don't get out...."

"Sure, I'll get out." Masset swung toward Cardigan. "But I'm coming back, and when I do, it'll be for good!"

He turned heavily and crashed off into the thicket like a ringy, old bull. Cardigan was just starting to get Masset's rifle when the sound came. It seemed far away, at first, and yet close up, somehow, filling Cardigan with a vague awe. He turned toward Florida; her mouth was open, and her eyes, staring at him, were blank with listening. The noise had died before her glance took focus with a perceptible jerk.

"What was it?" he said.

"Cat," she said, in a hollow voice. "Sounded like a cat."

"I never heard a bobcat squall like that," he said.

"Jaguar. Mexican ones. They come down out of the mountains like that." She seemed to twitch then, and something like shame came into her face, and her voice lost its hollow tone abruptly, coming out quick and hard. "Are we going?"

He had not moved yet when the scream rang through the brush, so akin to another scream that his own shout followed it instinctively. "Navasato," he yelled, and then realized the significance of his reaction, and jumped toward the *mogote* into which Masset had disappeared.

51

"Cardigan," gasped the girl from behind him, "Cardigan, don't go in there. Please!"

But he was already bursting through the thicket of chaparral, Masset's unintelligible cries driving him. He crashed into a small clearing on the other side of the first thicket, face scratched and bleeding, and the screams had stopped. Masset lay beneath a bunch of ripped, trampled mesquite on the other side of the open space, his face mangled beyond recognition, his shirt torn from his fat, bloody back. There was a rattling out in the brush, and then that ceased. Cardigan stood there, staring at Masset, hardly aware of Florida as she came out of the thicket behind him, and made a low, strangled sound of horror.

"I sent him into that," said Cardigan, a deep bitterness entering his voice. "I sent him into that."

"No, Cardigan." Florida's grasp at his arm pulled it down. "How could you know? It might have caught him anywhere. It wasn't your fault."

He didn't have to go down beside Masset to see if the man were dead, that was patent enough; but there was something else he wanted to see. Pinto Parker had said they were larger than any cat tracks he had seen. Cardigan struck a match for light and bent down. He was right. It gave Cardigan a strange, suffocated sensation to stare at the prints of the huge, padded claws. Florida was staring at them, too, and then she was catching at his arm again as he rose, a swift, breathless desperation in her voice, as the flame guttered out.

"You know what this means, Cardigan? Masset was right. I've sensed it all along, but now I know it. This *nagualismo* isn't just a rumor. It's too deliberate. We can't let it go any further, Cardigan. I can't go any longer trying to feel you out, and waiting for you to make your move. I've got to trust you, and you've got to trust me."

He sensed that what had just happened was bringing it out of her like this. "What do you mean?"

She had him by both elbows, staring into his eyes with a driven intensity. "You think I'm one of them, don't you? You think I'm just rodding a bunch of rustlers and smugglers?"

"It did look like you were top screw in the corral."

"You know that's not true." Her eyes were pleading with him.

"Do I?" he said warily.

"I told you that's got to stop." Florida's voice was rising. "We've got to trust each other, Cardigan. Why do you think I kept them from killing you that first time?"

"I really don't know."

"You *do* know," she almost shouted. "Will you quit evading me like this? There isn't any more time to play that game." She glanced at Masset, revulsion twisting her mouth. "You might be next, I might be next, Pinto might." Suddenly the warmth of her body was against him, and her face was pressed into his sweaty, burnt shirt front, and he could see the fight she was making to keep from crying. "Cardigan," she mumbled against him, "please, please, I'm at the end of my dally, and you don't know how long I've been doing this alone, in the brush, all alone, against all of it, and when you came, and I thought...I thought...." She twisted her face the other way against him, the hair drawn taut and lustrous across the top of her head. "Oh, Cardigan, please...."

Holding her like this filled him with a strange weakness he had never known before, and all his wary, suspicious control left him, and he spoke in a harsh, guttural acquiescence. "What do you want?"

There was a triumph in the way she lifted her face to him. "Who you are. I've got to know that, Cardigan. I've got to know where I stand now, whether there's anybody at all, or whether I'm still alone. I'm not, am I, Cardigan? Tell me I'm not. Tell me I was right about you."

The movement of her head away from his chest might have been what caused it. Suspicion returned in a swift inundation as he saw the triumph in her eyes. It might have been innocent triumph. He searched her face for guile, and found none. Yet he eased away from her, almost trembling with the realization of how close he had come. She saw what had happened, within him, and jumped backward like a cat in rage.

"You still won't trust me. You think they put me up to this? I guess I should have let them have you in the first place. You don't care. You know what Tío Balacar is up to, but you don't care. You'll just let him go ahead and do this. People think the *brasada*'s a dangerous place now? Wait till Balacar comes. What's gone on before will just be a Sunday school picnic compared with what it will be after he gets through. You told Masset he didn't know how big this thing is? I don't think you know how big it is. I don't think you want to know...."

"Florida...."

"Shut up," she spat. "I was a fool to think you were any different than Parker. You're just a couple of tinhorn rustlers looking for a place to hole up till it blows over about those Big Skillet cattle. You were right. You'll never make a brush hand. You'll never make anything. You...."

54

Perhaps it was the expression on Cardigan's face that stopped her. He had heard the sound before she did, because she was so deep in her rage. Now she heard it, and the angry flush seeped out of her face, leaving it pale in the moonlight. Cardigan's hand tightened around the butt of his Remington, and he raised the gun without being conscious he did it.

"Cardigan," breathed Florida, and took a step toward him, fear turning her eyes dark.

It came again, like the scream of a woman in mortal pain, weird and unearthly and terrifying. Then it ceased, and all Cardigan could hear was his own breathing. His burned, smudged face was greasy with sweat, and he could feel it dripping down his sleeves, from beneath his armpits. The first impulse to move seeped through him vaguely, and he was about to answer it when the brush clattered. Both of them whirled, and the hammer of Cardigan's Remington made a sharp, metallic click under his thumb.

"*Buenas noches*," said Africano, from where he stood beneath the chaparral with his two dogs. Cardigan stared at him blankly, unable to speak for that moment, and the girl stood with her underlip dropped slightly, making no sound. Africano's face bore no expression. "You heard *la onza?*"

"Yeah," said Cardigan finally. "We heard something." His voice took on a patient deliberateness. "What is it, Africano? What is *la onza?*"

Africano's eyes shone white as they dropped to Masset; then they rose again, meeting Cardigan's, and they held something he could not read. "*La onza* is a hybrid, *señor*. A cross between a bull tiger and a she-lion. There is nothing more deadly. There is nothing more terrible."

Cardigan jerked his gun to bear on one of the dogs as Africano started to move forward. "I'll kill those dogs if you bring them any closer, I swear it."

"They will not harm you unless you threaten me, *señor*," said Africano softly.

"How do you fit in with this *onza?*" asked Cardigan harshly. "Maybe Kamaska isn't as dumb as we think."

"If you refer to his belief in *nagualismo*, there is nothing stupid about that," said Africano.

Cardigan couldn't help bending forward sharply. "Then you know. You...."

"I know you had better get back to *Hacienda del Diablo* as soon as possible and never again get separated from your friend, Parker, as long as you stay in the brush."

"What are you talking about?" It was the first time Florida had spoken.

"*Tío* Balacar has come," said Africano.

VII

THE BLACK CHAPARRAL SURROUNDED THE COMPOUND of *Hacienda del Diablo* in endless undulations of skeletal malignancy, and the buildings huddled fearfully beneath a risen moon. One of the horses standing hipshot before the long porch snorted dismally. It was the only sound.

A yellow crack of light seeped from beneath the door, and drew a rectangle around each of the two shuttered windows on the north side. Weary from the long hike through the brush, Cardigan stood by the ghostly pattern of a cedar-post corral, watching the house.

"Any way we can get in without being seen?" he asked.

56

The quick shift of Florida's head to glance at him caused moonlight to ripple across the glossy toss of her long, black hair. "They might not have locked the shutters on my bedroom," she said finally. "There's no reason for any of them to have gone in there."

They skirted the fringe of brush till they were opposite the north side of the house, then cut directly across the moonlit compound. Cardigan was tense with waiting for some reaction from Florida, and it puzzled him, in a way, that she had made no objection to coming in this way, or had not tried to warn them. The heavy, oak shutters on her bedroom window opened with a loud creak, and Cardigan lifted a long leg over the low, battered sill. The bare, earthen floor of her room was as hard as cement, covered meagerly by a pair of hooked rugs he made out dimly in the soft light from outside. He passed her bed, a ponderous, hand-carved four-poster of Spanish origin, and reached the thick, wooden-pegged door. The handle of hammered silver felt cold to his touch, and it moved with less noise than the window. He cast one glance back at Florida before pulling the portal toward him. There was a tense, waiting line to the rigidity of her body. Then he turned his head, looking through the crack and down the short hall that led directly into the living room from this wing of the house.

He saw a broad-framed, thick-thewed man, with the flat hams and skinny, bowed legs of the inveterate horseman, his jack boots black and polished, a fancy gilt-edged sash about his heavy girth. His eyes were small and black and brilliant in the dissipated pouches formed by his puckered, veined, wind-wrinkled lids, and his thick lips moved with sensual mobility. His hands were surprisingly delicate and slender, and he kept moving them expressively while he spoke, as if the words were spawned and shaped and caressed by his supple, ceaseless fingers, rather than coming from his mouth. With his first sight of the man, Cardigan knew who he was.

"I understand your...ah...reluctance to commit yourself, *amigo*," he was saying, and he moved across the living room in a pompous, stiff-legged walk as he talked. "I have myself, at times, endeavored to enhance my financial position by just such means. We will dispense with the moral grounds for our objection to what you are doing, though you will admit there are those who would call your attitude far from honest. We will be merely expedient. Expediency is so much more logical a basis than morality. And you can see the obvious expediency here. You have tried to improve your monetary standing in this way, and have failed. Why don't you just admit your failure, and we can all be good *compadres* again and forget about it and take another drink together, and you will tell us where the Krags are."

Pinto Parker was seated at one end of the long table with a big jug of mescal before him, and he grinned thickly. "Don' know where any Krags are. I tol' you that."

Comal Garza had been standing a little farther down the table, and his pewter mug made a dull clank as he set it down on the furrowed boards. "I told you we were wasting time, *Tío*. We tried being polite before, and it failed. We would have gotten it out of him the other way if Florida hadn't interfered."

"No, no," said *Tío* Balacar, his smile placating and sly at the same time. "We want Lieutenant Dixon to work with us. We want him for our *amigo*. There are things

58

about those Krags we shall have to know before using them. Don't you see what a priceless asset an Army officer would be to us, Garza? We will never get any of that by antagonizing him. I'm sure if we could just make it clear to him"—he pulled a chair from beneath the table with a flourish, and put one foot up on it, leaning forward with his elbow on the knee of his white pants— "now Lieutenant Dixon, if you will only tell us what it is you want, perhaps we can come to an agreement. We agreed on a price in Brownsville, of course, but if you want more, say so, and maybe...."

"You got the wrong *hombre*," grinned Pinto foolishly, taking another drink. "Wait'll Card gets here. He'll tell you."

"Perhaps Cardigan will not be getting here," said Garza.

"Sure he will," slurred Pinto confidently. "Nothing can stop Card. Just a couple of cattle operators, see, *Tío*. Just running a bunch of cattle through. Let's have another drink. I haven't wet my whistle like this in weeks. Man needs to get drunk once in a while."

"You are already drunk, Lieutenant," said *Tío* Balacar, and Cardigan could see the brilliant pinpoints of light catch in his small, black eyes. He took his foot from the chair and paced about the table, rubbing his hands together, frowning. Then he turned back, speaking to no one in particular. "It seems we have failed to make the necessary impression on the lieutenant. We offer him logic, and he says he is just a simple *hombre* trying to get along. We fill him with liquor, and his tongue does not become any looser in the direction we wish. There is very little left."

"That's what I say," Garza said.

Parker blinked owlishly at Balacar, patently not

59

understanding the man's implication. Balacar moved around to the chair again, putting his boot up on it and leaning forward on his knee that way once more to peer intently at Parker. Carefully he took the glass away from him; then he put a hand on Parker's shoulder.

"Don't make us do this, *amigo.*"

"Do what?" said Parker, reaching for the bottle.

Garza slid in and moved the bottle away. "No, *amigo*, don't make us."

"I don't getcha," said Parker, lurching over the glass.

Balacar moved the glass daintily out of Parker's reach, then picked up the hand that Kamaska had used the nutcracker on, separating the swollen fingers from the rest. "It caused you some pain, eh?"

"Hurt like hell," said Parker.

"We would not want to cause you any more pain," said Balacar.

"I want another drink," said Parker. "Come on, Garza, let's toast to old Texas."

Balacar dropped the hand abruptly, swinging his foot off the chair to walk away from the table in those stiff strides. He stopped, facing the window. He slapped his hands together. "All right," he said, without looking at Garza. "Go ahead."

"No," said Cardigan, stepping into the hall, "don't go ahead. Just stay right where you are."

He had never seen Garza display so much emotion. The man's jaw dropped, and his oblique eyes were wide and blank. Cardigan's boots made a hollow tap into the room, and his lips were drawn back from his teeth in that mirthless grin.

"Did you think maybe the *onza* got me, Garza?" he said.

Tío Balacar had swung around, and, after the first

60

surprise, his glance crossed Garza's. "Cardigan?" he said.

"Cardigan," said Garza.

Cardigan moved across the floor without lost motion, his .46 swinging to cover what was necessary, and grabbed Parker by the arm. "Come on, Pinto, we're trailing out now."

"Card," laughed Pinto. "I told them you'd be back. They didn't think so, but I told them. Have a drink."

"Get up. I said we're going."

The cold, flat sound of Cardigan's voice sobered Parker momentarily, and he blinked upward in that owlish way. "I thought you wanted to stay."

"Yes." Garza had recovered his composure now. "Yes, Cardigan, you aren't going to leave us now, are you? *Tío* even brought some more men to help us with the *mestenos*. Meet Aragonza. He is the best *jinete* north of Mexico City, and they say a horse doesn't live he can't fork, and he's reported to be just as skillful with his gun."

Cardigan had already taken in Aragonza, standing slim and fancy in a long Durango serape and glazed sombrero by the window, and he knew why Garza had done it. "I can see how many men you got in the room without you pointing them out to me, Garza."

That pawky smile slid across Balacar's thick lips again, and he spread his hands out, palms up. "*Señor*, you misinterpret my *amigo*'s meaning entirely. We would not try to detain you forcibly if your desires lead you elsewhere."

Kamaska's restless shift across the front of the fireplace belied Balacar's words, and Cardigan hauled at Parker with a growing sense of urgency, knowing his one gun wouldn't hold them much longer. "Will you

61

come on, Pinto."

"*Pues*, you are so insistent, *señor*," said Balacar. "Is our hospitality that bad? Is it?"

"I don't think you have Florida to intercede on your behalf this time, Cardigan," said Garza.

"Watch it, Innocencio," snapped Cardigan, twitching his gun toward the man as he saw his hand slide toward his neck. "Parker, will you get up? Damn you, will you come on?"

"Whatsamatter, Card," said Parker, rising halfway, then falling back. "I don't wanna go. Look at all the *pulque* they got left."

"Don't you see what they're trying to do?" Cardigan almost shouted, and coming out with it openly like that must have been what set it off, because everybody started to move at once, and Cardigan slipped his arm clear around behind Pinto and yanked him upright, giving him a push that sent him toward the door.

"Cardigan," shouted Garza, and Cardigan turned toward him with the gun. Garza stood by the table, unarmed, and even as he realized his mistake, Cardigan had to admire the man's nerve, taking that chance. Cardigan's thumb was tight against the hammer, but he couldn't throw down, somehow, and he saw the triumph in Garza's face as he turned back the other way. It was too late; it had given them their chance, and Cardigan was not around far enough to recognize who it was when the weight was thrown against his arm.

He shouted with the pain of two vise-like hands twisting his wrist back on itself, felt the Remington drop. Then he saw it was *Tío* Balacar's sweating, sensuous face, jammed into his shoulders, and knew time to be surprised that the man's slender hands could hold so much strength. The man's position only allowed leverage on Cardigan's wrist from one direction and, when Cardigan whirled the other way, he felt his arm jerk loose. As he whirled, he let his knee come upward. Balacar's sick grunt was reward for the pain of that wrist.

Garza had been on the opposite side of the table from Cardigan, and he was not yet around it as Balacar reeled back into a chair with both slender hands gripping his groin. Cardigan made a loud, grunting sound, heaving that heavy table over on Garza. Kamaska and Innocencio had jumped Pinto, and he was on his knees beneath their combined weight, head bobbing down due to a blow from Kamaska's fist. It must have taken just about that long for comprehension to get through Pinto's drink-fogged brain, because his reckless shout rang out as Garza went down beneath the long table.

"Well, damn you," shouted Pinto, and the floor might as well have heaved up from beneath Kamaska and Innocencio for all the good their mad struggle did to keep Parker down. He burst from between them like a raging bull, smashing Kamaska in the face with a bony elbow and knocking him back onto the overturned table, butting Innocencio in the belly, swaying up onto spread legs with that wild grin. "It looks like the boys want to fight, Card. That'll finish the evening just right."

"Get out, Pinto, get out," yelled Cardigan, realizing this was their last chance, grabbing at Parker, and trying to whirl him toward the door. Then he saw Aragonza over at the end of the room with a gun in each hand, and the first shot drowned all other sound, and, before the echoes died, someone else was shouting.

"...at them, you *necio*, don't shoot at them. We want Dixon alive!"

It was Balacar who had yelled, and he hoisted himself

63

up out of the chair with one hand still at his groin and a sick, greenish hue to his twisted face, and Cardigan tried to shove Pinto out of the way. But Balacar crashed into Pinto, tearing him loose from Cardigan's grip and carrying him on over into the upturned bottom of the table. Before Cardigan could reach them, a heavy body struck him from behind, and he went to his knees beneath Innocencio. Down like that, he saw Pinto bring his knees up between himself and Balacar and lash out with them. It shoved Balacar off Pinto, and the upswing of Pinto's feet brought them past the heavy man's body, and Balacar screamed as both Pinto's sharp-roweled spurs hooked him in the face.

Cardigan knew of that *belduque* and, with Innocencio on top of him, jerked aside as he heard the man grunt. Innocencio's thrust went past Cardigan's shoulder, the long knife sinking deeply into the hard-packed earthen floor. Cardigan caught the man's arm and used it for a lever to pull Innocencio over him onto the floor. Innocencio jerked the *belduque* free to jab again, and Cardigan had to sprawl bodily across the man to block it. From that position he caught another glimpse of Pinto. *Tío* Balacar was holding his bloody face in both hands now and blindly trying to rise from where he had been thrown across the upturned table. Free of the man, Pinto had gained his feet, whirling to jump feet first at Balacar again. This time the spurs crunched into Balacar's hands, and rolled down his forearms, tearing the sleeves of his silk shirt from cuffs to the elbows, dragging deep, red furrows through muscle and flesh.

"That's Texas fighting for you, *Tío*," roared Pinto, still filled with liquor, laughing crazily, and launched a final kick at Balacar that struck the man's head and rolled him down the table bottom till he crashed into an end leg hard enough to crack it off.

Cardigan was still sprawled across Innocencio, and had just about realized it was Innocencio holding him down that way rather than him keeping the man on the floor, when a great, crushing weight landed on him from behind, and his head was driven into Innocencio's chest by a rabbit punch behind his neck. He had seen a man hit that way before and, through the fog of stunning pain, knew instantly who was on top of him.

"Kamaska," he gasped involuntarily, and then his blind struggle for the *belduque* was rewarded.

He had both hands on Innocencio's knife wrist, and had finally gotten it twisted around beneath his own chest, when Innocencio shouted with the pain of it, and the long blade was free. Sensing above him the stiffening of Kamaska's body for another blow, Cardigan grasped the knife's hammered silver hilt and lunged back over his shoulder, blindly.

"*¡Sacramento!*"

It came from Kamaska, and was so full of animal pain that Cardigan knew he had struck. The blade was held in a solid, fleshy way for a moment, and then jerked a little, and was free in his hand again. Kamaska's weight was slack enough on top of him for Cardigan to thrust himself from beneath it, slashing at Innocencio as the man sought to hold him. Innocencio jerked back to keep from having his face ripped, and Cardigan was free. As he got to his hands and knees, he could see Pinto again.

Garza had finally crawled from beneath the table, and his leap must have taken him into Pinto and carried both of them past Cardigan and Innocencio into the wall, because the two of them were up against the wall now. Whatever Pinto had done to Garza left him lying inert on the floor against the adobe *banco* that ran clear

65

around the room to form a bench against the wall. But Aragonza had jumped in from the other end of the room and had Pinto on his hands and knees above Garza, beating at his head with both those guns. No telling how many times Balacar's man had struck Pinto before this. Parker's blond head was red with blood, and he was dripping it all over Garza's face beneath him, and he was sobbing as he tried to make what was evidently his last attempt at rising. Aragonza grunted as he slugged again with the barrel of his right hand gun, and it knocked Pinto flat across Garza.

Aragonza must have seen Cardigan roll from between Innocencio and Kamaska with that knife, for Cardigan was still on his hands and knees, just stiffening to rise, when Aragonza turned from Pinto, and Cardigan saw his intent plain in his face. Maybe they wanted Pinto alive. He was the only one. Aragonza was an old-style gunslinger, pulling his gun hand up as high as his head so that when he let the weapon drop back, the weight of the gun itself would carry the hammer back beneath his thumb, and it would be cocked as the revolver came down. But as soon as he saw Aragonza's hand begin to rise, Cardigan knew what it meant, and his reaction was without thought. He tossed the knife while still on his hands and knees, throwing all his weight over onto one palm to free the other hand. It caught Aragonza just as his hand reached the level of his head and started to drop down again.

The hammer must have already started to cock from the weight of the dropping gun, because the knife, driving into Aragonza's forearm, hit it so hard the gun exploded at the roof. The weight of the big knife and the force of the throw carried Aragonza back against the wall the way a blow would have, pinning his arm

66

against the mud, the *belduque* sunk hilt deep through his wrist and into the adobe. Even as Aragonza went into the wall, Cardigan was whirling toward sound from behind him. Kamaska was getting to his feet, his hand clutched across one shoulder, blood seeping between the fingers. Innocencio had started to rise, but he seemed suspended there with his knees bent, staring at Aragonza in a stunned surprise, as if he found something hard to believe.

Cardigan flung himself at the man, his weight carrying both of them crashing into the overturned table where Balacar had broken a leg off. Cardigan came up on top of Innocencio, clutching at the smashed leg. There was a good length to it, and the wood came free when he yanked it.

"No," yelled Innocencio, "no," and then gasped wretchedly with the twelve inches of solid oak smashing him across the forehead. Cardigan still had the leg as he jumped to his feet, because he knew what was behind him. Kamaska was already coming at him. He didn't move fast this time, or slow. He came with both hands outstretched, in a lurching, deliberate walk, each step a little longer than the preceding one, each one a little quicker. Cardigan jumped out to meet him, knocking aside one arm with the table leg. Kamaska cried out with the pain, but did not stop. Cardigan had knocked his arm aside to come in against him, and this time his blow was across the top of Kamaska's head, with all the weight and force he could bring into it. He heard the crack of wood, and Kamaska dropped a full six inches. He stood there a moment against Cardigan, his knees bent, his one arm still outstretched.

Cardigan raised the leg, brought it down again. Once more the cracking sound. Kamaska dropped another six inches, his face buried against Cardigan's belly, that one arm clutched around Cardigan's hips. Cardigan brought it up for the third time. Then he held it that way, staring stupidly up at the short stub of wood in his hand. The leg had broken in two. He stood there a moment longer, dropping his head to look at Kamaska. Then he stepped back. Kamaska went to his hands and knees. Then he slid quietly onto his belly.

Cardigan swayed there, trembling, panting, his shirt ripped from his lean torso and hanging from his belt. *Tío* Balacar was sitting over on the *banco*, bent forward, with his elbows on his knees, and his bleeding face in his hands.

"I can't see," he said stupidly, "I can't see. Where are you, Aragonza? I can't see."

Aragonza was crying like a baby as he twisted one way and the other, still pinned against the wall that way, desperately trying to pull the knife free. At his feet, Comal Garza was stirring feebly beneath an inert Pinto Parker. Finally Cardigan's dim perception reached the hallway. Florida stood there holding Garza's gun.

Cardigan spat out a tooth. "Well," he gasped. "What are you going to do?"

VIII

A FOG HAD SWEPT IN FROM THE GULF COAST TO shroud the *brasada* in a gray oppression, the morning after the fight. Gaunt mesquite reached out of the viscid mist like helpless skeleton hands supplicating the unseen sky. The *cenzio* sprawling about the bunkhouse door blended its dead, ashen growth with the shreds of turgid vapor seeping into the room. Esperanza shuffled in from the kitchen with a bowl of beans, grumbling

68

through his flowing, longhorn *mustachios*.

"I don't see why you have to leave now. The whole *estancia* is yours. Everybody's afraid of you. You're the big *toro* of the pasture, and nobody comes within ten feet of you."

Cardigan was sitting at the table, wearing one of Esperanza's cotton shirts. "Would've left last night if Pinto was in any shape."

"An' leave the *señorita*?" said Esperanza.

"What does she have to do with it?"

"She don't want you to go."

"What did you do with those?" Cardigan pointed his fork at the beans.

"Those are on foot, *señor*. Boiled. Tomorrow we have them on horseback. Fried. You stay tomorrow and you see why we call them *nacionales*. *Sapodillas*. You should see my *sapodillas*. I make them for *General Porfirio Díaz* himself. Sweet, hollow pin cushions of puff paste, *señor*, as frothy as lather from the *amole*. I fry them in deep grease and make syrup to go over them hot. And *bishochitos*...."

"All right, all right, biscuits," said Cardigan impatiently. "Just bring the coffee and forget...."

This time the crash of gunshots did no more than make him jump in the chair. Esperanza stood there quivering with rage, hands filled with his smoking Colts.

"You don't like my *bishochitos*?" he shouted.

"I didn't say that...."

"You don't like my *bishochitos*. I make them for the whole Mexican army, but they aren't good enough for you. What are you, a *hidalgo*? *Sacramento*, no, just a loco *Tejano* who can't even ride through a mesquite tree without getting knocked off...."

69

"You want me to slit your throat?"

It came from the doorway, and it stopped the cook. He stood there a moment, staring toward Innocencio. Then he let the Colts drop back into their holsters.

"*Madre de Dios*, Innocencio, I was just telling him how I cook my *bishochitos*."

"Get back in the kitchen where you belong," said Innocencio, moving on in. He looked at Cardigan, grinning evilly. "Some *batalla* we had last night, no? I never see anybody throw a knife that way. Just a little flip, and it goes in so deep Aragonza can't get off the wall for fifteen minutes."

Cardigan shoved the bench back, rising. "Little Indian toss I learned in San Antone. I didn't want you to think you were the only one could use a pig-sticker around here."

Pinto Parker came from the bunkroom, his head swathed in white, cotton bandages Esperanza had put on the night before. He stopped a moment by the table to steady himself, grinning ruefully at Cardigan. Then he nodded toward the door. Cardigan followed him out, serpents of ground fog streaming about his legs. Pinto stopped by a big cottonwood to one side of the shack, turning toward Cardigan.

"You're leaving on account of me, aren't you, Card?" he said.

Cardigan shook his head. "I'm fed up."

"No," said Pinto. "If it was just you, you'd stay. There's something here. I know. But you're leaving because you don't want to let me in for something like last night again."

Cardigan shrugged his acceptance. "Just licking them didn't necessarily convince them you aren't Lieutenant Dixon."

70

Pinto was studying his face. "They were willing to have you killed at the bull-tailing the other day, but they didn't try anything on me. That's because they still thought I was Dixon. What would happen if they found out I'm not Dixon?"

Cardigan's eyes grew opaque. "They might cut *your* cinch."

"And that's why you're going," said Pinto. "To get me out of it. They've already tried to kill you, but you'd stay if it was just you."

"It's not your roundup," said Cardigan. "It wasn't from the first. I didn't look at it that way when the thing started. I hadn't known you long, and you were just a man I trailed with, and I didn't look at it one way or the other. Now, I've known you longer, Pinto. It's not your roundup, and I've got no right to rope you in on it."

"What if I want to be roped in?"

"We're still going," said Cardigan.

"The girl don't want you to go, Card."

"What's she got to do with it?" said Cardigan.

"She didn't interfere last night."

"What cows does that get you?" inquired Cardigan.

"It shows you she don't stand solid with Garza," said Pinto.

"You're still riding a muddy river."

Pinto's voice was intense. "You know what I mean. She wanted your help somehow all along. That's why she took a shine to you from the first. She sensed what I should have known. You weren't my kind. Just because you came in here trailing a bunch of wet beef didn't make you a tinhorn rustler like me. There was something else. She sensed it. She tried to get your help, but you wouldn't trust her because you thought she rode in Garza's wagon. Hasn't she proved different yet? It

71

was only her arriving when she did the first night that kept Kamaska from killing you. She tried to stop that killer bull at *Mogotes Oros* just as hard as I did. It was her told me something had gone wrong when she saw Garza and the others dropping back and letting you have the bull. And now, last night"—he reached out to grasp Cardigan's arm—"maybe she's in such a position she can't come right out against Garza, Cardigan, until she knows someone else is backing her. You can see how it would be for a gal, all alone like that. You can't run out on her, Cardigan, just because of me."

Cardigan bit his lip, meeting Pinto's eyes. "You'll go, anyway, Pinto?"

"The hell I will! What is it, Card? What is it you're after in here?" He was looking into Cardigan's eyes, and must have seen it there, for his hand dropped from Cardigan's arm, and he took a step backward, his voice sober. "All right, Card. You don't have to tell me if you don't want to. It won't make any difference. Not after what you did last night. Nothing would make any difference between you and me, Card."

The sound of someone's boots made a dull tap across the hard-adobe compound. It was *Tío* Balacar, moving toward them in that pompous, stiff-legged walk, the fringed ends of his silk sash ruffling against his polished jack boots. His face was blotched purple with some kind of local herb Esperanza had smeared on the deep gashes made by Pinto's spurs, and one of his eyes was squinted shut and twitching all the time. Aragonza was with him, a pinched, lethal look to his pale cheeks, as he stared at Cardigan. His right arm was bandaged beneath the sleeve of his fancy *charro* coat, and held in a black sling. Garza and Florida were following, and the woman was watching Cardigan with a repressed desperation in

72

her big eyes.

"Well, *compadres*," said Balacar and, although his thick lips held that pawky grin, Cardigan could see the corrosive hatred smoldering in his eyes. "That was quite a rodeo we had last night, eh? I haven't had such a *batalla* since my cadet days in the *Colegio Militar*. *Pues*, I understand you *Tejanos* do that every Saturday night just for amusement. I'm sure you're already laughing about it, eh? I understand you're leaving this morning, and I'd hate to have us part with a bad taste in our mouths."

"On the contrary," said Cardigan, and he saw hope leap into Florida's eyes, "we aren't leaving this morning," and saw the hope turn to a fervent thanks, "we're staying."

IX

A BUTCHER BIRD SAT PREENING ITSELF IN THE LEAFLESS *junco*. Mexicans said this was the only bird that would alight on the bush, for the *junco*'s thorns had formed Christ's crown. It was a somber belief, and seeing the bird, somehow, filled Cardigan with an apprehension. He recalled the first time he had felt that, riding the brush this way, just before Navasato had been killed, and turned to look at the rustling mesquite stretching dark and illimitable behind him. They had ridden after mustangs again, and it was the first time since they left *Hacienda del Diablo* that Florida had found a chance to speak with Cardigan. Balacar and Garza had drawn ahead slightly to scout for tracks, and Florida pulled her scarred, little brush horse up to Cardigan's dun.

"I think it was a mistake to come out this way," she said tensely.

"We've got to wait for them to make the first move," he said. "As long as Balacar wants to keep up a pretense like this, we've got to play along."

"It's like sitting on a powder keg," she said. "You can see it under *Tío*'s smile. The way Kamaska watches us. Garza's eyes. Your first slip is your last, Cardigan."

"I think they include you in with Pinto and me now, don't they?" he said, turning toward her. Their eyes met for a moment, and then he reached over and touched her hand. "Florida, if you want to tell me now, I'll tell you."

She grasped his hand and squeezed it with a certain desperate thanks at this evidence of his trust, and her words tumbled out in a swift, tense mutter. "You know who Balacar is?"

"I know he rode with Díaz in the 'Sixties. Turned revolutionist later on. Mixed up with gun-running down in New Orleans. Packs a lot of pull with the peons for what he did in the army. Is that what he's doing here?"

"Gun-running? You know it isn't. You know it's more than that." She glanced ahead quickly. Balacar and Garza were barely visible through the chaparral, talking in low tones. Florida twisted back in her rawhide brush-popper's rig. "You're right about him packing a lot of pull with the *peones*, though. Almost as much as Díaz. What do you think would happen if Díaz showed up here in the brush with five hundred Krag rifles and as many freshly broken horses?"

"He'd have just about that many men to use them within a week."

"The same with *Tío*," she said. "He was a fiery, popular, dashing cavalry leader, and his exploits in and after the war have become almost legendary among the Mexicans of the border. All he has to do is let it be known he's here and needs men to follow him, and they'll come flocking like so many buzzards to a dead horse. He already has the horses. All he needs is Lieutenant Henry Dixon and those Krags. As soon as he lays his hands on those guns, he'll send out word."

"You're a *revolutionario?*"

"It's no revolution," she flung at him. "Mexican politics don't affect me. And they have nothing to do with this. It'll stay right here in the *brasada*. Do you remember Cortina?"

"The Red Robber?" said Cardigan. "What Texan doesn't remember him?"

"Then you know what happened when he got going," she said. "He was leading a veritable army before he finished. The whole border had a regular war on its hands. You finally had to call on the United States Army. And it took them ten years to break Cortina's hold down here." She leaned toward him, eyes big and black. "It'll be worse with Balacar, if he's allowed to organize, Cardigan. You know what a terrible place this brush is. It's full of men in hiding, and very few law officers who came in after them ever went out alive. Think what it would be with an army in here, under a man like Balacar. Think what a terrible job it would be trying to smoke them out. It would be worse than any of the Indian wars. They could raid any town from here to the Red River. They could rustle cattle till cows stopped growing horns. It could well lead to another war with Mexico. You know how touchy the Cortina trouble left the whole border."

The scope of it staggered Cardigan. "Cortina was a piker beside this bird."

"It's been going on in the *brasada*, that way, since before Texas broke away from Mexico," she said. "But nobody ever had the nerve to try it on a scale like this."

He glanced around him, realizing what an impregnable fortress this harsh, impenetrable jungle would be for a force like that. "And they want your place for a headquarters?"

"It was the only spot in the brush big enough to corral that many mustangs," she said. "It would have been hard to steal that many horses anywhere, even over a period of time. Besides, rustling such a large number might have given away what Balacar intended in here, and he didn't want that until he was set. They did have to have horses, though. You know half the Mexicans in the brush and along the border don't own an animal. I didn't know exactly what was in the wind when Garza came to me wanting to use my ranch as headquarters for his *mesteneros*. He paid for a six months' lease for the use of my corrals and men. We'd just finished fall roundup and my crew was idle, so I didn't see any harm. By the time I realized something was going on, Garza had won over Kamaska and Innocencio. *Brazaderos* like them would give anything to ride with Balacar. And Aragonza had worked with Balacar before. I couldn't fight them openly, even when I did find out. I tried to reach Masset, but it was impossible. He's always thought I was mixed up with the rustlers in here. The *nagualismo* business starting about that time didn't help much. Two of Masset's deputies were killed that way, and he connected me with it."

"You could have gotten out."

She drew herself up perceptibly. "It's my *brasada*, Cardigan. My house. My land. Do you think I'd let them take it that way?"

The drum of hoofs turned him in the saddle. Kamaska had remained behind at the *hacienda*, and his horse was lathered with the hard ride from there as he pushed by

76

them on his hairy mule. He halted by Balacar and Garza, speaking in a hot, breathless way, glancing back at Cardigan. Garza nodded, said something, neck-reined his horse away. Florida caught at Cardigan's hand.

"Quick, you've got to tell me. Who are you?"

"Yes," said Balacar, and he turned back to them through the screen of mesquite. "Who are you, Cardigan?"

"Don't you know," laughed Pinto from behind them. "He's Lieutenant Dixon's brother."

A dull flush reddened Balacar's heavy-fleshed face, and he controlled his anger badly. "We have found mustang sign. We'll be riding."

He reined his horse in beside Florida, and Kamaska dropped back till he was just ahead of Cardigan, and they broke into a trot through the brush that way. Cardigan watched for them to come up with Garza, but the man did not appear. Aragonza was trailing, and kept dismounting to check the sign. They crossed a portion of brush that had been swept by the fire. There was a great stretch of blackened stubble, still glowing and snapping sullenly in places, reaching to a sandy river bed that the fire had been unable to leap. They plodded through the white sand and into thick brush beyond.

"Evidently a large cut of *mestenos* was driven this way by the fire," said Balacar.

None of them answered, and Cardigan gripped his reins more tightly with the thickening of the sullen antipathy that lay between all of them. Pinto was grinning blandly at Innocencio, and the knife-man shifted uncomfortably in his saddle, his forehead still red and lacerated where Cardigan had struck him with the table leg. Then a startled, crashing sound broke from the thickets ahead, and Aragonza shouted back at them.

"*¡Mestenos!* Head them off. They are cutting toward you. Head them off."

A mustang with great singe marks blackening his dun hide burst through mesquite with the berries caught like brown bubbles in his mane. His wild eyes rolled white as he saw them, and he turned on a hind leg like a roper, taking another direction through the brush. With a hoarse shout, Kamaska was after him. Another *mesteno* crashed into the open, and then three mares clattered in from the mesquite. Cardigan spurred his dun so that it nudged into Florida's pony before digging into its gallop.

"Don't get separated," he shouted in her ear, and then was past her.

He sensed her horse following behind him, and saw Pinto line out after Florida. Then he was into the chaparral, with the mares making a great crashing before him. Keeping his eyes open, as Florida had told him, was next to impossible. Every time a clawing mat of mesquite or a hackberry branch thrust itself out at him, his head jerked aside, and his eyes twitched with the violent instinct to shut. Yet he forced himself to keep them open, smashing hell-for-leather into the *mogote*, and found he could dodge the malignant brush with more ease than before. He ducked under a post-oak and, where, if he had allowed his eyes to close, he would have missed the *agrito* beyond that, and probably would have had his leg swept out of the stirrup, he spotted the thorny, crawling spread and swept his leg up to avoid it.

He neck-reined the dun violently to one side and scraped past the thick, shaggy trunk of a hackberry. Then he pulled up and turned the blowing animal, waiting for Florida. It was when his own noise had

78

stopped that he realized there was no sound behind him. He had purposely not gone far, only riding enough to penetrate the first thicket. An insidious fear fingered him. He was just touching his dun's flanks to send it back when the sound came. It stiffened him in the saddle, and he felt the blood drain from his face, and his lips formed the word soundlessly.

"*La onza.*"

With an abrupt motion, Cardigan kicked his dun back through the mesquite and into the clearing. It was empty. He opened his mouth to call Florida, then closed it. He turned the dun, a strange, clawing sensation tightening his vitals. Then it came.

"Card, watch out! Card, watch out! Card...!"

There was terror riding the hoarse, cracked shouts, and then agony, as the intelligible words became a wild, shrill scream, and that scream was so imbedded within Cardigan's memory by now that he raked his dun without thought and drove it toward the sound with all the coals on. He exploded through a mass of *granjeno* and ducked flat on his dun to tear beneath a low stretch of *chaparro prieto* and jerked aside from a clawing arm of mesquite. The screams had stopped by now, and he had smashed a straight line a hundred yards through the brush before he pulled his lathered dun up, trying to place the spot where the sound had just come from.

The brush was utterly silent, save for his dun's heavy breathing. He tried another tack through the mesquite, going slower. Finally he went back to the original clearing and started circling out from it. He lost track of the time it took him to find Pinto. He pulled through a stand of torn prickly pear into a small opening. Pinto was lying face down. Most of his shirt was gone, and the flesh across his back was ripped away so deeply the

79

white pattern of his bones was visible, and the ground beneath him was soaked with blood.

Cardigan got off his horse slowly, his face set in a stiff, terrible mask. It didn't matter what Pinto had been. It didn't matter that he hadn't known him long. All that mattered in that moment was the feeling of utter loss in Cardigan. The vagrant, poignant memory of a reckless laugh passed through him, and of a swaggering figure in the saddle, and of a cheerful Texas lullaby sung one night up by the Nueces when the going had gotten especially tough.

It must have been the sepulchral rustle of mesquite that caused Cardigan to turn around. Africano stood there, bare, leprous torso covered with fresh brush scratches, black chest rising and falling heavily. Cardigan drew a sharp breath, turning toward him.

"Africano...."

"Careful, *señor!*" It was a sharp command, but more than that, stopping Cardigan, was the guttural warning of the dogs.

"I don't have to touch you, Africano." Cardigan pulled his gun. His lips were flat against his teeth. "I don't have to touch you to kill you."

Africano was staring at Parker. "You think...me?"

"What else?" Cardigan's voice was brittle, and he was trembling a little now. "You've been around every time. *Nagualismo?* Go ahead. Go ahead and change back into that *onza* before I put a slug through your black brisket. I'd like to see you try."

"No, *señor*, no. I'm not *nagual*. Kamaska's loco. Just because I come from Yucatán? That was a long time ago, *señor*. I was a *niñito*, a baby. Garza is from Yucatán, too. This is my country, *señor*, my *brasada*. Do you think I'd let them take it, Balacar and the
80

others? I've been trying to help the *señorita*. When you came, I thought it was to get Balacar. I have tried to help you, *señor*...."

"By running around changing yourself into an *onza* and tearing people up?" said Cardigan bitterly.

"No, I tell you I am not *nagual*. Didn't I give you Balacar's brief case when I found it? Didn't I tell you of George Weaver? I was trying to warn you of *la onza* that night of the fire, but I got there too late. I used to work at *Hacienda del Diablo*, but Garza ran me off when I found out what they were up to and threatened to tell the *señorita* if they didn't leave. They have tried to find me and kill me ever since. And now she knows, doesn't she...?" Africano stopped abruptly, his black head raising, and then shouted. "*Señor*, behind you...!"

It was his own whirling motion that saved Cardigan, carrying him partially to one side. The hilt of the *belduque* tapped at his shirt as it hummed past him, driving into Africano's chest. The man made a gurgling sound and fell against Cardigan, knocking the Remington upward with its first shot. The slug shattered through the brush above Innocencio's head, where he stood across the clearing. Before Cardigan could jump away from Africano's body and throw down on his second shot, the two dogs had leaped past him, snarling savagely.

"Kamaska!" shouted Innocencio, trying to turn and run, "Kamaska," and then the ferocious animals were on him, and he went down with a pitiful shout beneath their snarling, slashing fury.

Kamaska came into the open from the other side, and Cardigan had his gun cocked, and he fired with the conversion held straight out at the level of his hip. The square, ape-like Mexican grunted, and reached out with both arms, and kept on coming toward Cardigan in that heavy, shuffling stride. Cardigan fired again, without throwing his gun up. Kamaska flinched, and kept coming. The Remington bucked with Cardigan's third shot. Kamaska made a sick sound with the impact of that one, and staggered a little, and then put his foot down in another step, grunting with the pain it caused him, and came on, grunting with each step. Cardigan's lips peeled away from his teeth in a grim desperation, and he dropped the hammer on his fourth one. Kamaska made no sound with that one driving through his thick, square belly. He took another step, his hands spastically spread out in front of him. His face contorted with the effort his will was making to drive him on that last step. His foot struck the ground with a solid, thumping sound. His thick, callused fingers touched Cardigan. Then they slid down the front of Cardigan's shirt, and Kamaska's weight almost knocked Cardigan over, falling against him, and sliding to the ground.

"*Señor*...."

It was Africano, trying to raise himself on an elbow, the *belduque* protruding from his chest. The dogs were worrying at Innocencio's body across the clearing, growling and snarling. Cardigan squatted down to Africano, and the man waved a hand at Pinto.

"You know...you know what that means?"

"It means you got what was coming to you and...."

"No, no, I'm not *nagual*." Africano licked lips flecked with blood. "I mean that they would kill Parker?"

"What do you mean, they?"

"They no longer think he is Lieutenant Dixon. They must have found the real Lieutenant Dixon!"

X

THERE WAS SOMETHING STRIDENT ABOUT THE UTTER silence of *Hacienda del Diablo* that caught at Cardigan. He hauled his dun to a stop just inside the fringe of brush, searching the compound for signs of life. Africano had died in the thicket there with Pinto Parker; and the dun was shaking and heaving beneath Cardigan, he had driven it so brutally to reach the spread. It came to him now with a shock that there were no mustangs in the corrals. Neck-reining the dun abruptly into the open, he spurred the flagging animal across the porch. His Remington was in his hand as he swung off the blown horse, and his heels tapped across the flagstones in a grim deliberateness. The heavy door stood ajar. Cardigan slid in with his back coming up against one wall and his gun covering the living room that ran the length of the front of the building. One man was in the room. He sat on the floor, slumped against the wall near the hooded fireplace, legs thrust out before him, head on his chest. The wall above his head was pocked with bullet holes that had dripped yellow adobe down onto his white head. Two big, stag-gripped Colts lay one on either side of him.

"Esperanza?" said Cardigan.

The old cook had trouble raising his head and focusing his eyes. "Cardigan," he croaked. "I thought you was dead. Balacar sent Innocencio and Kamaska out to kill you and Parker."

"Lieutenant Dixon?" said Cardigan.

"How did you know?" Esperanza made a vague movement with his hands, licking his lips. "Dixon came while all of you were gone into the brush. He said the two men who'd been guiding him had been killed

83

almost a week ago by some nigger, just before he reached the Comanche Trail. I figure it must have been Africano. Africano run Dixon's string of mules off into the brush and scattered them. That's how you and Parker must have come across the one Garza found you with. By the time Dixon got the mules rounded up, he was lost in the brush. He tried to find his way alone, but he said this nigger kept trying to kill him and get the mules again. Finally Dixon killed all the mules and cached their loads of Krags and started out alone to find us...." Esperanza trailed off, making that motion with his hand again. "*Agua*, Cardigan, *agua*. These holes in my *estomago* give a *hombre* a *diablo*'s own thirst."

Cardigan got a clay pitcher of water off the table, and Esperanza slopped it all over his chest drinking, finally pushing it away. "Kamaska lit out to tell Balacar the real Dixon is finally here, and they come back. They had to bring Florida in on the end of a gun. Garza claimed you and Parker had been taken care of, but Balacar sent Kamaska and Innocencio to make sure. He wanted them to bring your head back in a saddlebag. He said he wouldn't believe you were dead till he saw that. He said that's the kind of a *hombre* you are."

"Who let the mustangs out?"

"Florida. She wanted to stop Balacar from getting the guns, I guess. She's been against this from the beginning, only me and Kamaska and the others were too dumb to see that. Garza paid us extra *dinero* and promised us we'd ride high beside him as soon as they got those guns. We always thought Florida would be with them, but I guess they only wanted to use her till they got the mustangs broke. She got out somehow while Balacar and Dixon were talking and let all the horses loose, and that made them mad. They started

84

knocking her around, and I see what they really had intended with her all along. I'm her *hombre*, Cardigan. I been on *hacienda* with her grandfather and her father and her, and they can't do that. You see what I got for my trouble. Aragonza. I never see a man pull his gun so fast. I had mine already out before he started. *Madre de Dios*." He licked his lips again, blinking his eyes almost sleepily. Then, with a perceptible effort, he focused them again, reaching up feebly to clutch at Cardigan, his voice a hoarse croak. "You've got to get them, Cardigan. You got to stop them. Once Balacar gets those guns, there'll be no stopping him. He can get mustangs again. That ain't hard. Maybe it'll take him time, but he can get them. It's the guns."

He drew a long breath.

"The whole thing hinges on them. Once they're in his hands, the *brasada*'s going to burn from one end to the other. You think that was a good fire at *Mogotes Oros*? You wait till Balacar gets going. This whole border country won't be safe for a man like you to set foot in. They'll raze every town from here to Austin. There won't be a cattle ranch left south of the Nueces. And nobody'll be able to stop them, Cardigan, five hundred men with Krags under a soldier like Balacar in this brush. Nobody's been able to clean the brush of rustlers and killers in the last hundred years. What chance do you think they'll have with an organized army? And Florida"—his hand tugged at Cardigan's shirt with a spasmodic fear—"you got to stop them, Cardigan. Before they get those guns. She's with them and Balacar'll kill her as soon as he has the Krags for sure. The only reason he kept her alive was her influence with the *brazaderos* but, as soon as he gets those guns, he won't need her any more. From the description Dixon gave of the place he cached those Krags, I'd say Rio Frio."

"My horse is done," said Cardigan.

"There's some old brush ponies staked out behind the cookhouse. They ain't these mustangs, but they'll take you where you need to go."

Cardigan rose, took a step toward the door, then turned. Esperanza waved him on.

"Go ahead, go ahead. Ain't no use waiting to see me sack my kack." He took a gasping breath. "Make it before night comes, Cardigan. I heard *la onza* a while back. Make it before night comes or you'll have the *nagual* on you out there."

"I don't think so," said Cardigan. "I think that's already taken care of."

It was a stringy-backed, hammer-headed gelding no more than fifteen hands high, scarred from nose to tail by the brush and, once Cardigan touched its hoary flanks, the evil, little beast threw itself into a mad gallop, crashing through the *brasada* as if it hated every thicket personally, throwing itself broadside through *mogotes* of chaparral, driving tumultuously through a bunch of mesquite with its head down and little eyes glittering belligerently, dashing across open spaces in a driving impatience to be at the brush again. Cardigan had taken some wild rides in his day, but this sat the fanciest saddle. It was a constant battle to remain on the horse, ducking flat along its cockleburred mane or throwing himself off to one side, riding its rump, its neck, its flanks, not spending five minutes of the whole time sitting straight in the saddle. Yet, with all its apparent rage at the brush, the horse took him through *mogotes* the dun could never have negotiated, bursting thickets the devil himself would have gone around, penetrating seemingly impenetrable chaparral, crashing prickly pear so solid it looked fit to stop a herd of steers. And all the time it was Florida's admonition. Keep your eyes open, keep your eyes open.

There was a post-oak that batted his head and left him sick and dizzy and reeling in the rawhide-lashed brushpopper's saddle, and mesquite that caught at his face while he was off to the side and left his flesh torn and bleeding, and *agrito* that ripped his Levi's to shreds, and nopal that jabbed his hands and arms like bayonets. He seemed lost in a mad nightmare, filled with the roaring crash of brush and the clatter of chaparral and the squashing pop of prickly pear.

Esperanza had said Rio Frio, just south of where they had hunted *mestenos* that first time, and the best Cardigan knew was to drive in a straight line with the sun on his left. Soon he was fighting the brush as bitterly as the pony, flinging a curse at each jabbing *comal*, shouting a hoarse execration at every low-reaching hackberry branch. He had gotten the feel of it now, and was going more by sense than sight, his swing to the side automatic when a post-oak loomed ahead, his jerk up instinctive to avoid the clawing arms of *comal* before his face, riding like a drunken man, swaying and cursing and shouting and panting and bleeding.

He crossed a great, blackened stretch, where the fire had burned itself out in some pear flats, and ran again into the thickets. There was no trailing for him; he knew too little of the brush for that. He struck a wet creek finally and knew it to be Rio Frio, for there was no other water within miles, and turned down the dribble, fighting through cottonwoods and hackberries festooned thick with parasite moss and the constant pop and crash of brush as he burst through it to hear any sounds; and he came upon them in a mad rush, tearing through a screening thicket of *huisache* that grew down into the river, and almost running down Aragonza on the other side.

"Cardigan!" shouted Aragonza, jumping backward.

The man's first surprise kept him from any action, and, by the time he was ready, Cardigan had hauled his heaving pony to a stop and slid off and stood there, swaying and bleeding and panting, his legs spread out beneath him, his torso bent forward slightly. *I never see a man pull his gun so fast*! It was in Cardigan like that, what Esperanza had said, and he was waiting, with the knowledge. *I never see a man pull his gun so fast.*

"Go ahead," he said.

Aragonza went. His right arm was still in that black sling, but Cardigan had seen enough to know the man was as good with either hand, and, when the Durango serape flapped against Aragonza's *charro* vest with his blinding movement, whatever had been in Cardigan's mind was swept from it as instinct and habit reared up from his unconscious in an inundating wave. He felt his whole body sweep into motion, and that was his last conscious sensation till the crash of guns jarred through him. It must have been the jolt of Cardigan's slug striking Aragonza that made the man pull his trigger, spasmodically, for Aragonza had not lifted his gun high enough to be in line. With the smoking six-shooter still pointed at the ground, Aragonza sobbed in a strangled way and fell over on his face.

The brush pony had been spooked by the gunfire, and bolted for the mesquite, but the clatter of the men bursting into the open from there caused the animal to rear up and whirl back toward Cardigan. With all his concentration on Aragonza, Cardigan's awareness of

Florida had been but a dim one in those first moments, where she was standing on the far side of the clearing.

"Cardigan!" he heard her cry, and with the brush horse charging wildly at him, he threw down on the trio who erupted from the thicket behind Florida. He had to snap his shot at the first man he saw, and it was Comal Garza, coming out of the mesquite with berries dripping all over his shoulders, and that Ward-Burton hugged in against his belly as he snapped the bolt. Cardigan's gun bucked in his hand, and he had time to see Garza's face twist, and then the horse's shoulder crashed into him, spinning him around.

Desperately, Cardigan tried to keep his feet. He spun into a hackberry, hearing the horse thunder on into the *brasada* behind him, and then reeled off the tree and went to his hands and knees in the sand facing away from the hackberry, a foot behind his head. He flopped over onto his back with his gun in both hands. In that position, lying there flat with his feet toward them and the gun sighted down his belly through his toes, he saw Tío Balacar. Balacar must have been the one to fire that first shot, for he was still coming forward in a stiff-legged run, and he had already thrown his gun down for the second shot. Cardigan thumbed desperately at his own hammer, knowing his head would be blown off before he could ever fire.

He recoiled to the roar of the shot. Then he lay there, his gun still gripped in both hands, not yet cocked, realizing it hadn't been Balacar's gun that had made the sound. Tío staggered on forward a couple of steps, his face blank with a stunned surprise, and then a glazed opacity dulled the brilliance of his little, black eyes and, when he fell forward, one of his arms dropped across Cardigan's leg.

89

Florida was standing above Garza, with Garza's smoking Ward-Burton still held across one hip. She was not faced toward Balacar any more. She had snapped the bolt of the gun again, and her thumb was still over the breech where she had jammed in a fresh shell. The third man who had been running out with Balacar and Garza was halted, a frustrated rage showing in the way his mouth worked as he stared at the weapon, his hand still gripped on the flap of a holster at his hip, holding it open over the butt of an Army Colt he hadn't been able to draw.

Cardigan got to his feet, stepping over Balacar, slipping the Colt from the man's holster, and it was rather a statement than a question. "Lieutenant Dixon."

"Yeah," said the man sullenly.

"I'm Marshal Edward Cardigan, United States government, and I'm taking you back for desertion, theft of government property, and fomenting activity inimical to the government of the country, and that's tantamount to treason, and they usually hang a man for that."

Florida was staring at Cardigan, wide-eyed, and her words were hardly audible. "Marshal ...Edward ... Cardigan... ? "

"You can see why I couldn't tell you." He was turned toward her, and it was spilling out now, the way he'd wanted it to come for so long, the way he'd wanted to let her know she wasn't alone. "I didn't know whether you were with them or not, Florida, for sure. I couldn't take a chance. I had a job to do, and I couldn't take a chance. So much more depended on it than just you and me. The lives of so many men who would have died if I'd failed, men like Masset and Weaver and Smithers."

"Weaver was a marshal too?"

"Yes, the first one they sent in to find out what was

90

going on down here. Lieutenant Dixon was in the Quartermaster Corps at San Antone. Balacar reached him. It's usually money, in a case like that. Enough money. Dixon got assigned to a detail transporting those Krags from San Antone to Fort Leaton. At the Nueces, two Mexicans met the detachment and, with their help, Dixon got the guns into the brush. Two of the troopers were killed during the ruckus. Our office had word that Balacar was active somehow north of the border, and when the Krags disappeared that way, and with the reports Masset's office had been sending in about this *nagualismo* business going on south of the Comanche Trail, the government decided it was time for them to step in down here and try and clean it up.

"After Weaver disappeared, I was assigned. Instead of coming straight in, I figured it would be better if I dallied onto someone who knew the *brasada* and who would be accepted in here among the class of men who ran the brush. We had tabs on the local rustlers and border-hoppers working out of San Antone and other towns near the brush. In Brownsville I finally tied in with Pinto and Navasato to run a bunch of Big Skillet beef across the border. Pinto never suspected who I was till right at the last...."

He trailed off, and she looked up at him, sensing what was in his mind. "He wouldn't blame you, Cardigan. He didn't. He stuck, didn't he? Even after he began to understand how you'd used him."

"It didn't matter at first." Cardigan's voice was guttural. "He was just a two-bit rustler, and he was just someone who could get me in here. But you know Pinto. After being with him that way, riding with him, camping, fighting, drinking"—he moved his head in a helpless, frustrated way—"I can't help how I feel. It doesn't matter what he was or what he may have done. I can't help how I feel."

"He understood, Cardigan. He wouldn't have had you any other way. You're that kind. Pinto understood what kind you were and admired you for it, and whatever happened he never blamed you."

It was the rustling sound that made Cardigan realize how much of their attention had been focused on Dixon. Florida stood in front of where Garza lay, and it had hidden his movement just long enough. Both Florida and Cardigan whirled toward him, but he was already on his feet, and plunging into the brush. Florida tried to fire, but she hadn't shoved the fresh shell home hard enough, and the Ward-Burton jammed on her. Cardigan had put his Remington away, and it took him that long to draw it, and then it was Florida, shouting, "Cardigan, look out. Dixon. Cardigan...."

He whirled back, the Remington out, firing after Dixon as the man leaped into the mesquite. He heard Dixon cry out in pain, and then crash on through the thicket. Cardigan plunged after him.

Garza," called the woman. "What about Garza?"

"Dixon's the man I want," shouted Cardigan, smashing through some prickly pear. "Garza won't go far with that slug I put through his belly."

He was still shouting when the sound came. He stopped shouting, and stopped running, and stood there, with his mouth open. Bursting through the pear after him, Florida ran into Cardigan, almost knocking both of them over, and then, against him like that, she stiffened, and her fingers tightened on his arm. It rose above the *brasada* like the scream of a woman in mortal pain, weird, terrifying, unearthly. It was the same sound Cardigan had heard before Navasato, and Masset, and

Pinto. He felt a suffocating constriction in his chest, as the cry died, and Dixon must have stopped running somewhere ahead of them, for an utter silence settled over the brush.

"No, Cardigan," whispered the woman, "no, no, no."

"Cardigan." It was Dixon's shout, shocking them, coming shrill and cracked from ahead. "Cardigan, for God's sake, Cardigan! Help me, Cardigan! For God's sake, Cardigan...!"

Cardigan made an impulsive movement toward the sound that carried him halfway through a lane between mesquite thickets with the woman clinging to him, and then Dixon's screams had stopped, too. Gun gripped in a white-knuckled hand, Cardigan forced himself onward. Sweat was running down the deep grooves from his nose to his lips as he passed the mesquite and forced his way through thickly entwined chaparral. There was an open spot beyond the chaparral. Dixon lay there, face down. Florida stared a moment, then turned her face to Cardigan's chest with a small sob.

"I was a fool," Cardigan muttered thickly.

"A fool?"

"I thought Africano was the *nagual*."

Her face turned upward with a jerk, and her eyes were shining up at him in a wide fear. "You mean...Garza?"

XI

NIGHT TOUCHED THE *BRASADA* WITH ITS GHOSTLY hands, and the *chaparro prieto* stood in sinister silence along Rio Frio. From somewhere far off a coyote mourned through the darkness. And nearer, through the mesquite, back in the secretive pear, the sibilant, chuckling crackle of movement through the brush mocked them.

No telling how long they had crouched there, above the torn, dead body of Lieutenant Dixon. No telling how long they had waited. It seemed an eternity to Cardigan. His hand about the Remington was aching from its tight grip, and his palm was sticky with sweat against the butt. The woman, beside him, was still having those fits of trembling, her breathing coming out in small, choked spurts. She watched him intently with the fear in her big, dark eyes, and her lips kept forming his name, as if it were the last thing she clung to.

"Cardigan...Cardigan...Cardigan."

He couldn't blame Florida. He was terrified himself. A deep, instinctive, primal fear, that rose from the first fear the first man had felt for the night, and the unknown. He licked his lips, remembering the twisted horror on Navasato's face when they had found him that way.

"Cardigan...Cardigan."

He took a careful breath, trying to blot from his mind the picture of Sheriff Masset's bloody, rended body.

"Cardigan."

He almost shut his eyes to keep from seeing Pinto Parker, lying there, torn, shattered, dead.

"Cardigan."

And still the sound, quietly out there, circling them, stalking them. The rustle of mesquite that might have been the wind, only there was no wind. The faint sibilance of something brushing the curly, red grama. The barely perceptible crunch of prickly pear.

And the tracks, Cardigan. Hadn't Pinto said it? *Just like cat tracks. Only they couldn't have been. Cats don't grow that big in Texas, or anywhere.*

He tried to swallow past the thickening in his throat, and almost choked. He felt his fingers digging into the

94

flesh of Florida's arm, and tried to ease the grip. And still the sounds. A sibilant rattle. *Agrito?* A faint tapping. Mesquite berries knocked from a branch. A scraping whisper. Nopal?

"Cardigan, I don't think I can stand it...."

"Sh"—he put his finger across her wet lips—"it won't do us any good to move. It'll just give us away."

And the tracks, Cardigan. A jaguar, perhaps. Too big. Cats don't grow that big in Texas. Or anywhere. What is it, Africano? What is la onza?

There it was again. Mesquite? Oh, hell! He shifted his position to ease aching muscles. How could you tell if it was mesquite? How could you tell anything? What did it matter? It was out there. That's all that mattered.

La onza *is a hybrid,* señor. *A cross between a bull-tiger and a she-lion. There is nothing more deadly. There is nothing more terrible.*

"Cardigan...."

He squeezed her arm hard enough to make her wince, lifting his gun a little. It seemed to be nearer now. *From the right?* He turned that way slightly, cocking his head. *Or the left?* He began to shift back, and then stopped, the maddening frustration of it sweeping him. He bit his lips to keep from cursing, or standing up, or crying, he didn't know what. He realized he was breathing hoarsely, and tried to stifle it. Tears were running silently down the woman's face. She was biting her lips, too, and blood reddened the tears as they reached her chin.

"Cardigan!"

It came all at once, the crash of brush and that terrible, screaming sound that no cat could ever make and the woman shouting at him, and the bellow of his gun as he whirled and saw the huge, blurred silhouette of it, hurtling down on them. He caught Florida with a sweep of his free arm, knocking her back and aside, and jumped back himself to fire again, not throwing down this time, dropping his thumb on the hammer from where he held the gun at his hip.

He had a kaleidoscopic sense of evil, little eyes gleaming green as they were caught in the moonlight and white fangs in a great, velvety snout, and the blasting heat of stinking breath as the beast let out another of those unearthly screams. Then he was being thrown back by its terrible weight and impetus, all the air exploding from him in an agonized gasp. He had no conscious feeling of shouting again. With those terrible talons ripping at him, he felt the gun explode somewhere down by his hip.

He tried to get to his feet, crying out in pain as a swipe of the huge paw caught his upflung arm, tearing it away from his face. His impression of the animal was still blurred and unreal, and still going backward, he gained his feet, and managed a stumbling step on into the thicket, and jerked the Remington into line again to fire pointblank at the huge, snarling face before him. The screaming sound it made deafened him this time, drowning the report of the gun.

A great suffocation gripped him, and after that, nothing.

XII

IT WAS A VOICE. COMING IN FROM SOMEWHERE, Cardigan knew that, if he knew nothing else. It was a voice.

"It looks like my *onza* has eliminated Marshal Edward Cardigan now, too, my dear, doesn't it?"

"Your *onza*."

That was another voice, trembling, afraid, yet brave, with the kind of courage a man has who will go out to meet what he fears, or a woman.

"Then you're the *nagual*."

There was a laugh coming to Cardigan through succeeding layers of pain, now, that spread over him and spun through his brain. "My dear Florida, surely you don't believe that *nagualismo* rot. I'm no more a *nagual* than Africano was. The only rapport I have with *la onza* is that I've had the animal since it was a cub. It will do my bidding as Africano's dogs did his."

"Don't be fantastic. How can you train a beast like that? Even if it did exist."

"It does exist." The man's voice again. "And I did train it. Isn't that more logical to believe than the fact that I change myself from a man to an animal? They train ordinary cats, don't they? They train tigers to obey the whip. You'd be surprised what those Caribs can teach a jaguar. Why not an *onza*? You should see the beast, Florida. You will. It eats from my hand. Anybody else it will rend to shreds. It took time, of course, and patience. But so does a good horse."

"But why? Are you crazy?...a sadist?"

"No more than is a man who trains his dog to protect him. You'll have to admit it was an admirable expedient. There have been ordinary murders through this stretch of the brush for hundreds of years, but that didn't keep men from running it. You saw what happened with my *onza*. These Mexican *brazaderos* have enough Indian in them to know *nagualismo*. Even white men. Look at Masset. It kept them out of *Cañada Diablo*, didn't it? Every new kill by *la onza* was another brick in the wall of superstitious fear keeping the

97

brazaderos out of *Cañada Diablo*, and we could work here in perfect safety till everything was ready."

A growing acceptance was in the woman's voice. "Did Balacar know?"

"Nobody knew," he answered her. "I kept *la onza* chained in those caves south of Rio Frio. When we first heard Parker and Cardigan were coming through with a bunch of cattle, I let it out, thinking they were just rustlers. Then, after it had killed Navasato, I found that dead mule and the Krag with his body, and thought it meant one of them was Dixon. Africano had stampeded Dixon's mules, and this one must have been caught by the *onza* about the same time it found Navasato."

Cardigan was trying to squirm from beneath the ponderous weight of the animal lying across him now. He was sobbing with the agony in him. He wrested one leg from beneath the great, white-furred belly and rolled from under a bloody paw. The man was still talking from the thicket farther on.

"When Kamaska came, telling us the real Dixon had arrived at the *hacienda*, I told Balacar to go on, and I would take care of Parker and Cardigan. Tío must have sent Innocencio and Kamaska to make sure. He didn't know about the *onza*. If they hadn't bungled it, the *onza* would have had Cardigan there. When I realized Cardigan had escaped, I followed him with the *onza*. I reached you here just about the time he did, didn't I? And now it's just you and me. We can do the same thing Tío wanted. We can have an empire here. We can live like Cortina. Did you ever see his *hacienda*, Florida? Even his peons had silver-mounted saddles. Five hundred Krags and the men to use them and the *brasada*, Florida. Nothing can beat that combination."

"It's already beaten," she sobbed. "One man beat it.
98

Maybe he's dead now, but he beat it. You won't last the night out with that slug Cardigan put through your belly."

"Maybe you'd like me to call the *onza*, Florida."

"The *onza*?" Fear shook her voice.

"It will eat out of my hand," said Garza.

"This one won't eat out of your hand, Garza," said Cardigan.

He must have made a shocking sight, stepping from the thicket. His shirt was torn completely from his torso, claw marks drawing their viscid, red grooves from his collarbone to his belt, his left arm hanging torn and useless by his side, dripping blood off the limp fingers, the flesh ripped in a patch from his forehead.

"Cardigan," gasped the woman, and he had time to see the desperate joy in her face before she had hidden it against his chest, and he didn't mind the pain that caused him, as his one good arm encircled her pliant waist. He looked over his shoulder at the defeat in Garza's face, and he wanted to hate the man, for Pinto, and couldn't because there wasn't that much emotion left in him.

"The guns?" he said gutturally.

"Down by the river," said Florida, her voice muffled against him. "Dixon cached them under a cutbank. We've got to get you to a doctor, Cardigan, we've got to get you to a doctor."

"You come too?"

"Yes, you know I will. You can't make it alone."

"I don't mean...," he began. "Esperanza's dead by now back at your spread. All the others. Half the brush is burnt out by that fire. It will never be the same again."

She lifted her head to look at him, and understanding of what he was asking entered her eyes. What had

99

happened was still too strong within both of them for either to put this in words so soon, yet her answer encompassed all his questions, spoken and unspoken. "You know I will," she repeated.

SUNDOWN TRAIL

From the beginning in his short fiction for magazines Les Savage, Jr. often preferred to set his stories in the period before the Civil War and avoid the 1880s. Even the early Señorita Scorpion stories avoid the 1880s by being set in the 1890s. His first published story, "Blood Star Over Santa Fé" in **Frontier Stories** *(Summer, 43), is set in the period of the Mexican War, and his second, "Murder Stalks the Fur Trails" in* **Dime Western** *(8/43), has as its setting the period of the fur trade. "Sundown Trail," which was Savage's own title for this short novel, like his second published story occurs during the time of the fur trade; but coming later—it was first published as "Wolves of the Sundown Trail" in* **Frontier Stories** *(Spring, 49)—it has the added depth of character and historical background that had become hallmarks of his Western fiction. This short novel has been restored according to the author's typescript and appears now for the first time in book form.*

I

DUNCAN INNES ROSE FROM THE FIRE IN A DELIBERATE, unhurried way, picking up his Yerger rifle, and then he walked twenty feet into the trees. Here, in the black shadows outside the firelight, he dropped soundlessly into the screen of antelope brush, and began loading his gun. He could not tell if he had actually heard a sound outside of the fire—after so many years in the wilderness, a man's sensitivities reached a more impalpable plane than that—he only knew that sense of a foreign presence had been brought to him.

His narrow, long face had the sharp, cutting thrust of a tomahawk, turning back and forth, first toward the Tetons, towering in bleak, lithic omniscience to the west of Jackson Hole, then in the direction of the Snake, where it flowed out of Jackson Lake. It had taken him two days to reach this camp from the place the mountain men knew as Colter's Hell, and some heretics insisted on calling Yellowstone. His elkhides were pliable with wear and grease and dirt against his long, loose-jointed body. He was perfectly relaxed, though alert, holding the latent force of a watching cat. Finally there was the rustle of brush under the purple foliage of alders across the open space.

"Trapper?" called someone from over there. It held the hoarse, grunting bestiality of a bear. "I come peaceful. You out there somewhere?"

If you come peaceful, thought Innes, *why are you hiding?* After another long pause, the man must have realized his obligation. A shadow at first, a bulky, square-set shadow that moved like a bear, he shuffled forward on padded feet until light fell across his blackjack boots, his corduroy trousers, dark with grease, his coat made from the pelt of a cinnamon bear.

"Hell," he said, "you're as suspicious as a coyote. I'm John Ryker, and I come peaceful as a baby."

"Then tell your friends to show themselves," said Innes.

Ryker could not hide his mouth, parted in surprise. He clamped it shut, as if trying to mask the reaction. Then he chuckled throatily. "You got ears like some animal. Come on in, Wisapa."

The porcupine roach on the Indian's head and the black and white skunk fur, ornamenting his neck, marked him as a Dakota. A buffalo robe, worked with red and yellow quills, swirled around copper calves as he walked in and stood beside Ryker, leading a pair of saddle horses—one a buckskin, one a pinto—as well as a pack horse. His face was made up of bold, brutal planes, the flesh so swart it seemed almost Negroid. Innes waited another space, listening, sniffing, turning his narrow head from side to side. Finally he rose and moved into the clearing, keeping his Yerger on them.

"What's your business?" he said.

"No special business," said Ryker irritably. "Damn it, can't a man be sociable? I been up in the Wind Rivers all winter without seeing a white man. I heard there was a Scotchman trapping down this way. I come fifty miles just to smoke a pipe. Mountain men are usually a wary lot, but I never seen one suspicious as you."

"Maybe you're the one who should be suspicious," said the trapper. "You're John Ryker? I'm Duncan Innes."

Ryker's heavy beard was almost as cinnamon as his bearskin coat, but it did not quite cover the subtle alteration about his mouth. "Oh." He emitted the word in attenuated understanding. "Yes, I heard of you over in the Owl Creeks. The original hard-luck kid. I even saw the body of your last partner. Something like that's supposed to happen to everybody connected with you. Is that the story? If lightning don't strike them, they get smothered in a snowslide." The hearty, throaty chuckle bubbled out of him again. "Well," he said patronizingly, "suppose I ain't superstitious?"

Innes shrugged. "Suit yourself. I've tried warning people all my life. I'm tired of it. I killed a buffalo yesterday. I've got some *doupille* left if you want some of that."

103

"That's better," grinned Ryker. "We'll supply the potables. Wisapa, get that Monangahela from our possibles."

The Indian fumbled through the Mexican *aparejos* they were using for pack saddles, bringing forth a couple of the flat, wooden kegs of whiskey the traders brought up from St. Louis every year.

Innes squatted down, beginning to spit the backfat. Shifting firelight seemed constantly to change the gaunt, dour planes of his face. His long, thin lips were clamped tight as a jump trap. Sandy hair fell to his shoulders, filled with dark streaks from wiping greasy fingers in it for years. Ryker threw aside his bearskin to hunker down by the fire, warming his belly. He wore a red, wool shirt underneath, and Innes caught the glint of firelight on the brass butt cap of an immense Ketland-McCormick, thrust naked through the man's belt. Something sly in the man's glittering, little eyes kept Innes taut, close to his rifle.

When Ryker passed the Monangahela, Innes meant only to wet his tongue with it. But the only liquor he'd had for years was the acrid Indian *tiswin*, and he could not help drawing deep once he had the keg to his lips.

"There's supposed to be more than just that bad luck of yours," said Ryker. "A curse on your clan or something. I never did get the gist of it."

Innes found his painful reticence thawed by the fiery fumes of the Monangahela. "The Innes clan goes 'way back. I'm the namesake of Sir Duncan Innes, who fought beside The Bruce, back in Scotland. Alister Mor was one of those who opposed Bruce. In Twelve Eighty-Four, Bruce captured him and shut him up in Dundonald Castle on the Clyde. Sir Duncan Innes was put to guarding him. Alister pleaded with Sir Duncan to

104

release him before he died of fever he'd contracted in the battle, but Duncan refused. On his death bed, Alister pronounced a curse on Duncan, promising nothing but tragedy and death to any by the name of Innes, or any who should have association with them, until the clan Innes was exterminated...."

He stopped, realizing the release he had allowed himself, and the firelight seemed to change his eyes from a deep-pooled blue to a sudden opacity that glittered like the reflection of sun on ice. Ryker grinned, handing him the whiskey again.

"Now, don't start getting touchy just because you've opened up to a stranger. A man needs to talk once in a while. That's probably your trouble. Surely there's no harm in telling someone his tales."

Innes shrugged, taking the keg. *What was the difference? The man was right.* He lifted the whiskey for a toast.

"Thumping luck and fat weans," he said, and choked on the burning liquid.

Ryker sent Wisapa an oblique glance. "So the curse came true?"

Innes nodded. "A bitter feud naturally arose between the Inneses and the MacAlisters," he explained. "Sir Duncan's son was killed on his wedding night by a group of MacAlisters. Sir Duncan's wife was carried off by a Viking sea raider. They both drowned in the North Sea. Sir Duncan's daughter had an idiot for her first baby. I could keep going on all night. Five hundred years of it, and not one Innes has escaped. After the Disarming Act in Scotland, a lot of Inneses and MacAlisters sailed to America, along with thousands of others. My grandfather settled in Virginia. A Tory named George MacAlister led a bunch of Hessians to my grandfather's plantation, and they burned it to the ground. Grandfather killed George with this very Yerger I'm carrying, and had to flee to Kentucky to escape his kinsmen. My father was born there and grew up to be a drunkard. He murdered my mother in a fit when I was sixteen. Grandfather killed him for it and in turn was hanged for murder."

"Lord," said Ryker, huskily. "That's quite a story."

"You don't believe it?"

"I didn't say that," snorted Ryker. "Won't you let me express a little amazement? I've lived among the Indians too long to doubt anything like that. You'd be surprised at the crazy things I've seen. I'm as superstitious as they are, I guess."

"You speak awfully smooth for having been out here that long," said Innes, squinting at him suspiciously.

Ryker shrugged. "I come from college people. I'm not ashamed of my education. I even got Wisapa talking English as good as that of most white men on the frontier." He paused, studying Innes. "If that feud is still on, you'd better not go around Hoback Cañon. A man named Roderick MacAlister runs a trading post there."

"I heard of him," said Innes. "The son of George MacAlister was hunting my family in Kentucky. That's why I headed West after Grandpa was hanged. I can't see any sense in going on with this feud. I don't know whether Roderick MacAlister followed me or just drifted out this way. More than one of them did that. There's another MacAlister working for H. B. C. over on the Missouri."

"Suppose you found a man willing to be your partner, Innes?"

"He'd be a fool," said Innes. "If you saw the body of my last partner, it must have been in a tree. I left him

106

with the Shoshones, and that's the way they bury their own. His name was John Donn, and he was drowned in the spring breakup on the Wind. Another man threw in with me last summer, and the Crows got his scalp two weeks later. It happens to anybody connected with me."

"Knowing all that, suppose a man still wanted to throw in?" said Ryker. "Those Shoshones in the Wind Rivers told me you'd been there, too, hunting for Lost River."

"Wasn't me," said Innes.

"Don't be like that," said Ryker. "They even told me that toast you made when you drank their *tiswin*...thumping luck and fat weans. A big Scotchman with a piece of parchment, hunting for Lost River."

"I told you it wasn't me," said Innes. "I haven't seen the Big Horns since 'Thirty-One."

Ryker leaned forward, his voice taking on a sarcasm. "Surely you've heard the Lost River story."

"Something about a Franciscan priest in the Seventeen Hundreds, wasn't it?" suggested Innes.

Ryker's voice thickened with that sarcasm. "Fra Escobar. Seventeen Fifty. He was an expert cartographer and kept an extensive journal on all his trips. These journals are preserved in documents of the Roman Catholic Church in Madrid and Mexico City. There's a legend that he got as far north as Colter's Hell, but historians don't hold with it, because there's no journals or maps to prove it. On all his travels, a Negro servant named Juanito accompanied him."

Innes could not help but glance at the dark Indian. The man nodded. His voice startled Innes, and the fluency of his English.

"Wisapa means Black Son in the language of the Dakotas. It is a story of my tribe that a white medicine man came into the Powder River country with a black servant many generations ago. When he left, an unmarried squaw had a child who was almost black. This child was my great grandfather."

Ryker pulled a small, leather-bound book from his coat, handing it to Innes. The paper was brittle, yellow parchment, with faded, partly obliterated writing in old Spanish upon it.

"Black blood wasn't the only thing Escobar and his servant left with the Dakotas," said Ryker. "He must have lost his journal there, too. It was one of Wisapa's fetishes, when I first met him, handed down through his family as good medicine. Turn to page fifty-three, about the tenth line, Rio Perdido. It's under the date of March tenth. Escobar says he's come upon the headwaters of a sizable river that was unknown even to the Indian guides, in a valley so close to being inaccessible that he stumbled into it by the merest chance. In one hour, sitting at breakfast, he counted ninety-eight *castores*...that's beaver, in Spanish...at a single pool alone."

Staring at the faded book, Innes could not deny the tug of excitement such a bizarre tale brought. "That's a dream. There aren't that many beavers left in all the mountains west of the Missouri. It's getting trapped out, Ryker, and you know it."

"But this river hasn't been found," said Ryker. "Trappers have been hunting it for years. With Wisapa's help, I've tried to find it. But the landmarks Escobar mentions aren't clear enough. The Indians had different names than he gave them, and a lot of them have probably changed since then anyway. Escobar drew maps for every other trip he made. He must have drawn one for this. Ninety-eight beaver in one hour at one spot,

108

Innes. Think how that place must be crawling with plews. A man could get rich in one season."

"If you're still thinking of me," said Innes, "I told you I don't have any map."

Ryker's thick, hairy neck grew red, but he kept his voice low. "You'll never get it with that map alone, Innes. Together, we could find it."

"I told you. I don't have any map, damn it."

"Yes, you do. Give it to me."

Innes did not realize how much the whiskey had affected him until he tried to focus his eyes on what Ryker held in his hand. An iron pan resolved itself. A flat lock plate. A goose-necked hammer. A Ketland-McCormick.

"I tried to do it the friendly way, you'll have to admit that," said Ryker. He jerked the pistol. "Search him, Black Son."

The Indian threw off the robe, revealing the fancy buckskin covering his body, and rose softly to move toward Innes. Innes made a forward shift, as if to rise, but a wave of that pistol held him. Its threat was clearing his head some now. He could hear his own breathing. *Damn fool, to trust anyone even a minute.* The Indian stooped to pull off his slipover elkhide shirt. Innes reached up and grasped a wrist, lunging to one side with the grip. Innes heard the click of that goose-necked hammer, cocking under Ryker's thumb, but the shot would have hit Wisapa.

Innes tried to throw himself with the falling Indian, keeping the man between himself and Ryker, but Wisapa twisted in his plunge, and Ryker was leaping to his feet, reversing the pistol. Innes whirled toward him, trying to rise. Wisapa's hand hooked in his elbow, pulling him off-balance. Ryker slugged with the clubbed

109

gun.

It struck Innes in the face, and he fell backward with pain blotting out all perception. He felt the blow of the gun once more and knew he was lying on his back because there was pressure there. He heard Ryker snarl something, and felt hands pawing over his body. His moccasins were ripped off, his shirt, his pants.

"It's not on him," said Ryker. "Look in the pack saddle."

Stunned by the blows, Innes knew he could not hope to fight them. If they had gone this far for the thing, wouldn't they just as soon kill him? He had been a fool once tonight. No use laying himself open again by stupid heroics. Ryker had picked up his rifle in one hand and stuffed the pistol back in his belt. They were both going through his pack saddles now. Innes's feet were near enough to the fire. Summoning all his concentration in a supreme effort to overcome the daze of pain, he squirmed till his feet were right in the fire, and then swept them toward the horses. A shower of blazing sparks and popping sounds flew at the animals. They reared, screaming wildly. The Indian pinto charged right into the men bent over the pack saddles. Innes stumbled to his feet, plunging for the trees. He heard Ryker shout something from behind. He was in darkness when the shot came. The lead slug rattled through the purple flowers in the alders above his head.

He was dizzy and weak, and he reeled through chokeberry, ripping his bare legs, crashed into a cottonwood, gagged in the resinous scent of poplar. Somewhere ahead he could hear the rush of the river. He was going downslope. He could hear them behind, gaining on him. He fell in dark, loamy earth, rose to run again, swaying, stumbling, trying to shake the pain and giddiness from his head. There was a flash of white water in the darkness ahead. His feet sank in saffron sand. He knew he could not run much farther.

Spring floods were carrying all kinds of débris down the swollen river. Buckbrush floated past, soggy and matted. An uprooted aspen, still bearing clouds of yellow foliage, came into his vision. He waded out and caught at it.

Swirling water pulled him down. The sucking force of the tree caught his arms. He sank down into the sweet-smelling leaves, gasping painfully, and felt the tree gather speed. Deep water clutched at it, and for a moment he thought it would roll him off. But the foliage gave the trunk the stability of outriggers, and he was still solidly aboard as he passed out, that one last thought forming dimly in his mind, before all thought fled: *Thumping luck and fat weans, hell!*

II

THE YOUNG WOMAN HAD IMMENSE, DARK EYES, AND the whitest skin Duncan Innes had ever seen. Her hair was blue-black as a Hawken barrel, caught up in laughing, tufted, windblown curls all over her head, making a wild, dancing frame for her strange, little, elfin face. Her mouth kept curling up at one corner in a smile, half compassionate, half mocking, as she bent over him. He tried to rise, but she pushed him back down.

"You'd better lie still for a while," she said. "I'm Nairn. My billie found you floating by our house on a tree yesterday afternoon. You're pretty sick."

"Your billie?" he muttered.

"My brother," she laughed. It was like tinkling glass. "Brahan."

111

"Nairn? Brahan?" Innes did not speak the names very loudly, because something was beginning to work in his consciousness, something dark with foreboding. He tried to find its logic. It was the Snake he had thrown himself into. Could he have been carried as far south as Hoback Cañon by that tree? Something inside him started crawling.

"I'm Brahan," smiled a curly, black-haired, young giant beside Nairn. "And this is Elgin, my older brother. And Roderick, my father."

"Roderick MacAlister?" asked Innes, in a cold, dead voice.

Brahan's father must have been in his middle fifties. He was the biggest man in the room. Both Brahan and Elgin were over six feet, but Roderick topped them by the full length of his massive head. The deep, weathered lines of his open face were as stone-like, as uncompromising as the granite crags of the Tetons. His eyes were so blue they looked black, and he wore his mane of white hair down to his shoulders. His laughter at Innes's question shook the room.

"Aye, Lalland, how did ye ken a bouk like me was a Vic-Ian-Dhu?"

"You'll have to forgive father," chuckled Nairn. "He's been here forty years, but he still talks like he came right out of Loch Shin. He called you a Lowlander, and he asked how a man like you knew he was...."

"I understood him," said Innes thinly. He was staring at the tartan Roderick wore, the hated colors of the MacAlisters. He could hear his grandfather cursing its red and green sett now; he could hear the Gaelic invective heaped upon its coat of arms by his father in a drunken rage.

"What's your name, trapper?" asked Elgin.

Innes got up before speaking, because he knew what would come when he told them, and something in his face kept Nairn from trying to push him back down. He saw that they were in a bunk room at the rear of a log building, its walls hung with the stuffed heads of bears, a huge moose thrusting its mossy antlers from the rear, the puncheon floor covered with bearskins and buffalo robes. He himself was draped in a red Hudson's Bay four point, warm and woolly against his bare hide. A silence had fallen in the room as they watched him. For a moment he thought of giving them a false name. The negation of that went through him so violently he shook his head with it. Despite the resignation the tragedies of his life had molded into him, some fierce pride of those ancient Celtic Highlanders still flamed within him.

"I'm Duncan Innes," he said.

There was a moment when all the sound in the world seemed to have stopped. Even his own breathing. He could see the diffused blood sweep into Roderick's face until the flesh looked crimson. A great pulse started a tom-tom beat across the man's temple. Innes grew taut, waiting for that roar of ancient Celtic rage to fill the room. It did not come. Roderick turned without a word and moved toward the door.

"Father," said Nairn. "Where are you going?"

"To git my claymore." Roderick could hardly force the words from his mouth. "An Innes should be killed with nothing else."

"No, Father...." The young woman jumped after him, catching an arm. "You wouldn't...you can't...he's sick. Can't you see, a MacAlister would have more honor than that!"

"I have my honor." The shout was coming now, as

113

deafening as the ice breaking up on Ben Nevis. "I won't allow an Innes in my house."

"No, Father…."

"Aye, aye," bellowed the man, swinging her off his arm so that she fell against the wall. "I'm ard-righ here. I'm high-chief. Do ye question my dictates?"

"Nairn's right, Dad," called Brahan, going after him. "You can't do it to a sick man. Can't you forget this feud? We're in a new country now. We have no right to carry it on. This Innes never did us any harm."

"His grandfather killed my father in Virginia," bellowed the man. "My own father died hunting them down. I'll do the same before I let one stinkin', crawlin' ferlie of them remain alive."

He was in the other room now, the stamp of his feet shaking the floor, and Nairn and Brahan had followed him out. Innes could hear them pleading with the old man. He stood shakily, holding the blanket up about him, gripping the pine bunk post with the other hand, searching the room for some weapon. Elgin MacAlister stood near the rear wall, watching him closely.

He was a man about thirty, taller than Innes, with some of his father's massive size in his great neck, like a brazed tree trunk set on his shoulders, and the immense body structure of his thick-hewed wrists and great knobby hands. But the ceaseless animal movement of woods running or trapping seemed to have melted off all superfluous weight, until his frame bore the gaunt, drawn refinement of a timber wolf. His face, too, did not bear the full stamp of Roderick's stubborn, unbending integrity. It was more narrow through the jaw and brow, something almost sardonic in the tilt of his black brows.

"Never mind looking for a weapon," he said. "Nairn will argue him out of it. She's the only one who can

114

handle Dad. It's unfortunate, in a way. I think you should be killed."

Innes looked sharply at him. "Isn't that unreasonable? Just because I'm an Innes? I never saw you before. I never did you any personal harm, and you never did me any, and, if we met under other circumstances, there would be no cause for a quarrel."

"But these aren't other circumstances," said Elgin. "To a true Scot, the honor of his clan is as precious to him as his own name. It doesn't matter that Sir Duncan Innes killed Alister Mor over five hundred years ago. I could feel no more cause for vengeance if it had been you killing my brother yesterday. If you don't see it that way, you aren't worthy of being called a Scotsman."

"Oh, now, Elgin," pouted Nairn, coming into the room with a tray of food. "Here we've just got Father quieted and you start. Can't we have peace? I've brought Innes some food. Let's toast to a new day in the history of our clans, a day of friendship and good will. Here's health to the sick, stilts to the lame, claise to the back, and brose to the wame."

The brose was potage made by pouring boiling water over oatmeal that was stirred while the water was poured, and the wame was the belly that Innes soon filled. With the oatmeal were square cakes Innes had heard his grandfather call bannocks, and a broth Nairn said was broo. Brahan came into the room while Innes was eating. He bore the candid, open honesty of his father in his red-cheeked face, with none of the older man's stubbornness. Like a big, clumsy puppy in his movements, he seated himself casually on the floor beside the bunk.

"Father's cooled off now, I guess," he said. "Tell us how you happened to be floating down the Snake in

115

such a naked state with big weals on the back of your head, Innes. Did somebody rob you?"

"Just as well," said Innes somberly. "A man named Ryker was trying to get a map from me that I never had. He said a Scotsman had been up in the Big Horns with an old Spanish map, hunting for Lost River."

Brahan looked in a surprised way at his sister. Then he reached inside his red wool shirt to pull forth a roll of buckskin. When he had opened it, there was a dirty, faded piece of parchment.

"That was me, last spring," he said. "I saved the life of a Franciscan father down near Santa Fé two years ago. He gave me this. I told him I didn't want pay for such an act, but he forced it on me. Said it had been in the possession of the chapel at Chimayo for a hundred years. It would do a fur man more good than a priest. Dad didn't take any stock in it. But I was trapping north last spring, and I turned aside for a couple of months."

"Did you find Lost River?" asked Innes.

"No," frowned Brahan. "But I found plenty of evidence and stories among the Indians up there to prove this isn't too far off the track."

"And you're a damned fool for showing anything like that to an Innes," said Elgin. They all turned to him, and an empty, uncomfortable silence filled the room. "What's the matter," he asked mockingly. "Am I not even welcome among my own kin? Time was when an Innes would never have crossed our threshold. Now, one comes in and takes my place!"

"Oh, don't be bleth'rin' like that, Elgin," sighed Nairn. "Can't we treat him like a human being? Can't you forget all that?"

"No," said Elgin, looking at Innes. "Never."

III

THE DAYS PASSED TOO SWIFTLY FOR INNES AFTER that. Because of Nairn. She brought him all his meals and sat often late into the evening, talking with him, sometimes in the buckskin skirt of the trading post, sometimes dressing up for him in the plaid and arisaid of her clan. She took up one of Brahan's shirts for him, and found a pair of elkhide leggin's with all the fringe cut off by some trapper for whangs. She talked brightly the first day or two, keeping him amused with her news of the early spring rendezvous on the Green that Brahan and Elgin had attended, with light chatter about her own history, her childhood, her trip West with her father, the founding of the Hoback Post.

But he sensed a definite attempt to keep it impersonal, a maternal desire, perhaps, to shield him from anything somber or depressing during his convalescence. It was ironic, in a way, for that would indicate that she felt any discussion of his own past could be nothing but somber. Finally, however, on the third evening, she could not control her natural curiosity. She sat beside his bunk in the silence that had fallen, and he could feel her eyes on him. He lay on top of the blankets, arms behind his head, listening idly to the sounds Roderick made in the front room.

"You're a strange, morose sort of man," she observed then. "More like the old Highlanders than most third-generation Scots. Yet you don't even speak like a Scotsman. What makes you this way?"

"Maybe I'm naturally that way," he murmured.

"I can't believe it," she said. "Not to such a degree. Only an animal that has been hunted and hounded and cheated and hurt all its life is suspicious and secretive.

117

You remind me of that, a lot. Is it the curse? Has it followed you that closely?"

He looked darkly at her. "Most men would ridicule it."

"I'm a Scot, Innes," she said. "And a MacAlister. I've heard it all my life. I've seen it work. My father showed me the ruins of your grandfather's plantation when we were passing through Virginia. I was ten when we heard a man named Innes had murdered his wife in a drunken rage in Kentucky. I was with Father when he traveled there, seeking your people out of vengeance for George MacAlister."

She caught at his arm, bending toward him. "It can't go on like that forever, Duncan. It's got to stop somewhere. Maybe this is the place. The first time an Innes has been in the house of a MacAlister for over five hundred years. You don't know how hard it was to win Father over. I didn't realize I had that much influence on him. But it's happening, Innes. Let me help you."

He turned part way on his side to find that she had bent toward him so closely that his own movement brought their faces to within an inch of each other. The smell of her was too much like heather, the look of her too beautiful. He realized how long it was since he had been this close to a woman. A man got lonely, and the craving took on an intensity that was painful sometimes. A tremor ran through his body, and he found it hard to get the word out.

"Why...Nairn?"

"Why?" She shook her head from side to side, lips parted with the word, as if trying to find the answer herself. Her breath warmed his face, full of a faint, seductive scent. Almost as if it were not his own

118

volition, his arm went about her, and he rolled over until the upper part of his body was against her, his legs slipping off on the floor to give him leverage, bending her backward in a kiss. She took it with no resistance, a growing eagerness in the way her lips ripened against his. When he finally took his mouth away, they were both breathing heavily. She stared up into his eyes for a long time, without speaking. Finally it came in a husky murmur.

"Now, do you have to have a reason why I should want to help you, Innes?"

He turned violently toward the wall. "Go away, Nairn. Before it's too late. Nobody's ever been associated with me who didn't suffer for it. I couldn't do that to you."

"Maybe it's already too late, Innes."

"It can't be," he said viciously. "Forget what happened. It could happen to any man and woman. Just a kiss."

"It's more than that to me, Innes. The kiss is just a proof of it."

"No," he said, in a tortured, almost incoherent way. "Not with me. I've kissed a lot of women. Never meant anything." He turned his head away.

"Then why does it bother you so?" she said.

"It doesn't," he said. He wouldn't face her. "Go away, will you, Nairn. Leave me alone. Please."

She left him, then, there in the darkened room, and it was the first time he had ever wanted to cry since he was a child. He had never craved anything so badly— and had never seen so little hope of attaining it.

He tried to avoid her next morning by getting outside. But she found him down by the creek. The wide, frank depth of her eyes on him was a challenge. He tried to avoid it, skipping rocks, hunting for beaver sign, pointing out the tracks of a pronghorn to her. But all the time, her eyes were on him that way, and he could read the feeling in her easily enough, because the same thing was in him. The men felt it that night at supper, and it was a strained half hour, with Roderick leaving the table in a surly mood. Innes retired early to escape her, but could not sleep. The next morning he told her he had to leave.

"Why?" she said in a small, hollow voice.

"If I stay much longer, I won't be able to leave. I couldn't do that to you."

"You're talking about your feelings for me now."

Her voice was stronger.

"No...."

"Yes. Why don't you say it out loud, then, instead of beating around the bush? I'll say it, if you won't, Innes. I love you."

The shock of it stopped him for a moment, and then his voice left him in a guttural, strangled sob. "No, Nairn, you can't let yourself...."

"I can't help myself."

"It's just being around so close to me. A stranger. Something new. You don't get many men here. Just your brothers. When I'm gone, you'll see."

"I should be insulted," she said. "You don't know how many men have courted me, Innes. One came three hundred miles. I've known enough men. I never felt anything for the others. I do love you. I told you. Do you love me?"

The quiet, candid depth of her gaze went clear down to the bottom of him, and he thrust his head from side to side in a tortured way. "No, Nairn, I can't let myself...."

"It's time you stopped running from that curse," she

120

said. "You've been running from it all your life. You ran from Kentucky when your mother was killed. You haven't stopped anywhere along the way to fight it."

"But I have. I have, you don't know how many times...."

"Then stop again. We're already fighting it, Innes. You're living in the house of a MacAlister."

"With Elgin waiting to kill me and your father hoping for one false move?" he said bitterly.

"Are you afraid of them?"

"No," he muttered.

"Are you afraid of me?"

"No."

"Do you love me?"

He stared at her, the contortion of his face twisting all its flat, hard planes out of shape. He couldn't tell her. He couldn't suck her in like that, draw her down, lay her open to what so many others had suffered. The conditioning of a lifetime blocked him off from it. He drew in a warped, rended breath. Then, slowly, he forced a grin onto his face, emitted a harsh, cynical chuckle.

"Don't be a *fule*, kid," he said, mocking her with the Scottish word. "Sure I'm thinking of the curse. I'm trouble, and you can't get out of it. But not because I love you. I'm fond of you. I'm grateful to you for what you've done. And for that very reason I'm leaving. I'd do the same for a dog. I'd kick him away from my campfire for fear a bolt of lightning would strike him there or a MacAlister would shoot him for being with me." He saw the stricken look fill her eyes and squint them, as if with the shock of pain. He turned swiftly away, unable to bear it, and walked swiftly to the door. The front chamber comprised the store of the trading

121

post, with a long plank set on barrels sufficing for the counter. It was filled with scents of acrid, black powder and sour leather and stored pelt. Roderick was standing behind this plank, and he must have heard them, for he put his two massive hands on the board, and it groaned as he leaned his weight forward onto them.

"So you're leaving," he said. "Good riddance to the devil, I say. You're going that way, with not another thing from me."

"Dad," said Brahan, from the doorway, "at least give him a coat and some food."

"Shut your trap, you crawlin' ferlie!" shouted Roderick. He beat one hand on the plank, causing it to clap sharply against the barrels at either end. "I'd rather he left feet first, but I gi'e me word to Nairn. Just remember that, ye ree, chuffle-mouthed brak of an Innes. Gin ye leave that door, the promise is over. Gin ye ever show up again, I'll take me claymore to ye!"

"Guid swats," murmured Elgin. He sat in a dark corner, peeling an apple, and Innes had the feel of the man's sardonic eyes on him all the way out. Brahan followed, slipping out of his heavy coat of Scottish plaid.

"Here. It's spring, but you'll need it. I've got a rifle and some shot if you'll wait a minute."

Innes started to protest, but the young man was already in his clumsy, puppyish run toward an outbuilding where he slept, returning with an old Jake Hawken and a shot pouch and buffalo horn.

"I'll pay you back somehow," Innes told him gratefully.

"Don't insult me," said Brahan, laughing, clapping him on the back. "We're brother Scots, aren't we?"

That warmed Innes unaccountably, and he felt

122

himself turn his face away in a paradoxical, typically masculine gesture of embarrassment in the face of sentiment. *How strange a man got when he stayed away from his fellows*, thought Innes. Here, the most he wanted to do was thank Brahan, and yet he could find no words to do it with; he could only find an embarrassment so deep it blocked up his throat. Brahan put a hand on his shoulder and told Innes he would accompany him to the mouth of the cañon.

They set out toward the trail along the river bottom. Before plunging into the thick willows, Innes glanced back once. Nairn stood in the doorway. Her face looked small at this distance, doll-like, a cameo of lost, hopeless pain that twisted his insides till he thought it was a cramp.

Spring was ripe in the land now. Scarlet cones covered the upper tips of the spruce, and they stood like flaming pyres against the darker green of pine and fir. The aspen crowded the sandy banks of the Hoback River with fluttering jade, and the red-blossomed balsam poplar filled the air with its honeyed scent. The rusty coat and double-prong antlers of a muledeer flashed through the willows, and great, soft eyes peered at the two men for a moment. Finally they reached the columnar ochre cliffs forming the cañon mouth.

"You want to keep an eye out for Ryker," Brahan told Innes. "I was down to Bridger's Fort while you were sick. He was there with that Dakota of his. I even had a few words with him."

"You didn't have a fight?"

"No," said Brahan. "But I told him he picked the wrong Scotsman when he thought you had the map. The next time he wants a look at it, he'd better hunt up the MacAlisters."

"You fool!" said Innes. Then he quieted, staring narrow-eyed at the man. Finally he brought himself to speak. "You did that…for me?"

Innes saw the same embarrassment in the young man he had felt earlier. Brahan shrugged, grinning self-consciously. "You won't be bothered any more."

"But you...," said Innes, "you've laid yourself wide open. He might try it again."

"We have a saying in our house," Brahan told him. "It's ill getting the breeks of a Highlandman. In this case, Ryker will have to get the britches off three Highlandmen. Dad and Elgin and I may have differed over what to do with you, but when it comes to a fight, we stand as true as a Lock Liel oak."

Innes started to say something, broke off. Brahan must have sensed his inhibition. The youth thrust out a hand, and Innes took it gratefully, feeling in the firm, strong grip all he could not express vocally, knowing Brahan understood, now.

Without speaking again, he turned and made his way over the pale buffalo grass to the sparkling confluence of the Hoback and the Snake. He ducked into timber, hunting a ford, and was deep down an avenue of spruce when he heard the sharp report. He halted, thinking it might have been ice breaking up on the heights. But that did not suffice, somehow. In a dark, Celtic premonition, he turned back. He was running when he reached the edge of timber, turning up a slope that brought him out on a bluff above the spot where he and Brahan had halted.

The men must have been a quarter mile up the cañon. Two of them were dragging Brahan's body from an open glade into timber. A cinnamon bearskin caught the sunlight in ruddy tints. There was no thought in Innes's

124

mind at that moment. He was flooded with a terrible, blinding anger that clogged up his throat with hot blood and started the pulses across his temples to pounding like drums. He threw himself down the bluff, sliding through shale and chocolate earth, landing heavily on the slope below. Then he began to run, loading his rifle as he went, in a thoughtless, mechanical way. He was sucking in great, painful breaths from the long, punishing, uphill sprint when Ryker's head turned. They had dragged Brahan within a few feet of the willows. Ryker dropped the slack body and wheeled. Apparently he had not stopped to reload after shooting Brahan, for he plunged into the trees without trying to fire.

Innes took a snap shot at the disappearing bearskin coat. Wisapa followed Ryker, and the two of them were gone. No woodsman in his right sense would have run after them, crashing through the underbrush like that, but the rage was still so roaring in Innes that he had no caution. He ran for a hundred yards without even trying to cut sign and found himself at the river. Then, gasping painfully for air, vision swimming with exhaustion, he realized he had about played out his string.

They were nowhere in sight. He backtracked, trying to pick up their sign, but his own passage had obliterated whatever tracks they had left. It would have taken him an hour to unravel their sign from his for any distance. He finally went back to Brahan, sobbing with the terrible frustration of his defeat, hands working on the rifle with an awesome rage filling him.

The youth had been shot through the back, and was dead. His shirt and pants had been searched, and Innes knew why. A few feet into the open, he saw the large sheet of tanned buckskin Brahan had wrapped the map in. Then the steady plod of running feet entered his

125

consciousness, driving him upright. Elgin and Roderick appeared on the river trail, coming at a steady dogtrot that any woodsman worthy of the name could keep at for hours. Innes's figure, rising up beyond the band of willows, must have caught Elgin's eye, for he turned, and then plunged toward Innes. He halted when he was near enough to see Brahan on the ground. Roderick came up, staring at his son.

Then, in ominous silence, the two men began moving forward again. The red fireweed swished at Elgin's buckskin leggin's. The blue asters whispered around Roderick's laced boots. The river made little chuckling murmurs in the distance. Innes watched them in a strange, petrified tension, unwilling to think, a horror growing in his eyes as he saw what lay in Roderick's face. Elgin knelt beside Brahan, feeling for his heart through the bloody shirt.

"Dead," said Elgin in an empty tone. He turned to look up at Innes, a curious lack of emotion in his voice. "We heard the shot from the post. I told him he was a fool to show you that map."

Roderick made a small, animal sound in his throat, and started walking toward Innes. "My son," he said. "Ye killed my son, Innes. I might hae kenned it. An Innes. And I took ye in, Innes."

He kept saying the name over and over again, as if it were a curse, something blasphemous. His great, knobby hands lifted in front of him. Innes stepped back, raising the gun with an instinctive, defensive gesture.

"No, MacAlister," he said. "No. It was Ryker."

"Who's Ryker?" said Elgin, rising from the body.

"Stop, MacAlister," shouted Innes. "Let me explain."

"Ye'll do yure explainin' to the de'il," roared Roderick, and jumped at him.

126

In that last instant, Innes realized he had been too deep in his anger even to reload the gun after that first shot. He did not think he could have fired anyway. One of Roderick's fists knotted up and lifted for a blow. Stumbling backward, Innes brought the Jake Hawken across in front of him to block it. The man's fist hit the rifle where the iron barrel joined the stock. There was the sharp splinter of wood, and the gun broke into two pieces, and that fist came right on through to smash into Innes's chest.

Innes heard the hoarse, agonized exhalation he emitted. The pain seemed to fill his whole being in that instant. He had a sense of his whole body crumpling up. But instinct was still jolting him, and with the conditioning of countless other battles like this he rolled his body to one side and hit, going over and over on the ground, away from Roderick.

He had a dim vision of Elgin, stooping to grasp the barrel half of the rifle and lunging after him with the deadly iron pipe raised as a club.

Coughing in a deep, sick way from the pain of that blow in the chest, Innes made a feeble attempt at rising to his knees. Roderick was coming at him again, and would reach him before Elgin. With that flashing glimpse of their two faces, Innes got an instantaneous impression of the crazed, insane light filling Roderick's eyes, and the cold, calculating lack of emotion in Elgin's.

Then he had twisted around, not yet fully risen, to dodge Roderick's next blow and lunge in under it against the man's legs. The length of his torso thrown against the man's knees upset Roderick, and he fell across Innes. As the giant Highlander went down, one of his great, clawing hands caught Innes's arm, pulling

Innes back down off his knees onto the ground.

With both of them wallowing across the buffalo grass, Innes saw Elgin leaping around to put himself in position for a blow. In a terrible, feeble desperation, Innes caught at Roderick's arm, hooking in under the elbow and pulling the man's great body across him. Roderick came willingly, clawing for a grip with his free hand, gasping Gaelic curses. Elgin could not abort his blow soon enough, and the length of the barrel struck Roderick across the thick muscles of his upper back. His sick grunt of agony beat hot and fetid breath across Innes's face. His massive body sagged heavily against Innes.

Innes caught the rifle barrel before Elgin could lift it again. Elgin tried to pull it free, and Innes used the opposing force of that to pull himself from beneath Roderick's great, stunned body. Roderick pawed feebly at him. Innes kicked the man's hand free. He felt the rifle barrel slipping out of his hands, with Elgin's savage jerk, and let go completely.

Taken off-guard, Elgin stumbled backward, trying to regain his balance. Innes threw himself at the man, butting him in the stomach. Elgin gasped and went down. Innes went with him, straddling him, beating at that dark, sardonic, mocking face with all the strength left in him.

He heard Roderick's groaning behind him, and knew he was trying to rise. Then he heard Nairn's voice from the river, and turned to see her stumbling up the trail. She must have been left behind, unable to keep up with her father and brother in that dogged run, for she was gasping, her face flushed with the terrible exertion, her arisaid torn by brambles, her black hair wild about her face from the wind. She caught at the low branch of an alder and took in the scene with one swift, understanding glance.

"He killed Brahan," groaned Roderick, now on his hands and knees, shaking his head like a great, dazed bear. His shirt was bloody across the back where that blow had caught him. "He killed my son."

"No, Father," said Nairn desperately. "He couldn't have. He wouldn't do that."

When Innes got up off of Elgin, the man rolled over, pawing at his face and moaning softly, trying in a weak, half-hearted way to rise. Roderick saw Innes get up and started coming to his feet.

"Don't, MacAlister," Innes cried at him. "I don't want to fight you like this. Damn you. I didn't kill Brahan. I don't want to fight you. There's no reason for it. Don't, please...!"

With a small, despairing sound, Nairn threw herself in front of her father. He tried to swing her out of the way, but she caught at his torso, winding her legs into his. Still dazed by that blow, he tripped again and went down on her. Innes heard her cry of pain as his weight pinned her to the ground, but before he could reach them, Nairn had squirmed from beneath Roderick, throwing herself across him to hold him down.

"Leave, now," she sobbed at Innes, her face flooded with tears of utter desperation. "Please go. You'll have to kill him to stop him, and if you don't do that, he'll kill you. Oh, please, Innes, get out, go away, while you've got the chance."

Innes stared for that last minute at the pitiful, sobbing figure sprawled over the gigantic Scotsman. A terrible despair shook his whole frame. He heard the sibilant brush of Elgin getting to his feet behind him and knew that he did not have the strength left to face them both

129

again. The sound he made as he turned away to plunge into the timber was hardly human.

It seemed as if he had been the repository for all the tragedy and death his clan had known for the past five hundred years, and it had lurked somewhere down in the dark depths of his unconscious, waiting for the culmination of this moment, to sweep up and inundate him with the terrible, devastating, final defeat of his inheritance.

IV

THE SUMMER SUN MADE A BRILLIANT GLITTER ON THE ice fields of the Wind River. The trunks of aspens traced their delicate silver columns against the dense green of pine on the slopes. Goldenrod looked like patches of yellow sunlight against the curing buffalo grass filling a glade. There was a furtive, darting movement amid the spruce at the edge of this meadow.

It was a man, crouching in the yarrow, plucking at wild strawberries in swift desperation. There was not much humanity left to him. All the marks of the wild, hunted animal stamped him. He had no shirt, and his scarred, gaunt torso was burned the color of mountain mahogany by the sun. His feverish, sunken eyes were never still in his narrow skull, shifting back and forth like the dance of light on water. His mouth was hidden in the matted, sandy beard obliterating the long, bitter line of his jaw. He had been wild and shy enough originally. Now, few would have recognized him as the Duncan Innes of four months ago.

There was a snap of underbrush from across the glade, and Innes leaped back into the brush, crushing the berries in his hand till the juice ran red as blood
130

from between his fingers. Deep in the thicket, still running, he turned to look over his shoulder. A brown bear had ambled into the glade, rooting for wild onions. Innes halted himself with great effort, making an angry, snarling sound, and dropped on his hunkers to stuff the crushed mass of strawberries ravenously into his mouth.

The juice dripped into his beard and ran heedlessly onto his chest. The hair on the top of his head was almost white from the sun, and almost black on the sides and back from using it to wipe his hands whenever he ate. He added to that now with a swipe of wet fingers across it.

He caressed the bare blade in his belt for a moment, considering the possibilities of getting the bear with that. It had been two weeks now since he'd had meat. The last had been a rabbit, caught in a deadfall after days of patient trailing and waiting. He shook his head finally, realizing how foolhardy it would be with only a knife. There wasn't even a hilt on it. He had found it in a rotting trapper's cabin over in the Shoshones. How long ago had that been?

He looked over the glaciers above and behind him. There were no known trails over the Wind Rivers. He had followed a game trace made by mountain sheep, and had gotten through by chance. He shivered with the memory of the freezing night, clambering over ice fields, almost falling into a crevice so deep he had not been able to see the bottom. There were many lucid moments like this, when his mind would work with some logic. But there were other periods he could not remember at all, when he must have run like some animal, aimlessly, thoughtlessly, sleeping when he felt the need, eating when he could find food. Brahan still came to his mind, occasionally, and he felt a resurgence of that terrible defeat. Mostly, though, it was an apathy. He felt no desire for anything beyond the fundamental necessities.

When his shirt had fallen apart, he had not cared about mending it, or getting hide for another. He found within him a growing aversion to human beings, almost a fear. He had assiduously avoided a party of trappers sighted two weeks before. And beneath it all, haunting him, driving him, harrying him till he could never stop moving, like an animal running from the hounds, was the knowledge that he was being followed. He knew Scotsmen, and he knew Roderick. The man would not let the death of his son go unavenged. The man was on Innes's back track somewhere, stubbornly, ungivingly, patiently, sifting out his sign and plodding along after him, inexorable as the curse itself.

Innes rose and started downslope once more. In his mind was a vague idea of reaching the valley before nightfall. It would be somewhat warmer, farther from the ice that never melted up there in the glaciers. Beyond the glade, his eye unconsciously picked up a sign in the earth beside a fallen tree trunk. The print had no heel. A moccasin. It was too deep and clear to have been made in dry earth.

How long ago was the last rain? He could remember one two weeks ago. He was safe, then. He rose and swung on down the hill, an aimless, loose-jointed motion entering his body. Within sound of the river below, he came across more sign. It was a broken arrow shaft. It looked like it had been made from a shoot of early berry, and had two wavering red lines painted from the feathers down either side. That would be Dakota. A strange apprehension filled him, and he began to look for those prints again. He found them.

132

Suspicion of years formed a premonition in him, and he began following the prints. The sign cut to a ford in the Wind River.

He crossed through the freezing, knee-deep water, cut more sign on the other side, went on in dripping leggin's. It was still old sign, and it was what fooled him. He almost stumbled into the man. The first sight of him caused Innes to drop into service berries at the very edge of the glade. The rattle caused the man to turn his head toward him in a swift jerk.

Recognition closed Innes's throat off against breath. It was Wisapa. The Dakota lay in a buffalo robe, propped up against a mossy boulder at the edge of the park. His face was even more haggard than Innes's, great, black hollows beneath the oblique cheekbones, the eyes sunken till they seemed to be staring from the sockets of a skull. There was so little flesh left that Innes could see the formation of the man's teeth through the skin.

The two of them stared at each other for a long time, without speaking. Innes saw the Indian's parfleche bag opened on the ground, its effects scattered over the earth. Beyond that was Innes's old Yerger. The Indian must have taken the rifle from Innes's camp back there in Jackson Hole, when Ryker had first jumped him.

Innes worked back into the thicket. His first impulse was to run. But the puzzle of this held him by a tenuous thread. He made a complete circle of the park. The only other sign he found was of heeled boots and three unshod horses, going out to the east, and they were as old as the sign he had seen before.

Finally he circled back to where he was nearest his rifle, but still in cover. He had moved so silently the Indian had not heard him approach this second time, and sat staring straight ahead. Sniffing the air, cocking his ears, waiting for a painfully long time, Innes at last rose and darted out, scooping up the gun and shot pouch and powder horn from where they lay on the ground, then ran back into timber.

He started to load, when, unaccountably, the thought came into his mind. This was the same gun with which his grandfather had killed George MacAlister back in Virginia. With a strangled sound in his throat, he almost flung the Yerger from him. Would it never stop haunting him? No matter which way he turned? Not just the MacAlisters themselves. Everything he did. Every move he made. It caused him painful effort to retain the piece and load it.

"All right," he said from his covert, "I've got it loaded now. If you don't want a chunk of Galena in you, tell me what this is."

The man stared at him in utter silence. As weak and haggard as he looked, his eyes were filled with bitter, black defiance. Innes kept going over the signs, trying to obliterate his unreasoning suspicion with the logic of it. There just couldn't be anybody else around. With the memory of Brahan, his finger kept twitching against the trigger. It was no more than the Indian deserved. Then a new thought struck him. Wisapa had a bow, and no Indian would waste precious lead on game. Innes reached into his shot pouch. He had carried extra bars of Galena lead in his possible sack, but there had been only fourteen molded balls in his tiger tail pouch. He counted them carefully. There were thirteen in the pouch, and the one in the gun.

"Ryker shot Brahan?" he said.

The man's eyes had been on his hand in that pouch, and the Indian must have realized what he was figuring.

134

But there was no answer.

"You might save your life," said Innes.

Still no answer. Finally, Innes squirmed in behind the rock, trying to remain in cover, and caught Wisapa beneath the armpits, dragging him back into the shelter of timber. Here he threw off the buffalo robe. Caked blood covered the man's buckskins. They had been cut away from the hip, and a crude buckskin bandage applied. When Innes lifted this off, the ghastly, swollen infection of the wound sickened him.

A sense of purpose he had not held for months filled his movements now. He went into the clearing, scrambling through the parfleche bag for the flint and steel he hoped was there. He found some, and gathered up dead wood for a fire. There was a brass trade kettle still lashed on an *aparejo* that had been thrown from a horse. Innes pulled the kettle from the pack saddle and filled it with river water. While it was coming to a boil, he hunted for black root along the river bottoms, gathering a double handful. Putting as much as he could in his mouth, he started chewing on it, while he cleansed the wound with the boiled water. Then he rubbed the pulpy poultice of black root into the infection.

He marveled at the Indian's stoicism. The pain would have been unbearable to a white man in that weakened condition. Bandaging the wound with strips torn from the *aparejo*, Innes dragged Wisapa in close to the fire, getting enough wood to keep it going should he be gone all night. He piled this within reach of the man, and set off for some game.

That was easy for a man with a gun. He found a buffalo wallow torn apart by rutting bulls, and followed fresh sign into a meadow where a great, shaggy beast snorted as it saw him. Innes maneuvered for a heart shot. The detonation of the gun was followed by the beast's roar of agony. The buffalo shook his head, staggered from one side to the other. A great gout of blood spurted from its shaggy coat. It steadied itself, lowering its short-horned head, and rushed for Innes. He turned to leap aside, and the beast ploughed blindly by. It ran for a few yards beyond, then halted again, and with a low, rumbling groan fell on its side.

He skinned it, cut steaks and backfat and shortribs, cleaned the intestines and looped them over a stick. All this he put in the bloody hide, gathered up the four leg ends, and carried it back to camp.

When Wisapa saw what Innes had brought, a strange, puzzled light tempered the bitterness of his eyes. Innes cut up the steaks to season a broth he made in the trade kettle. He found pemmican in the parfleche bag and thickened the broth with this. He fed it to Wisapa slowly. Then he toasted the intestines over hot coals till it was crispy brown, and fed it in small pieces to the Indian. This was a delicacy almost as cherished as beaver tail to an Indian. Finally Innes cooked two great steaks for himself, eating the first one almost raw. After the meal, he hunted in the *aparejo* for some fleshing materials to clean the buffalo hide. He found the tools in a little, buckskin bag. There was the leg bone of a wolf, serrated on one edge, for scraping the hide. He staked the great, shaggy skin out, and began fleshing.

"Why are you doing that?" asked Wisapa.

His voice was stronger, and Innes gave no sign of his surprise at this abrupt overture. "If we're going to stay here long, we'll need some robes," he said. "Winter isn't too far off, and that ice field across the river doesn't help any right now. Looks of that wound, I don't think you can travel much for a while."

"Perhaps, never," said Wisapa. "I have not been able to move from the hips down since Ryker shot me."

Innes lifted his head to stare at the man, and all the pieces dropped into place. The Indian had lain there, like that, paralyzed, starving, for almost two weeks.

"You didn't shoot Brahan, then?" said Innes hopefully.

"No," said Wisapa. "Ryker came into this country many years ago, trapping and trading with the Indians. It is how I got to know him. I had worked for Hudson's Bay since I was very young. It is how I knew English. Ryker engaged me as an interpreter, and finally as a partner. He convinced me that it would ruin the country for anyone but him to find Lost River. If another trapper discovered it, more of his breed would flood in. The trapper always opens the door for the settler, and with the settler, war. The Indian always loses. But Ryker promised if I helped him find Lost River, he would keep its secret. He also gave me his word there would be no killing over it. After we met the young MacAlister at Bridger's Fort, and found out they possessed the map, Ryker and I camped above Hoback Cañon. He said he would try to make a deal with Roderick, but he kept putting it off. We were on the bluffs when you came down to the mouth with Brahan."

"But how did you know it was Brahan who had the map?" asked Innes. "He just told you at Fort Bridger that if you wanted it, look up the MacAlisters."

"The older brother was in our camp once," said Wisapa. "I think he betrayed Brahan in return for a share of Lost River."

The emotion flooding Innes caused him to tremble, sick at his stomach, and then that resolved itself into a hate for Elgin he knew would never die. He gestured at the Indian's legs, speaking gutturally. "How did this happen?"

"When Ryker killed Brahan, my face was turned from him," said Wisapa. "We quarreled here, and he shot me. He must have thought I was dead. He went through the *aparejos* on my pack animal to get what he needed and scattered the rest on the ground like that, and left me lying in the clearing." He paused, staring at Innes. Finally he spoke again, in a quiet resignation. "Ryker has the map, not I."

"I didn't think you had it," said Innes.

"Then why are you saving my life?" asked the Indian.

"Is it inconceivable to you that I just can't go off and let you die?" asked Innes.

The Dakota stared at him for a long period without answering. "That is a very simple reason," he said, at last. "Perhaps that is why it is such a good reason. It is not many white men I have called *kola*."

"What's that?"

"In my language, it means friend."

A faint, strange warmth pervaded Innes. It was the same feeling he had felt when Brahan called them brother Scots. Then, with a bitter, habituated response, he choked it off.

"Don't make the mistake of doing that," he said. "Anybody who calls me friend is as good as signing his own death warrant."

V

SUMMER WANED. THE RED HAWS BEGAN TURNING brown, and the fireweed was losing its flame. Innes built them a dugout against the bluff near the clearing, and for weeks applied the black root to draw the infection

138

from the wound. It was a slow, painful process, with Wisapa delirious and close to death much of the time, but, when the first wedge of geese honked south from Bull Lake, the wound had really begun to heal.

The paralysis remained, however, and in mid-September Innes built a travois upon which to lay the Indian and, taking the place of a horse, hauled him the twenty-some miles to Warm Springs Creek. Here, on a rolling sagebrush bench, was a geyser, known to the Indians for its curative qualities. With the wound healed, Innes could bathe the man daily in its warm, bubbling water, and massage his legs for several hours after each bath. The first snow bore down the branches of the spruces beneath the ledge until they looked like great, white umbrellas, but Innes did not let it prevent their bath that day, and a Chinook melted the banks before nightfall.

Wisapa could move his legs by now, and was gaining weight. More snow came, turning the slopes white, and this was how Innes saw the tracks.

He had come from the dugout they had built just under the ledge one morning, looking about for signs of game to replenish their larder. He sighted what he thought were *wapiti* tracks south of them, emerging from snow-blanketed timber, crossing a park, and disappearing again. He told Wisapa he would be back soon, and slipped into the buffalo coat he had made for himself.

The wind was coming from the southwest, and, heading south toward the track, he climbed to the ridge where he could sight the animal. He was close enough to the tracks then to see that they were made by only one pair of feet. He dropped to his hunkers beside some fir, realizing how much his suspicion, his wariness had been dulled by these last weeks with the Indian.

Had the man seen him? How could he help it? The dugout was in plain view from the park those tracks crossed, and he had been standing at the door for a long period. An awesome prescience filled him with a knowledge of who this was as certainly as if he had seen the man. His belly began to constrict with that cramping pain. He could get out now. He didn't want to face this. He didn't want to kill. There was no sense to it. And he would have to, if he stayed—he knew that. It was stupid. It was animal. There was utterly no reason for it. Yet, if he stayed, it was either kill or be killed.

Then, get out. He glanced down at the dugout. There would be no returning to it. It was too much in view. He would be a perfect target. And Wisapa, after all these patient weeks? The man was still sick, barely able to move. He would be alone. Or would they let him survive? After they found an Innes had befriended him? His head turned from side to side in that painful, frustrated way. His every instinct was to run. He didn't think he had ever wanted to do anything so badly in his life.

The sound of the shot filled the cañon. His horrified eyes stared at the furrow in the snow a foot from his elbow. Then he sprawled downslope in a desperate, blind run, hunting for better cover. The detonation had shattered against a granite uplift of a high ridge behind this one, sweeping back across the valley to strike the other slope in a hundred echoes, multiplied to a thousand by the crags and rock faces on that side, till the valley seemed filled with roaring, laughing, clapping explosions.

He went belly down behind a granite ledge, hands working with the feverish skill of the countless other times he had loaded that Yerger. He dumped powder down the barrel without bothering to measure it in the charge cup. He had long ago used up his linen patches, and he fumbled a buckskin patch from his shot pouch, greasing it with bear tallow from a trap in the stock of the gun, clapping it onto the ball of Galena lead.

Ramming this into the barrel, patch between the ball and powder, he searched the timber vainly, below and above, for movement that would give the gunman away. He called to the man in a final desperation.

"MacAlister, damn you, don't do this. I don't want to fight you. I didn't kill your son. Do you hear that, Roderick? I didn't kill Brahan. I don't want this. I don't want to shoot you. Don't make me. Please, don't do this…!"

He stopped as he sighted movement. It was above him now, in the cedars, stunted and twisted by the wind. Below him was that park, fifty yards of open snowfield in which he would be a perfect target. Yet this rock ledge was not high enough to protect him. He could not run. It was shoot, or nothing.

"MacAlister, please, I'm begging you. Can't you hear me, Roderick? I don't want to fight you. Damn you, I don't want to fight!"

The flash of light on gun metal stopped his shouting and brought habituated reaction. Without conscious volition, he brought his own gun up, and felt the velvety pressure of the trigger. Curly maple jarred his face as the stock bucked into him with the explosion. He was still partly deafened by it when the other man's bullet hit the top of the granite shelf in front of Innes, screaming off in a ricochet. Sharp rock chipped into Innes's face. The cañon was filled with those laughing, clapping echoes again.

Then, from the trees up there, a figure staggered out into the snow. He had no rifle, and he was holding his belly with both hands, doubling over more and more as he stumbled through the deep drift downhill. Finally he was jackknifed so low Innes could see the back of his neck, and the man over on his face.

Innes waited for a long time with reloaded gun, searching the surrounding terrain. Finally he rose and made his way to the man, rolling him over. It wasn't Roderick. It was Elgin.

Innes dropped to his knees beside the man, that awful, bitter despair filling him again. The dark face still mocked him, staring up in sardonic death. Knowing it had been Elgin who betrayed Brahan to Ryker, Innes could feel no sense of vengeance, no vindication. He could feel nothing except the black, sinking, overpowering knowledge that this was only further fulfillment of the curse. Now Roderick would be hunting him on two counts.

"Damn you," he told Elgin between his teeth in a desperate, sobbing way, "damn you."

VI

WISAPA HAD THE WISDOM AND UNDERSTANDING NOT to try and penetrate the somber, uncommunicative mood that shrouded Innes. They hardly spoke all day long, and the Scotsman spent most of the day and half the night searching the forest for sign. It had become an obsession with him. More than once he rose up in his robes in the middle of the night and asked Wisapa if that were not Roderick MacAlister standing in the doorway.

He still tended the Indian, however. The bitter chill of full winter gripped the valley now, and the streams were iced over, and game was scarce. The two men were on a diet of jerked meat and pemmican Innes had prepared for this contingency. Then, one day, a band of Shoshones appeared, traveling south. Innes had a good store of buffalo robes, and quill work Wisapa had worked on during his convalescence, and, for this, they traded a couple of mangy ponies. Innes had not meant to use the horses as soon as this. It was the word the Shoshones dropped, just before they left, that gave him the impetus.

They said a giant Scotsman had been sighted in the Wind Rivers. With him was a young woman. They were traveling eastward.

The next day Innes set to work on a buffalo saddle for Wisapa that would carry him comfortably. He finished it that night, and they left the dugout with dawn, with the Indian riding an old beef-steak paint, and their robes and food packed on the weedy mare. The Dakota country was east of the Big Horns, and it was a bitter, grueling journey. They reached Tensleep Creek, named that by the Indians for the number of days it took to reach from Colter's Hell. From the heights above Tensleep gorge, they could see over onto the eastern slopes, and, though Wisapa allowed no expression to reach his face, there was an excited gleam to his eyes as they ranged over home country. Toward evening, they caught sight of a trapper's cabin snuggled into a cairn halfway down the cliffs into the gorge. There were tracks over the snow, too. Neither of the men cared to stop, however—Innes being driven by his haunting fear of Roderick, Wisapa wanting to reach his people as soon as possible. Innes did not notice when the fairly warm, west wind began to shift, but Wisapa pulled the horse up sharply.

"We had better seek cover, *kola*. That shifting wind

brings a blizzard in this area quicker than you would believe. That cabin?"

"There's no point in turning back that far," said Innes.

"More point than you realize," said Wisapa. "You don't know this section as I do. The blizzards are violent and deadly."

Reluctantly, Innes wheeled in the other direction. Already the chill of the wind was penetrating his buffalo coat. Soon sleet began to fall, and they were pushed heavily along by the force of the growing storm at their backs. At last visibility was such they did manage to find a trail down. He felt a tug at the lead line in his hand, and whirled to see the mare slipping over. His own shout was muffled as he made a last, vain effort to drag the kicking beast back onto the shelf, and then he had to let go, and the horse toppled off with a wild whinny that had no sound in the blizzard. Sickly, Innes turned back to Wisapa, lifting him off the other animal, for fear the same thing might happen to the Indian. He half carried him the rest of the way down.

Reaching the cabin, he tried to open the door, but it would not give. Apparently it was barred from within, and he began to throw the weight of his body against it, feeling the give of rawhide hinges. Then it was thrown open, and he found himself facing a short, massive bear of a man holding an immense Ketland-McCormick in one fist.

"Don't beat the door down," said Ryker. "I wouldn't keep a dog out in a storm like this. Come in, my friends." He chuckled ironically, hoarsely, deep in his throat. "Both my good friends."

Dazed by the storm, Innes could do nothing but stare at the man. Then, answering the imperative wave of Ryker's pistol, he carried Wisapa in. Innes lowered him

144

to a sitting position against the wall. The Indian had not taken his eyes from Ryker, and they had a wide, unblinking glitter to them that started disturbing the man.

"Where's the others?" asked Ryker.

"What others?" said Innes, watching that pistol.

"You know what others," said Ryker, glancing in a quick, nervous way at Wisapa, then edging to the door to look out. "I saw tracks on the other side of the gorge this morning."

"We didn't come in by that side," said Innes. "What are you doing here, anyway? Tensleep can't be Lost River."

"Close to it, if the map's right," said Ryker. He had to lean all his weight against the door to shut it, and stood that way, without having dropped the bar into place, his body trembling to the buffeting wind beating at the portal. "I built this cabin when the snow started. Been using it as a base to hunt the Lost River ever since."

"Did it strike you," said Wisapa, "that he can only shoot one of us with that pistol?"

"Now wait a minute!" Ryker turned the gun on Wisapa in automatic reaction, then jerked it back to Innes, as the trapper shifted his weight faintly. "Wait a minute. I let you in, didn't I?"

"And you'll kill us when you're good and ready," said Innes. "You already tried to kill Wisapa once."

Wisapa turned himself about and dragged himself bodily into a standing position against the wall.

Innes saw what he meant to do, and moved around onto the other side of Ryker so they would approach him from two different directions. Ryker looked from the Indian to the trapper, apparently unwilling to believe their intent. Under ordinary circumstances, Innes would have thought it a foolish thing to do. But it was a certainty in his mind that Ryker did not intend to let either of them live. It might as well be this way as any. And knowing the implacability of Wisapa's purpose, it just wasn't in Innes to let him do it alone. Wisapa started dragging himself down the wall, and Innes took a step toward Ryker. That it was still inconceivable to Ryker showed in his twisted face.

"Don't be crazy," he said, trying to laugh, yet brandishing the gun from one to the other. "There's no need for me to kill you. I'll cut you in for shares. We'll find it together, and I'll cut you in for shares."

"Like you did Brahan?" said Innes.

The sudden, full shock of realizing they meant to go through with it stamped a bestial contortion on Ryker's face. He twisted from side to side, turning the gun on Wisapa, cocking the flat, goose-necked hammer with a desperate hook of his thumb, sweeping the big, brass-bound weapon back toward Innes.

"No, listen. Don't be crazy. This is crazy, Innes. I'll kill you…."

"Only one of us, Ryker."

"And it'll be you, Innes."

"Will it, Ryker?" said Wisapa.

Ryker whirled toward him. His eyes widened, glittered. The gun jerked higher. Only one more step.

The door shuddered suddenly beneath a heavy, buffeting weight, knocking Ryker forward so hard his gun went off at the floor. Innes jumped at him, grabbing the gun arm. Ryker twisted beneath him, rolled to the floor, wrenching the gun arm loose to beat at him with the heavy weapon. Wisapa threw his body across the arm, pinning it to the floor.

Screaming curses, Ryker doubled up his legs to kick

146

out from beneath Innes. A foot caught Innes in the belly, and he slammed against the wall. Wisapa tried to stop Ryker from rolling over on him, but the bearded man possessed immense strength. He left that one arm beneath Wisapa and reached around in a bear hug with the other, putting his weight atop the Indian. Then he caught the roached hair and beat the Dakota's head into the puncheon floor.

Gasping in pain, Innes threw himself back at Ryker, clawing him off Wisapa. For that one instant, he was on the man's back. He thrust a knee into the small of it, hooked desperate arms around Ryker's neck, heaved upward.

Ryker's body bent like a bow in the leverage. There was a loud, snapping sound, like a breaking branch. Ryker's body formed no more pressure for the grip; it was like bending a limp sack. Innes released him, letting the lolling head drop to the floor. The mouth gaped; the eyes were open, glassy. The man was dead.

Innes was trembling heavily. He realized it must be reaction. At the time, moving in on Ryker with the gun, he had felt no particular emotion. But it must have created a terrible tension, for he felt so weak and shaken now he could hardly focus his gaze. Then he saw what had come against the door. It was open now, with the howling blizzard piling snow and sleet a foot high across the threshold. The girl crouched there, staring in horror at them through eyes streaming tears from the wind. The name left Innes in whispered shock.

"Nairn."

"Innes," she said gutturally.

"Those were your tracks Ryker saw across the gorge."

"We were following you," she panted. "We've been

following you for months. Dad tried to leave me at several posts, but I came after him every time. I didn't realize we were this close behind. We found that dugout on Wind River and figured it was yours. And the grave…."

"You know who it was?" he asked. They were crouched there, staring at each other in some sort of dazed spell, oblivious to the shouting gale, unwilling to move.

"Elgin," she said in a small voice.

"I had to kill him, Nairn," he almost sobbed.

She stared at him a long moment, an indefinable expression twisting her face. Then it smoothed out, and she was looking at him in that wide-eyed way.

"I still love you, Innes."

"You can't." His shout was animal, guttural. "I killed your brother. Don't you hear? You can't love me."

"I do, I do!" The spell was broken now, and they were both stumbling to their feet. She caught at him. "I do love you, Innes, and you've got to get out of here. Father's behind me somewhere. He'll be coming in. We were about a mile beyond the cabin when the blizzard started. I lost him on the way back. You've got to leave. He's not the same, Innes. He was bad enough to begin with. He would have killed you at the first if I hadn't stopped him. But now he's crazy. He's possessed with it, Innes. He thinks you killed his two sons, and he's possessed with it."

"No!" His shout was sharp, edged, and he released her, backing up against the wall. There was a strange determination in his face. "You asked me once to stop running, Nairn. It's no use. It follows me wherever I go. Ryker wasn't just a man, killing and stealing and hunting for a fortune in furs. He was part of the curse. It touches everybody who comes near me. I can't escape it by running."

"Please, Innes, Father'll kill you."

"Let him. What's the difference? I don't care any more. I'm through running. You're the only thing I ever really wanted, anyway, and I can't have you, so what's the difference? Do you hear that, Roderick? Come on, kill me. I don't care."

"Innes! You're getting as crazy as Father. Don't. Please. Get out. Please."

"No!" His wild shout lifted above the storm, and he raised his head to roar into it. "Do you hear that, Roderick? I'm through running."

"Aye, Innes, I hear it," said Roderick MacAlister, appearing out of the storm like a ponderous giant. He swayed there a moment in the doorway, staring ghoulishly at Innes. He was muffled to the chin in a plaid mackinaw. Ice had formed on his brows, giving them a hoary, frosted look. His eyes were red-rimmed and gleaming with a feverish, fanatical light. Innes had seen the same look in Cheyenne Sun Dancers at the peak of their crazed orgies, when the terrible tortures of the ceremonies had robbed them of all reason.

Roderick reached back for the hilt of his claymore where he had slung it in a case behind his back.

"Father," screamed Nairn, throwing herself on him. "Roderick!"

"Out of me way, ye ree loun. I'm goin' to kill this Lalland Innes," said Roderick. With one arm he swept her aside, yanking the huge sword from its scabbard and swinging it down before him. Innes stood back against the wall. He could feel fear in himself. He wouldn't deny that. Yet his bitter resolve to stop running from something that had haunted him all his life kept his body spread-eagled against the logs.

"Brahan, Innes," said Roderick, moving toward him. "Elgin. That was Elgin, wasn't it? That grave back on the Wind River. He was trailing you. He left even before I did. My sons, Innes, both my sons." He stopped a couple of paces away from Innes, breathing heavily, a sly, waiting, expectant look on his face. As Innes made no move, surprise showed in those little, red-rimmed eyes for a moment. Then he drew in a great, gasping breath, and let the shout go. "Thig Ris, Innes, Thig Ris!"

The sword made a dull glitter in the dusky light. Innes could not inhibit his responses. They jerked him aside uncontrollably in the last instant. The blade struck the log wall with a clanging shudder.

"Thig Ris," bellowed MacAlister, "at it again," and heaved up with his prodigious blade. Innes did not see how Nairn came in. She caught her father's arm, screaming at him.

"Let go, ye whingin' wean, let go. I'm killin' an Innes."

It was with his sword arm he swept her back. Perhaps it was the pain in her cry that penetrated his fogged mind. Or the horror filling Innes's eyes, staring at Nairn, as she staggered back with the blood spurting from the wound that blade had made in her side. She struck the wall and collapsed in a heap. Roderick dropped his sword and staggered over to her, falling to his knees. He cradled her limp body in one arm, pawing at the blood covering her dress. At first, calling her name, his voice was a sobbing contrition. It began to grow louder as she did not answer. He felt for her heart.

"Nairn," he screamed finally. "Nairn, answer me, say I haven't killed ye. Yure own father, Nairn...he couldn't kill ye...tell me I haven't!" He let her sink back, his

150

hand slipping away from her heart, a brassy film covering his eyes. Then, with a great, maniacal scream, he heaved to his feet. "Nairn," he howled, like a bereft beast, "Nairn, Nairn, Nairn!" His voice was lost in the storm as he lunged out the door, screaming it over and over.

"Roderick," shouted Innes. "Don't. You'll go off the cliff...!"

It was impulse more than anything else driving him out after the man. It couldn't have been thought. The last few moments seemed to have shocked all capacity for that from him. He stumbled out into the blizzard, catching sight of the gigantic, plunging figure ahead of him. Roderick seemed to halt for a moment on the edge of the cliff. Innes shouted at him again. Then his figure was gone.

Innes staggered to the bluff, staring downward. He wondered, dully, whether the man had fallen, or had deliberately cast himself off. He sank to his knees, eyes still turned down into the gorge.

Murk hid the bottom, hundreds of feet below. It seemed to draw him, pull at him. *Why not?* There was nothing left for him. He knew now for a certainty that Roderick had thrown himself off, deliberately. And he could understand why. It was the logical thing when there was nothing left in life. It would be so easy. He squinted his eyes shut against the sight of Nairn's dead body back there in the cabin, of Elgin's dead body, of the pain in Brahan's dead face, of John Donn lying there in a Shoshone grave, of the chain of tragedy and death that he had left on his back trail.

And now it was over. He would finish it. He could face no more of it. Slowly, inexorably, the defeat inclined his body forward.

151

"Kola!"

Innes jerked, straightened, seemed to lift from a trance. When he wheeled about, he saw Wisapa, dragging himself down across the trail. Innes turned reluctantly back to the man, shaking his head.

"The woman is not dead," Wisapa told him. "I stanched the blood. It's a bad wound, but, if we can get her to my people, I think she will live. You saved my life, *kola*. You can save hers."

Innes's heart leaped against his ribs with painful force. He ran past the Indian, into the room where Nairn lay on the floor, covered by a robe. He dropped to his knees beside her, catching a pale hand in his. She looked up weakly.

"Something must have snapped in your father when he thought he had killed you," said Innes, answering the question in her eyes. "He ran out. The cliffs...."

She closed her eyes, a poignant grief pinching her face, whitening it. Her breast lifted beneath the robe with the breath she took. Finally she spoke, carefully.

"You're not to blame, Innes. He brought it on himself. As much as he meant to me, it's the truth."

"You'll be all right," he said. "We'll get you to Wisapa's people."

"Of course, I will. You'll stay with me, won't you, Innes? It's over, now. You've beaten the curse." She must have seen the way he squinted his eyes and shook his head from side to side, for she lurched up, catching feebly at his arm. "Yes, you have. You stood up to it. You stopped running. You refused to perpetuate it. And you won. There's no reason for it to go on. We're together, aren't we? An Innes and a MacAlister. That in itself refutes the whole thing."

"She's right," said Wisapa. He held up the map and

152

journal of Father Escobar that he must have found on Ryker. "You have these now. We can find Lost River. With you, I know it will not harm my people."

Innes took the book and map. Ryker must have been building a fire in the fireplace when they entered, for the coals were still glowing. Innes put some more wood on, and, when the flames began to leap, he threw the map and book on it.

"That way you can be sure your people won't suffer," he told Wisapa. "We couldn't really wipe the slate clean with those around. It's what started all this trouble."

Wisapa bowed his head humbly. "You are a greater man than I thought, *kola*. When I tell my people what you did, you will have their lifelong respect. It is something few white men can command."

That vagrant smile caught at Innes's lips, flashing across them like sunlight on dark waters for a moment. He moved back to Nairn, taking her hand. Then he looked into the flames, licking about the little, leather-covered book, and for a moment the mysticism of his Celtic blood asserted itself, and he spoke to the fire with all the naïve sincerity of a savage propitiating some ancient god.

"Do you see this, Alister Mor?" he said softly. "An Innes and a MacAlister joined. That's something you never believed would happen, isn't it? I think that's something all your curses in the world can't harm."

"I *know* that's something they can't harm," smiled Nairn.

THE CURSE OF MONTEZUMA

In 1843 William H. Prescott completed his epic history, **The Conquest of Mexico**. *The early chapters of this history recorded most of what was known of Aztec culture and the Aztec empire, and no historian since has been able to write of the Aztecs without referring to Prescott's monumental work. Les Savage, Jr., obviously availed himself of it when he came to write this short novel and united the milieu of the Aztec empire with his own legendary characters, Elgera Douglas, better known as Señorita Scorpion, and her compadres, Chisos Owens and John Hagar. Chronologically this story occurs shortly after* "The Secret of Santiago," *third and last of the short novels collected in* **The Legend of Señorita Scorpion**. "The Curse of Montezuma" *was first published in the spring, 1945 issue of* **Action Stories** *and appears now for the first time in book form.*

I

Wave the parrot plumes again.
The guáchupin *now burns.*
Quetzalcoatl comes to reign.
The Serpent-God returns.

THE THREE MEN SAT HUNCHED OVER IN THEIR SADDLES with backs to the wind that mourned down off the ridge like the plaint of a lost soul, fluttering the brim of Elder Fayette's hat against its crown with a constant, slapping sound.

154

"Can't you turn that hat around or something?" said Orville Beamont nervously. "Gets on a man's nerves."

Fayette's hard mouth curled at one corner contemptuously, and he didn't answer, and the hatbrim kept on flapping.

"When's he coming, anyway?" muttered Beamont angrily. "He promised he'd be here before night."

"Don't say it like that," insisted Abilene, trying to light a cigarette for the third time. "He ain't a devil or something. He's human, just like you or me."

The wind rose to an unearthly shriek, whipping Fayette's hatbrim into a mad tattoo for a moment, and then died to a soft whine again. Beamont suddenly stiffened. Fayette's mare whinnied and tried to bolt, and he caught it with a savage jerk on the reins.

"*Buenas noches, señores,*" said the man who had appeared so silently from the blackjack timber above them. "Have you been waiting long?"

Orville Beamont let out a gusty breath. "You! I thought it was him. Isn't he with you?"

The man was on foot, wearing a dark-blue, hooded cloak the Mexicans called a *capuz*. His shiny *mitaja* leggin's gleamed dully as he came on down toward the three horsebackers, something serpentine in the lithe, sensuous movements of his slim body. He had a narrow, vulpine face beneath the hood of his cloak, and the slender, pale hands of a conspirator, and he kept rubbing his long forefinger against his thumb in an oily, habitual way, like a usurer who saw the promise of another gold piece.

"No, he is not with me," said the man. "We were all to arrive separately, if you recall. *Pues*, you have not prepared for him. A fire, *hombres*, a fire. After all, it is not every day you meet the reincarnation of

Montezuma, returned to free his people from their servitude."

Fayette snorted. "Keep that tripe in your own duffel bag, Ortega. We didn't want to show any light with a fire."

"You are farther into the Guadalupes than any white man has ever been, *señores*, and there is no possible danger of anyone seeing you," said Luis Ortega urbanely, and turned to Abilene. "If you would be so kind as to get some wood?"

Abilene looked at Fayette. Fayette shrugged, then edged his mare over to an outcropping of rocks, and dismounted, kicking away the matted undergrowth until he had hollowed out a place for a fire. The dark-faced Ortega laughed softly and ran his slender hands up and down the gold-hilted cane he carried, looking up the cañon toward the sombrous peak, El Capitán.

Abilene came back with his dally rope hitched around his saddle horn, dragging a dead cottonwood log. It was rotten enough to split with a Bowie knife he took from his saddle roll. They banked kindling against the rock, out of the wind. The light flared under Abilene's match, catching redly across the impatient line to Elder Fayette's hard mouth. Beamont had been standing nervously by his horse. He jerked around suddenly.

"Whassat?"

The Indians had appeared without sound. They stood like silent ghosts, just outside the circle of firelight.

"All right, all right," said Fayette. "Come on in."

"*Señor* Fayette," hissed Luis Ortega, "you do not speak to the Lord Montezuma in that fashion. I warned you...." He turned to the pair of Indians, and Fayette thought a mocking note had entered his suave voice. "We thank Quetzalcoatl for your safety, *Tlatoani*

156

Montezuma. Please accept our humble companionship and join us."

Fayette's eyes narrowed, studying the Indian who stepped into the light. He was a huge man, well over six feet tall in his rawhide *huiraches*, his tremendous shoulders and great, broad chest swelling a mantle that hung to below his knees. At first Fayette thought the cloak was of vari-colored cloth, then he realized it was feathers, feathers of a dozen different hues, catching the firelight in a bizarre pattern. The second inscrutable Indian spread out a gold cloth, and Montezuma seated himself cross-legged without a word. He held his great head up, the haughty beak of his nose throwing a deep shadow over the curl of his arrogant mouth.

Luis Ortega picked up a handful of earth, kissed it, threw it into the flames. "Xiuchtecutli, the Fire God. May he consume the *guáchupin*."

Beamont's thin head jerked toward him. "*Guáchupin?*"

"The *guáchupines* are descendants of the upper class Spaniards who have been ruling Mexico since Cortés conquered the Aztecs," smiled Ortega softly. "The *guáchupines* are the tyrants who will be annihilated in the all-consuming fire of Xiuchtecutli, now that our Lord Montezuma has returned."

"All right," said Fayette. "All right. How about the business? Does he speak English?"

Montezuma had been sitting silently, heavy-lidded eyes staring blankly into the fire, as if he were lost in reverie. His voice startled Elder Fayette, deep and hollow.

"I speak all languages. I am *Tlatoani*. I am a supreme ruler. I am Montezuma."

Standing out in the darkness by the horses, Abilene

157

spat. Fayette glanced his way a moment. He couldn't see him very well, but he knew how the supple hands would be hitched into the cartridge belt of that Beale-Remington Abilene wore. Orville Beamont spoke in his nervous, spiteful way.

"We didn't come here to discuss Aztec mythology. Let's get down to business."

Ortega turned toward him. "*Señor*...."

Montezuma stopped Ortega with a wave of his bronzed hand, looking at Beamont. The Indian's eyes seemed focused for the first time. They held a strange, glittering intensity. Beamont flushed angrily. He wiped the back of his hand across his mouth in a jerky gesture, eyes shifting before Montezuma's black glare.

"You do not believe Montezuma has returned?" asked the Indian.

"I didn't say that...."

"You do not believe Montezuma has returned." It was a statement this time, and it held something final. "You are an unbeliever."

"*Señores*," said Ortega swiftly. "We did not come here to quarrel. It would be wise of you, *Señor* Beamont, to watch what you say. *Tlatoani* Montezuma, forgive the *Americanos*. They are ignorant."

"Their ignorance is no excuse."

"Look," said Fayette. "Let's scrape the fur off and get down to the hide. You're going to do a job for us, and we're going to pay you. That's simple enough. You want to hear what the job is, or shall we call it a sour deal?"

Ortega's words slipped from his flannel-mouth, as sly and furtive as his eyes, and he rubbed his forefinger against his thumb in that way. "*Pues*, of course, you shall not call it a sour deal. Who else could do the job? You have tried, and failed. *Por supuesto*, if you will use

158

a certain amount of tact, we shall come to an amicable agreement." He turned obsequiously to Montezuma. "It is this, my lord. For a long time now, *Señores* Fayette and Beamont, and certain of their constituents, have had...ah...shall we say...ambitions concerning the Big Bend. Unfortunately, there are those in Brewster County who do not sympathize with these ambitions. Elgera Douglas, for one, the heiress to the Santiago Mine. Chisos Owens, who is the friend of every *peon* this side of the Rio."

"Peons," spat Orville Beamont. "That's just it. A whole bunch of small-time peon *rancheros* holding little spreads and controlling all the water. What chance has a big operator?"

"Your cattle don't seem to be dying," said Ortega slyly.

Beamont jerked his hand in a nervous gesture. "That's not the idea. Fayette and I haven't got enough cattle now to put in your left saddlebag. And it won't do us any good to get more if we don't have the water for them."

"Ah, yes." Ortega's voice was insinuating. "You wish to expand. What a laudable ambition."

Fayette squatted there without speaking, letting Beamont go on, watching him with a faint contempt in the curl of his lip. Perhaps Orville Beamont sensed the sly mockery in Ortega's voice. He rubbed the back of his hand across his mouth, speaking jerkily.

"Yeah, yeah. We've tried to put through legislation for a fair division of the water. But the Douglas girl and Chisos Owens have Brewster County sewed up. Sheriff Hagar's their man. Alpine's the county seat, and whatever legal measures we've tried to take there, Hagar's stopped."

Montezuma looked up. "Legal measures?"

Beamont wiped his mouth. "Yeah...uh...the legal measures we...."

"I don't think you know what legal measures are, *Señor* Beamont," said Montezuma. "Are you a hypocrite as well as a thief?"

Beamont's voice was shrill. "Listen...."

"Why not speak the truth?" interrupted Montezuma, staring blankly back into the fire. "Alpine is the county seat for Brewster. It is the shipping center for all the Big Bend. A lucrative plum for any political machine that could break the hold that the Douglas-Owens faction has on the county. In a cattle country, the man with the most cattle can invariably gain political control. And in a dry cattle country, such as the Big Bend, the man who wants the most cattle must have the most water. As long as the Douglas-Owens faction is in power, the small *rancheros* will be protected, and the water rights will be equally divided so that no one man, or group of men, can get the upper hand."

Fayette's laugh was harsh. "How well you put it."

Montezuma didn't seem to hear him. "Whatever political measures you have tried were certainly not legal, *Señor* Beamont. And the other measures? Terrorism? You thought you could drive the *rancheros* away from their water with your raids. I understand Elgera Douglas can handle a gun. Was it she who put a stop to that? But not before several small *rancheros* had been murdered, eh? Pablo Otero's two sons. Sheriff Johnny Hagar is still looking for their murderer. Wouldn't he be surprised to know you are the man he wants, Orville Beamont?"

Beamont jumped to his feet, watery eyes wide. "You're lying. How did you know? You're a lying son-of-a...."

160

Montezuma's gaze swung to him, focusing suddenly in that strange, glittering intensity. "I am a *Tlatoani, Señor* Beamont. A supreme ruler. I know all. You led those raids on the *peones*. It was your guns that killed Otero's two sons!"

"You're a liar," screamed Beamont. "You're no *Tlatoani*. You're just a damn', greasy Indian, lying in your filthy teeth…."

The gunshot deafened Fayette. He saw Beamont stiffen. He saw Beamont claw at his skinny chest. He saw Beamont fall over onto his face in the fire.

For a long moment, nobody moved. The mahogany color left Elder Fayette's heavy-boned face until it was dead white beneath his soft-brimmed hat. He hadn't seen Montezuma draw the gun. He couldn't see it now. The Indian sat in that utter composure, his eyes looking into the flames without seeming to be focused on anything. His hands lay on his knees, empty. The only man with a gun out was Abilene, standing back there in the darkness by the horses, the Beale-Remington gleaming fitfully in his hand. But he hadn't fired. Fayette had caught the movement of his draw an instant after the shot. Finally, Fayette spoke between his teeth.

"Why did you have to do that?" he asked Montezuma.

Ortega took a sibilant breath. "The life of any man is *Tlatoani* Montezuma's sovereign right to take, or save."

The two Indians came from the darkness like wraiths. Fayette wasn't aware of them till they stood over the body, tall and stalwart in gilt-edged loin cloths and plumed bonnets, as like as two barrels of a scatter-gun. Without a word, they lifted Beamont and carried him out into the darkness.

"Now," said Ortega smoothly. "Shall we go on?"

161

Fayette looked toward him. Luis Ortega smiled, shrugging his shoulders, and his words were oily.

"Come now, *Señor* Fayette, you cannot tell me Beamont's death bothers you so much. He was a contemptible *borrachín*, of small value to either you or us. I have no doubt you planned to eliminate him."

Fayette lowered himself to a squatting position again with a slow, deliberate control over his weight that was surprising in such a heavy man. He looked into Montezuma's blank eyes.

"Sort of up to date, isn't it, for the reincarnation of Montezuma to carry a hide-out?" he said thinly. "All right. All right. Just don't try it on me, *compadre*. You haven't got enough lead in that cutter to stop me before I'd kill you so dead you'd never reincarnate."

"*Señor*…," Ortega began.

"Shut up," said Fayette. "I'm talking to Montezuma. You claim you can get rid of Chisos Owens and *Señorita* Scorpion? All right. I don't think you can, but I'll give you a crack at it. Elgera Douglas's Santiago spread is down in the Dead Horse Mountains. The only way in or out of the Santiago Valley is through a mine shaft. Beamont tried to get in three times when he was raiding down there, and couldn't do it. I've paid to have the girl nailed on the outside, more than once, but she can handle a gun better than any man in Texas, and she's a wildcat, and she still wears her boots sticking straight up."

"You have the payment?" asked Montezuma.

"You'll get your payment," said Fayette, "when you prove you can do the job."

"Getting rid of the girl and Chisos will pave the way to your control of the Big Bend," said Montezuma. "But you'll not be through fighting when they're dead.

162

Johnny Hagar is as dangerous as either of them. This Chisos Owens, is he really as strong a man as you claim?"

Fayette nodded his head toward the lean, silent man standing out by the horses. "Abilene's been with me a long time. I never thought I'd see the man he couldn't take care of. He couldn't take care of Chisos Owens."

Montezuma stared into the fire. "I have been hunting a man such as that for a long time. I shall need him in the days to come. It would be a crime to waste him by killing him. Why not turn his strength into our strength?"

"I'd give anything to have Chisos Owens riding in my wagon," said Fayette. "But you can't buy him."

"I did not mean that," said Montezuma, and his voice held a brooding portent, and he was looking into some infinity beyond the fire, his eyes blank and glazed. "There are other ways, *Señor* Fayette, other ways."

Surprise crossed the harsh planes of Elder Fayette's face for the first time. "What do you mean?"

Montezuma began to speak.

II

As Mictlantecutl in Hades rules
So I will rule above.
And turn strong men to traitor-fools
Who betray the ones they love.

THE NORTHER THAT HAD BEEN BUILDING FOR A WEEK now swept into the Santiago Valley with all its fury, howling dismally outside the sprawling adobe ranch house, bending the willows in the small *placeta* behind the building until they brushed against the earthen roof top with a mournful, scraping insistence, as if seeking the safety inside. Elgera Douglas sat in the huge, oak armchair by the roaring fire at one end of the long parlor. Her blonde hair fell shimmering and unruly along the curve of her cheek, flushed from the heat of the blaze. There was something wild in the arch of her eyebrow, a tempestuousness in the piquant curve of her pouting, lower lip. She sprawled in the chair like a boy, the length of her slim legs accentuated by the tight-fitting, *charro* trousers, gaudy with red roses down their seams.

She stiffened suddenly as the man entered the room from the hallway, her blue eyes flashing in a startled way, like a doe surprised at a pool.

"Were you thinking, *Señorita* Scorpion?" said Lobos Delcazar, his white teeth gleaming in a grin. "About Chisos Owens, perhaps?"

She tossed her head. "Never mind. Have you looked at the guards at the mine?"

"Not yet," said Lobos. "But you have nothing to worry about. Nobody can get into this valley. Two men in that mine could hold off an army."

Since the mysterious raids had been sweeping the Big Bend, and Pablo Otero's two sons had been murdered, Elgera had hired extra men to guard her spread. Lobos Delcazar had been recommended by Johnny Hagar, and deputized for the job. He was the cousin of Ramón Delcazar, who was Chisos Owens's best friend. He was a big, swaggering man, Lobos, wearing a Mexican dragoon's coat with red cuffs and collar over his white, silk shirt. To show off a waist as slim as a girl's, he wore a broad, red sash, tied on the right side and hanging down his legs so that the fringed edge touched the top of his polished Blucher boots. There was something ceremonious in the way he slipped a reddish bean from his pocket, passing it to his mouth.

"What are you eating all the time, Lobos?" asked Elgera. "*¿Fríjoles?*"

Lobos laughed, brushing his finger across his mustache affectedly. "No, *señorita*, not beans. Peyote."

"*¿Raíz diabólica?*"

"Ah, *señorita*, some may call it the devil weed," he said, and his red sash twitched as he moved toward her. "But, in truth, it is a boon to mankind. It makes life a gorgeous dream." He bowed low to her. "Many of the Mexicans use it. Perhaps you would let me inculcate you into its sacred mysteries."

He was almost leering, and she caught the slight dilation of his black pupils, and then the faint glaze that passed across his eyes following the dilation. She had seen it before, and somehow it made her feel that beneath all his affected ostentation Lobos Delcazar was not quite so colorful or gallant as he seemed, or so harmless.

"You'd better go out and see about changing the guards," she said, and rose from the chair.

He pressed a brown hand to his heart, and she thought his voice sounded mocking. "You would send me away so soon, *carisma!* All the *hombres* in Alpine talk about the wild girl of the Santiago, and now, when I finally see her, she sends me out into the storm."

Señorita Scorpion hitched her gun around. "Lobos."

He straightened slowly, and took a step backward. His eyes were on the gun, and his grin was suddenly forced. It was a big Army Model Colt, with black, rubber grips, and it hung against her slim thigh heavily.

"*Perdóname*," he said. "I did not realize it was that way. Would you really use that gun on me like they say,

165

señorita?"

"What do you think?"

He had recovered his composure, and he brushed his mustache with a finger, grinning broadly. "*Dios*, I think you would. *Sí*. I think you would. I'm going, *señorita*, I'm going right now. I hope you will forgive me. I am an impetuous fool. *Adiós, señorita.* It breaks my heart. *Adiós*...."

Laughing, he turned and swaggered to the door. The fire was almost swept out by the gale as he opened the portal. He had to turn and lean his weight against it to close it.

Elgera turned back to the chair angrily. Yet, as she sank into it again, she couldn't help comparing Lobos with Chisos Owens. Lobos was the kind of man who should appeal to her, really, the handsome swagger, the dash, the wildness. But, somehow, it was always Chisos, big and slow and stubborn, patiently waiting for her. The blue of her eyes deepened, staring into the fire. If she could only be sure how she felt for Chisos. She knew she loved him, yet there was something wild and untamed in her that rebelled at the thought of settling down.

She was still sitting there when the wind once more almost extinguished the fire. Elgera turned in the chair to see her brother bursting into the room. He was tall and lanky, Natividad Douglas, with jet black hair and blue eyes, long legs bowed slightly in greasy *chivarras*. He ran to the chair without shutting the door behind him, grabbing Elgera by the arm.

"You've got to get out," he shouted above the screaming norther. "Something's gone wrong. They've gotten through."

She was out of the chair, jerking loose from him.

166

"Who's gotten through?"

"I don't know," he yelled. "I was coming from the bunkhouse down by the river and saw them riding out of the mine."

Above the wind, she heard the first, faint shots, then the dull tattoo of hoof beats. Someone yelled from far away, the sound warped by the storm. Elgera pushed by Natividad, breaking into a run for the hall door.

"Not that way," he called. "You'll be caught...."

She ran down the hall to the right wing of the house, boots pounding the hard-packed, earthen floor. The wind struck her like a wall when she tore open the rear door, driving her against the outside of the house. She bent almost double, long hair streaming behind her as she struggled away from the building. The slope rose behind the *hacienda* into the *Sierra del Caballo Muerto*—the desolate Mountains of the Dead Horse, lifting their jagged, red peaks up to surround the Santiago completely. The only way in or out of the valley was through the shaft of the ancient Santiago Mine that opened out above the house. Elgera could hear the shouts and gunfire more clearly now. A ridden horse passed her far to the right, racing down the hill toward the river below. Other riders clattered by on her other side, missing her in the darkness.

Two of them hauled up on sliding haunches by the corrals above, and one man jumped off his mount to unlash the let-down bars. Elgera ran toward them, drawing her Army Colt. The one still mounted caught sight of her. He wore some sort of long cloak that whipped about him as he whirled in his saddle to fire.

She began shooting now. The one on foot turned from the bars, trying to get a rifle from the boot on his rig. Elgera's second shot caught him, and he fell back against the cottonwood post. His horse bolted, spooked by the gunfire. The mounted man had to stop shooting and fight his own frenzied horse, wheeling and plunging it on up the hill, trying to turn it back.

The slope shook as more horsemen passed Elgera, farther out, whooping savagely, going on down toward the bottom of the valley. A red light flared up behind her. They had set fire to the house.

She reached the corral before the man above had gotten his horse turned around. She ran past the one sagging against the bars, thinking her shot had finished him. She was tearing at the top bars when he threw himself on her from behind.

"*Miquistli!*" he screamed, and she caught the flash of his huge knife coming down on her.

Elgera whirled, throwing up her gun. The blade clanged off the Colt's barrel. The gun dropped from her stunned fingers, and the man's sweaty, fetid weight was against her, streaked with ochre and vermilion, black teeth showing beneath lips peeled back in a snarl. Gasping with the pain it must have caused him, he struck at her again. She jerked to one side beneath him. The cottonwood bar shuddered as the huge knife struck it near her shoulder.

Elgera threw herself forward, grabbing the man about his legs. They rolled into the grama grass. The girl fought savagely, clawing, biting, kicking. She came on top of him and rammed a vicious knee into his stomach. He choked and doubled up, trying to jab upward with the big knife he still held. But it was too long a weapon for close work, and she caught his wrist.

"*Miquiztli!*" he bawled again, jerking away from beneath her.

She was thrown off balance. He rolled over on her.

168

She held his wrist in a desperate grip. He tried to jerk the knife from between them before his full weight descended on her. But he didn't quite make it, and he came down on her heavily, and his body stiffened suddenly. He sprawled out on her, his gasp hot in her face. She struggled from beneath him, seeing that he had plunged the strange knife into his own body by rolling onto it.

The wind caught at Elgera as she ran toward the corral again, scooping up her gun where she had dropped it, jamming in fresh loads. Other horsemen had spotted the corral, and a bunch of them was wheeling toward it. But Elgera knew she could do nothing on foot, and she ran in among the squealing, kicking remuda of *Circulo S* horses, seeking her own palomino. There was no time to stop for saddle or reins. Reaching the big, golden stallion, she ripped off her long bandanna and grabbed the horse's creamy forelock, jerking its head down to knot the handkerchief around its jaw in a hackamore.

The riders were wheeling outside and shooting into the corral. A big mare screamed and reared and went down beneath the other frenzied horses. Elgera jumped aboard her palomino, cutting around to the rear of the corral where it was clear. She pulled the animal about and began firing her gun into the air. The thunder of shots behind them drove the remuda forward out the gate. The press of their hurtling bodies smashed against a section of the fence nearest the opening, taking it with them. And riding their tails like an Indian was *Señorita* Scorpion.

She had one, long leg hooked across the palomino's broad, bare back and was bent forward, lying along its left side, as she pounded out. The riders had to break

169

away from the point of the herd, and they were still milling around on either flank as the girl passed them. One wild-eyed horsebacker tried to follow her, gun stabbing the darkness. She turned, fired, and saw his horse stumble and fall, pitching the rider over its head.

Elgera rode with the stampede into the junipers on the slope above the house, then cut down through the trees, skirting the burning building. The majority of the raiders had gone on down into the bottom of the Santiago where the *Circulo S* cattle were. Already, a greater thunder than that of the stampeding horses was beginning to roll up to the girl.

She passed one of her own men, sprawled out where he had been caught running across the ford of the river, his face and torso lying in the sandy bank, his feet sunk in the water.

She splashed to the other side and raced past the bunkhouse. It was a blazing holocaust, a few remaining timbers reaching up through the flames like blackened bones. A riderless horse passed her going the other way. Then she crossed the bed ground of the cattle, and saw the tail of the stampede ahead. She couldn't understand why they were driving the herd northeast. The way out of the valley was to the west, behind her. The only thing ahead of her....

A strange, feral look crossed her face as she realized what did lie ahead of her. She bent forward on her horse, screaming at it in the wind. The stallion stretched out beneath her, lathered flanks heaving as it poured on the speed. A motte of poplars swept by it in a shadowy pattern, and she broke into the open *sachaguasca* flats beyond. Then she saw the first of the riders ahead. Some of her own men were still going, their guns spitting redly, now and then.

Elgera passed another body, sprawled on the ground, catching the impression of a paint-streaked face staring blankly upward. She fought her horse around the flank of the herd, bent low. The singular golden color of the animal was lost in the darkness and billowing dust, and the riders must have taken her for one of their own. She passed half a dozen of them, and they didn't look twice. Then ahead, on the swing, she saw her brother riding a big black. He was firing across the sea of horns at a dim rider far to the front.

"Natividad," screamed the girl. "Get up to the point. They're stampeding them toward the cut. Can't you see? They'll go over the cliffs!"

Natividad turned in his saddle, waving his gun. They were charging up the steepening slope through crackling sagebrush, and it looked like one smooth incline forming a flank of the jagged range that towered ahead, but there was a big cut that ran traversely across the shoulder of the mountain, not a quarter mile in front of the herd, a cut deep enough to finish every animal running, if they went into it.

Elgera's palomino passed Natividad's black, and she dropped over to hang on one side as she brought up with the next man. He glanced back at her, twisted around to fire. Over the humping withers of her palomino, she shot the rider from his saddle.

Four more horsebackers had been galloping farther out on the flank, and they quartered in through the dust as they saw their man go down. Elgera shifted her gun across the palomino's back, throwing down on the man leading the quartet.

Then she stopped her Colt there, with her thumb holding the hammer back, and her mouth opened in a soundless cry. The man across her sights wore a strange,

171

gaudy cloak that flapped away from shoulders like a range bull's. His sun-bleached eyebrows and stubble beard gleamed pale-blond against the face colored like old, saddle leather from the sun. He was close enough by now for her to see the fiendish grin that drew his lips back against teeth stained black. There was something savagely eager about the way he raised his six-shooter to fire at her.

"No," she called helplessly. "No...."

The man's gun flamed again and again. She didn't know which bullet struck her shoulder. It was as if a giant hand had torn her from the palomino. Screaming agony blotted out most of her consciousness when she hit. Through the awful pain, she was aware that she bounced and rolled, with the cattle thundering all about her, the ground shaking and rumbling beneath her.

Someone wheeled a horse above Elgera, jumping off. She felt hands lifting her up. She tried to aid as she was dragged out of the path of the running animals. A pair of steers shook the ground in front of her. The man dragged her toward an uplift of sandstone. A big heifer charged by behind. Then she was laid gently down, sobbing and shaking with pain and reaction. It was her brother, bending over her, breathing heavily, tearing her ripped, bloody shirt away from the bullet wound in her shoulder.

The sound of running cattle gradually died, and the dust settled softly back to earth, and it was ominously silent. In a little while, a cavalcade of horsemen passed them below, picking up the black horse Natividad had left behind, then going on back toward the burning house.

"Did you see who was leading them?" she queried. "Did you see who shot me?"

172

Natividad shook his head. "No, Elgera, all I cared about was getting you out of there."

She put her face against her brother's chest and began to cry again, and it wasn't because of the pain, now, and her voice had a dull, hopeless sound.

"It was Chisos Owens," she said. "Chisos Owens."

III

The Gods of Night are from Atzalan.
The Señores de la Noche *are nine.*
Their sacred sword is the macapan;
Their powers of darkness mine.

THE NORTHER HAD BLOWN ITSELF OUT, LEAVING A sombrous pall of yellow dust above Alpine. The hitchracks of the county seat were full of horses, huddled together as if they sensed the strange foreboding that seemed to have settled over the town, their tails fluttering in the last vagrant gusts of biting wind that mourned across Second Street.

Elgera had gotten her wound tended by Dr. Farris. Now she stood in the sheriff's office down Second Street from Main, watching Johnny Hagar apprehensively.

It was said, in the Big Bend, that Sheriff Johnny Hagar would be grinning when he came face to face with the devil himself. He wasn't grinning now. He stood in front of the girl, turning the strange sword over and over in his hands. It was made of some tough wood, about three feet long, with sharpened pieces of obsidian attached to the flat blade for cutting edges.

A man walked past the open door, head bent into the wind. His boots made a hollow sound on the plank walk.

173

"Crazy knife, isn't it?" said Elgera nervously. "The Indian who attacked me at the corral used it. You know most of the tribes, Hagar. I thought maybe you could tell me where it comes from."

Johnny Hagar studied the knife silently. He was a well-proportioned man for his six feet four, broad shoulders filling out his flannel shirt, twin, ivory-handled Peacemakers riding slim hips in an arrogant, reckless way. He kept his curly, black hair cropped close, accentuating the youth of his clean-shaven jaw and straight, frank mouth. The only thing that might have indicated his true sophistication were his eyes. The faint wind wrinkles at their corners gave them an older, worldly wise look. Or perhaps that look emanated from the eyes themselves. He had been around.

"You were wiped out?" he said finally.

"I'd sunk most of my cash in the herds," she said, "and improvements on the spread. They ran every cow I owned off the cliff. Whatever else I had was burned in the house and outbuildings. My uncle and brother were guarding the mine. You know how the lay of that land is. They could have held it against all the cavalry from Fort Leaton. Only somebody coming in from behind could have gotten past them, or someone they trusted enough to allow close in. Chisos Owens...."

She broke off, turning toward the window so Hagar wouldn't see the tears welling in her eyes. *Yes, they would have trusted Chisos Owens with their very lives. It must have been pitifully simple for him.* She shook her blonde head angrily, seeing that most of the huddled mounts at the hitch rack in front of this office bore the Teacup brand. Across the street in front of the Alamo Saddlery, a little knot of dusty cowhands stood talking in low tones. On the corner of Main and Second, by the

174

Alpine Lodge, were others.

"I see Fayette's in town with his whole army," she said. "Is that how we stand?"

"Our position isn't so good," said Hagar, "and he knows it. I think he's getting ready to push something. If it was just a matter of stacking my guns against Fayette, I wouldn't worry. But you know it's never been that. As long as Chisos and you were the strong hand in this county, and backed me, whatever play I made was all right with the county commissioners. But with Chisos out from under now, and you financially wiped out, Fayette will pump the first wrong move I make, and start putting pressure on the county board, and the courthouse gang, and I'll be out of office."

She nodded dismally. "I'm afraid we've got too many people in this county who blow with the wind. Mayor Cabell. Judge Sewell. More than one county supervisor I could name...."

"*Sí*," said Ramón Delcazar. "And right now, it looks like the wind has shifted to Elder Fayette. It looks like he will get his water from us small *rancheros* without any more trouble, eh? It used to be Chisos who protected us. And now, with him doing this, what chance have we? I still can't believe it. My best friend. Chisos Owens. Burning the very house he helped me build. Butchering my *pobre* cattle. Leading the attack on you, Elgera."

He shook his head morosely, sitting on the desk with his bare feet on Hagar's swivel chair. He was Lobos Delcazar's cousin, a slim young Mexican with the tails of his white, cotton shirt slapping outside his cotton trousers, and a pair of black-butted Forty-Fives strapped around outside of that.

"Montez came in yesterday from Persimmon Gap,"

175

said Hagar. "Same story. Five hundred of his cattle run off. Spread ruined."

"Lobos," said Ramón. "You say you couldn't find his body?"

"No," said Elgera. "The last time I saw your cousin was just before he went out to change the guards at the mine. We found several of my own hands dead, and three of those raiders. Natividad and I hid in the rocks until they left. He's still down at the Santiago with the wounded. All I brought north with me was that knife, Hagar."

"I'm sorry to see it," the sheriff said, looking at the sword. "I heard they were rising again, somewhere up in New Mexico. I didn't think it had to do with the raids that have been sweeping the Big Bend. I sort of thought Fayette and Beamont were behind them. Do you know what a *macapan* is, Elgera?"

"*Dios*," said Ramón, jumping off the desk. "Is that a *macapan?*"

"Who's rising again?" asked *Señorita* Scorpion. "A *macapan?* What are you talking about?"

"The Montezuma cult," said Hagar somberly. "Not many people know about it. In Eighteen Forty-Six, when the United States went to war with Mexico, the Mexican government wasn't very sure just how loyal their northern province of New Mexico was. In order to strengthen that loyalty, the officials in Mexico City sent to New Mexico a manuscript claiming that, when Cortés had conquered the Aztecs of Mexico in Fifteen Twenty-One, he had married an Indian princess named Malinche. According to this manuscript, Malinche was the daughter of the Indian emperor named Montezuma, who ruled the land to the north. Thus, as part of her dowry, she brought to Cortés the province of what is now New Mexico. The whole story was a fabrication, of course, designed to prove to the Indians of New Mexico how much they owed allegiance to Mexico. In reality, Malinche was Cortés's mistress, hated by the Aztecs."

Ramón was watching Hagar with a strange intensity. "How can you be sure of that, Juanito?"

"It's a historical fact," said Hagar. "Also, there was no northern emperor named Montezuma. Montezuma II was in reality the ruler of the Aztecs at that time, and his death was brought about by Hernando Cortés. The Mexican government twisted these facts for their own use. The upper-class Spaniards who ruled Mexico after Cortés were known as *guáchupines*. These tyrants have been hated bitterly and traditionally by the Indians of New Spain for the last four centuries. Cortés was the first *guáchupin*, and, when he caused Montezuma to be killed, it made Montezuma a martyr, and his name became the symbol for all *guáchupin* tyranny. The Mexican officials in Eighteen Forty-Six knew how much sympathy the Indians had for the symbol, and used it in their document, not only to prove how conclusively New Mexico belonged to Mexico, but in a hope that the name would sway the Indians."

"It swayed them all right," said Ramón. "But not the way the Mexican government had planned. The manuscript had no effect as propaganda. You will remember that the *Americanos* took New Mexico with hardly a shot fired."

"What this manuscript really did," said Hagar, "was to start a strange, new religion almost overnight, known as the Montezuma cult. The Papagos applied the name Montezuma to their Elder Brother, a god that had existed long before Hernando Cortés was born. The Pecos Indians claimed Montezuma had been born in

177

their village...was supposed to have worn golden shoes and walked to Mexico City, where the *guáchupines* confiscated them so he couldn't walk back. The *Pecosenos* kept a sacred fire burning night and day in their kiva, awaiting the return of Montezuma."

"And they use this sword...this *macapan?*" asked Elgera.

"A *macapan* is the sword of the ancient Aztecs," replied Hagar. "I found out a lot of this from Waco Warren. You know him, Elgera. One of my deputies. Half-breed Comanche boy. He claims there's something going on in the Guadalupes. The Indians know a lot more about those things than we do. I'd take his word. If they are rising again, it's too bad. No telling who belongs to them and who doesn't. Could be all around us, and we wouldn't even know it. Most of the peons down here have Indian blood in 'em. Get them soaked in red-eye and thinking they're descended from the Aztecs, and you have a Montezuma on your hands. I don't like it. Fanatics have tried to use the symbol of Montezuma before to unite the Indians against the white man down this way. You can understand how dangerous it would be, used by the wrong man...," he broke off, and his eyes darkened as he looked past Elgera, and his voice was suddenly brittle. "Oh, hello, *Señor* Ortega."

Ortega carried a gold-handled cane over one arm, and rubbed his hands together in an oily way when he spoke. He was the kind of man whose words hid from each other.

"*Buenos días, Señor* Hagar," he said sibilantly. "My...ah...consignment was not on the afternoon train. We thought perhaps that you could throw some light on the matter."

"Hell, Ortega," said Elder Fayette, shoving past him.

"You beat around the bush too much. Say it straight. The rifles have disappeared, Hagar. By your order, it seems."

Fayette reminded *Señorita* Scorpion of Chisos Owens in that moment, standing with a stubborn, inexorable look to the forward thrust of his bulky shoulders. Teacup riders filled the doorway behind their boss, and spilled out across the sidewalk into the street, and Mayor Cabell had difficulty getting through them. He was a dowdy, little man in a rumpled Prince Albert, his gray hair fringing a bald pate. He cleared his throat.

"Yes, Sheriff," he said pompously. "Disappeared. *Señor* Luis Ortega is the Army contractor, as you know. Or do you? Yes. Five hundred Henry repeaters, Hagar, consigned to Fort Leaton. That's a lot of guns to disappear. Yes, a lot of guns."

Hagar suddenly grinned. "Isn't it, Mayor? You must be mistaken. Those guns were never under civil jurisdiction till the Army picked them up here at Alpine. I'm the only one with authority to issue any order releasing them. And I certainly didn't do that. There was an armed guard aboard the train, and I had two deputies down at the station, waiting to hold the rifles till a troop from Fort Leaton came after them with the wagons. Nothing short of the U. S. Army could have gotten away with those guns."

"The sheriff of Terrel County," said Fayette heavily, "got a wire, ordering him to unload the guns at Sanderson and hold them there for the troop from Fort Leaton. The wire was sent from here, under your authority, Hagar. Soldiers arrived at Sanderson, with the wagons, accompanied by one of your deputies, and took the guns."

"Yes." Mayor Cabell cleared this throat. "Yes. Took

the guns. And now, a Captain Maryvaille is here with his Army wagons, and a troop of cavalry, expecting to find the Henrys waiting. He says Fort Leaton did not send any troop to Sanderson, and they have not received the guns."

"Perhaps," said Luis Ortega urbanely, "you can enlighten us, *Señor* Hagar."

The Teacup riders shoved in farther, and Elgera suddenly felt a strange suffocation. She turned from Fayette to Hagar, fists closing. A tall, young captain pushed his way through the crowd, slipping off a white glove. His forage cap sat on his clipped, blond hair jauntily, his arrogant face was flushed.

"Is this your sheriff, Mayor Cabell?" he asked in a loud voice. "I demand you put him under arrest immediately."

"Ah, *Capitán*," interposed Ortega. "Surely we can settle this unfortunate error without such...ah...drastic measures. After all, if Sheriff Hagar made a mistake...."

"Diverting government supplies *is* a mistake," said the captain, fixing Ortega with his cold, blue eyes. "You're the contractor? I should think you'd be the first to want the culprit attended to. And you, Sheriff. What in thunder did you plan to do with that many guns? I can't understand it."

Hagar turned calmly and took a big ring of keys off a peg on the wall, then chose one carefully, and inserted it in the lock on the barred door that opened into the corridor between the cells at the rear. At the other end of the corridor was the back door leading into an alley. Elgera began to edge between Hagar and Fayette. If Hagar wanted it that way, all right.

"What are you doing, Sheriff?" demanded Cabell.

"I'm unlocking the door," smiled Hagar, watching

them. "Is this your frame, Fayette?"

Fayette glanced imperceptibly at the Teacup riders behind him. "Frame?"

"Frame-up," said Hagar, opening the door unhurriedly. "I never sent any wire to unload the guns at Sanderson. The only way it could have come from this office was that one of my deputies sent it without my authority. Who did you reach, Fayette? Waco Warren? I don't think you could buy him. Nevada Wallace?"

Hagar had moved so calmly, so obviously, that none of them had realized his intention at first. Suddenly Fayette sensed it. He jumped forward.

"Don't let him get through that door. The back way...!"

The sudden scuffling surge of men stopped as soon as it had begun. Fayette stood where he had taken the leap toward Hagar, a dull flush creeping into his heavy face. Elgera hadn't actually seen the movement of Hagar's hands. Somehow he held his guns now, and he was grinning easily, and backing through the door.

"I don't know what this is about," he said. "I'm not going to take any frame-up sitting down. Don't try to follow me."

"Drop your iron, Johnny!"

As if jerked by a string, Johnny Hagar whirled and fired at the huge, yellow-haired man in the rear door before he had finished shouting. It was Nevada Wallace, and his gun went off at the roof as he staggered backward into the alley, grabbing at the hand Hagar's slug had smashed.

Elgera threw herself at Fayette, tripping him over onto her own body as he jumped for Hagar again. The others swarmed past as she fell beneath Fayette's great weight. Desperately she caught at the captain's boot. He stumbled and kicked her hand free, and threw himself into the hallway as Hagar swung back. Elgera struggled to get out from under Fayette, a sea of kicking, shuffling boots surrounding her.

"Get those guns," the captain shouted.

A Peacemaker boomed, and someone grunted sickly. Fayette got to his hands and knees above Elgera. She clawed at him, trying to kick his legs from beneath him again. He hit her in the face. Then he was off her, throwing himself into the struggling mass of men. She could see dimly that all but two were in the hallway fighting Hagar now. Mayor Cabell still stood between her and the door.

"Please." He cleared his throat. "Please. Johnny was the best sheriff this town ever had. Be careful. Yes."

The light from the front door was blocked off, then, by the second man's body. He seemed to bend over Elgera from behind as she struggled to her hands and knees, dazed from Fayette's blow. She realized suddenly that the man had placed himself so as to hide her from the mayor, and she tried to jump erect. She caught a blurred view of *mitaja* leggin's, and heard his voice soft in her ear.

"I...ah...regret this exceedingly, *señorita*."

There was a sudden, shocking pain. There was nothing.

Ⓥ Ⓥ Ⓥ Ⓥ Ⓥ

"I am glad to see you are regaining consciousness," the cultivated voice was saying. "It was an execrable thing to do, but necessary, you must agree. They would have put you away with Hagar, I think. Perhaps for aiding and abetting his escape, or trying to. The charge wouldn't have mattered. They just wanted their paws on you."

Into her vision swam the narrow, vulpine face of Luis Ortega. The hood of his cloak was thrown back, and his queued, black hair lay like a slick skullcap over the top of his thin head, gleaming in the light of an oil lamp on the marble-topped table.

"You are in the Alpine Lodge," he said. "The Teacup riders Fayette left out in Second Street were very solicitous when I told them you had been...ah...incapacitated in the struggle. They even offered to accompany me to the doctor's office with you. A whole lot of them. They said they would wait outside. I did not know the doctor was such a good *amigo* of yours. It simplified matters...and that alley his back door opens onto. *Gracias a Dios, señorita*, you are now hidden from them right under their very noses."

"Why?" said Elgera, and the springs squeaked as she swung her legs to the floor.

"Why?" he repeated. "Perhaps *you* will elucidate."

"Why did you get me out of it?" she asked. "What do you want?"

"Aha," he laughed softly, tilting his head back. "You are a singular judge of character, *señorita*."

She moved unsteadily to the window. The two-story Alpine Lodge stood on the northwest corner of Second and Main. She was on the second story of the side facing across Second to the Mescal Saloon on the southwest corner of Main and Second, and the sheriff's office farther down Second. A couple of Fayette's Teacup hands stood in the door of the sheriff's office. Another came out of a building farther down the street, looking toward them and shaking his head.

Elgera's eyes were caught by movement on Main. Two more Teacup men had come out of Si Samson's livery stable on the other side of the street, and stood looking up toward the brick depot at the north end of town. Luis Ortega's oily voice startled her, coming from directly behind.

"*Sí*, they are looking for you, *señorita*. Perhaps it was Fayette's meaning to get you and Hagar both out of the way at one blow, eh?"

She turned angrily. "Fayette was connected with that business about the guns then?"

Ortega shrugged his shoulders, and his words slid unctuously through a secretive smile. "You ask me? Perhaps many men are connected with it, *señorita*, whom you would never suspect were connected with it, and then again, perhaps many men whom you would suspect were connected with it were not connected with it at all."

"I would suspect you were connected with it," she said, "in more ways than just that of the government contractor who doesn't seem at all worried about the money he stands to lose by the theft of his guns."

A mock hurt look tilted his brows; he held out his slim hand, opening his mouth as if to protest. Then his mobile lips slipped into that sly smile, and he began to chuckle sibilantly.

"*Sí, señorita, sí, sí*. Perhaps you are *correcto*. Let us say that I am an *hombre* who is not averse to making a few *pesos* on the side. And it is a fact that the more sides an *hombre* looks on, the more *pesos* he is likely to find."

"Saving me was one of those sides?"

"Ah, *señorita*, you do me an injustice," he said. "What *caballero* wouldn't throw his life at the feet of such a *carissima*? You can have that free of charge. But, shall we say, there are other...ah...services I could render you...."

184

She turned away from the window. "I was ruined in that raid on my spread. I couldn't pay you for anything, and, if I could, I wouldn't."

He held up an ingratiating finger. "Ah, perhaps your cattle were killed and your home destroyed. But you have some...ah...liquid securities left. Not enough to do much against Fayette, perhaps, but enough, I'm sure, to propitiate the sordid god of gold that I have the unfortunate weakness of worshipping."

She started for the door. "Thanks for helping me. I'm sure there's nothing I could want from you."

"Before you throw yourself to Fayette's dogs," he said, and it stopped her, and he began rubbing his thumb against his forefinger. "I see I must come to the point. How much would you give to find *Señor* Chisos Owens?"

Elgera felt the blood drain from her face. *Chisos?* A wild look flashed in her eyes. She moved toward Ortega in a swift, tense way, like a cat about to leap.

"You know where Chisos is?"

Ortega took a step backward, holding up a hand. "I have certain connections, shall we say, that would assist you immeasurably in finding him. I am sure the Alpine National Bank would honor your check for...ah...ten thousand, yes, ten thousand dollars, made out in my name, if you would care to have access to those connections."

The shot outside was flat and muffled. There was another one. Someone yelled downstairs, then the thud of feet came from the hall. Elgera had started for the door again when in burst Waco Warren, one of Hagar's deputies, the half-breed Comanche with his buckskin leggin's tucked inside old, cavalry boots. He must have been falling when he thrust the door open. He hung onto

185

the knob, and the portal swung in with his weight, carrying him on around with it till the door smashed against the wall. He went to his knees there, with his head against the panels and his back toward Elgera, his fist still closed desperately on the knob.

"Elgera," he gasped, trying to rise. "They're taking Hagar away. Nevada. Fayette's man. Said they're taking him to Terrel County because the crime was committed there. You know that's a lie. They won't take him to Sanderson...."

She hadn't yet reached the deputy when someone else ran in the doorway. A gun bellowed. Waco grunted in a sick, hollow way. He jerked on around, and his shoulder brushed Elgera's outstretched hand as he fell on his face with his legs all twisted up under him.

Elgera didn't know just when she had drawn her gun. It must have been the reaction to the shot. She stood there with the big Army Colt leveled at the man in the doorway, and she had gotten it out soon enough, she realized, to have him covered before he even began to raise his own Forty-Fives from where they had been pointed at Waco Warren.

"Don't lift them any higher, Ramón," she said, and she was turned now so she could see Luis Ortega. "In fact, you'd better just drop them."

Ramón Delcazar's mouth opened slightly. Then his Forty-Fives made a metallic thud on the floor, one after the other. Ortega was bent forward with his gold-handled cane gripped in both hands, as if he had started to do something with it. He straightened with an effort. His chuckle was weak.

"*Por Dios, señorita*, my eyes must be going bad in my old age. I did not see you draw that gun. How did it get in your hand?"

186

"Why," asked Elgera whitely, "did you have to do that?"

Ramón looked surprised. "I thought Waco was after you...."

Elgera didn't look at the dead man, lying on the floor. She was trying to keep from feeling the horror of it. She was remembering how Hagar had said they would be everywhere, now, if the cult was rising again, and that there would be no telling who belonged, and who didn't.

"Oh," she said. "You thought Waco was after me. Are you part Quill, Ramón?"

Ramón nodded. "*Sí*, my grandmother was a Quill. A pure-blood Indian of Mexico. And that makes me...."

He stopped suddenly, a strange look crossing his face. Elgera backed across the room and shoved up the window overlooking a shed roof that slanted down into the alley behind the Alpine Lodge.

"*Señorita*," said Ortega, "what about our... ah... arrangement?"

The girl threw a slim leg over the sill. "I don't think I want your connections to help me locate Chisos, Ortega. I have some connections of my own, and they only play one side of the game at a time. Don't follow me for a while. I'd very much like an excuse to kill you, either of you!"

IV

In TONALAMENTE, the BOOK OF FATE
All things are decreed and written.
For Chisos Owens it is now too late.
John Hagar shall next be smitten.

THE CAMPFIRE WINKED SMALL AND LONELY IN THE malignant darkness that cloaked the Barrillas, and that pressed in on Hagar with a frightening intensity as he sat cross-legged before the softly snapping flames, trying not to look at the circle of faces surrounding him, silent, inscrutable, waiting. Farther out, he could see the circle of wagons with U. S. Army showing vaguely on their blurred white tilts.

"You were the deputy with that troop of cavalry who got the rifles at Sanderson?" said Hagar thinly.

Lobos Delcazar was dumping coffee beans from a paper sack into a tin cup. He still wore his blue dragoon's coat with the red cuffs and collar, and his fringed sash twitched at his Blucher boots with each movement. He showed his white teeth in a grin.

"Sure, Hagar, that was me. I didn't have any trouble, as your deputy. We timed it nicely, no? I fixed the guards down there at the Santiago so Chisos Owens could get through without any trouble, and left even before he got there, on my way to Sanderson to meet my troop of cavalry and pick up the guns."

"Oh," said Hagar. "It was you who fixed the guards at the Santiago? We sort of had Chisos pegged for that one. Why didn't you just shoot the girl in the back, too, while you were about it?"

"Do you think I am the kind who shoots women, Johnny?" said Lobos, looking hurt, and then he grinned. "Besides, Elgera is too good with an iron. I don't think even you could edge her out. Why should I take chances with a wildcat like that when it wasn't necessary? Chisos Owens was supposed to have taken care of her. Nevada tells me he slipped up, though."

Nevada Wallace stood uncomfortably to one side, the firelight glinting on his curly, yellow hair. The Peacemakers didn't have their rakish threat, somehow, on his thick hips; they looked ponderous and
188

ineffectual. He must have coveted them for a long time. They were the first things he took from Hagar. He had taken the sheriff east, toward Sanderson, until they were out of sight of Alpine, then turned north into these mountains. The hand Hagar had wounded in the jail was bandaged. Nevada kept moving it around as if it hurt him, and his mouth took an ugly twist whenever he looked at Hagar.

"The girl hit town this morning," he said sullenly. "Fayette tried to get her when we hooked Johnny, here. She got away somehow. I think that Ortega had a hand in it."

Lobos poured water from a five-gallon Army canteen into the coffee pot, sighing. "*Sí*, I suppose Ortega did have a hand in it. He has a hand in 'most everything, it seems. Like that gun deal. Ortega found out Elder Fayette would pay him twice as much for those Henry repeaters as the Army would. The Army had already given him his payment, however…an outrageous price, by the way…and he didn't want to lose that. They could hardly demand a refund, though, if the guns were diverted by a party who could not possibly be identified with Ortega, could they? He was quite willing to sell the guns again, under those conditions."

"What did Fayette want with the guns?" asked Hagar thinly.

"He wanted to give them to us," said Lobos, and laughed. "I see you are confused. We wouldn't have fooled with Ortega or Fayette, understand, but we wanted those five hundred Henry repeaters, and were in no position to take them by force. Thus, we contracted to do a little job for Fayette, in return for his getting us the rifles. Ortega, as a government supply contractor, had access to a number of uniforms. Thus, Fayette's riders became a troop of cavalry. I couldn't use my own boys there, could I? Even that short-sighted Sanderson sheriff would have smelled some bad beans if I'd showed up with a bunch of Indians in U. S. cavalry uniforms. Nevada was the one who wired to unload the guns at Sanderson. There you have the whole little conspiracy. Fayette gets his job of work done. Ortega gets two prices for his guns. We get the guns. We even get you, as sort of a bonus. Nevada gets to be sheriff. Ah, how happy everybody is."

Very clever, thought Hagar, and he could feel the frustrated anger building up in him again. He had tried to control it all the way from Alpine. It was boiling near the surface now. He wondered how much longer he could hold it in. Very clever. So they had it all sewed up. Him all sewed up. Everything all sewed up. He put his manacled hands in his lap suddenly and knotted them together till his fingers hurt.

Outside the circle of wooden-faced Indians, a dozen white men were stripping off yellow-striped cavalry trousers and blue coats. Abilene came walking over, Elder Fayette's right bower, a lean, taciturn man who had ridden with Nevada and Hagar from Alpine. He was constantly rolling wheat straws, and Hagar guessed it was as good a way as any to keep his fingers supple for the big Beale-Remington he wore. Abilene studied the cigarette he was building, speaking in a toneless, impersonal voice.

"I'll take the Teacup boys back now. Coming, Nevada?"

Hagar looked up sharply. "Yeah. Go ahead, Nevada. You should make a good sheriff. I guess you've been with me long enough to learn all the little tricks. Tell Cabell hello for me. Tell all my friends hello. I must have a lot of friends in Alpine."

"Shut up," said Nevada sullenly.

"I thought you were my friend, Nevada," said Hagar. "That's funny, isn't it? I thought all of you were my friends. Lobos and Cabell and Ramón Delcazar and Waco Warren and you, Nevada...."

The yellow-haired man dropped his good hand to the white butt of a Peacemaker. "I said, shut up."

"Your trust is childish," laughed Lobos. "Fayette reached Nevada a long time ago. Promised him a spot in his set-up. Nevada's always had his eye on your job, and your guns. You should never trust anyone, Hagar. Look what Chisos Owens did to *Señorita* Scorpion. The girl will be the next one to turn on you...."

"Don't talk about her," said Hagar between his teeth.

"Why not?" said Lobos. "Women are the ones you should trust the least. I would rather turn my back on a sidewinder than a woman. And that wild girl. *¡Caracoles!* She is the worst of all. She is just a little...."

Hagar's face twisted, and he grunted with the effort of coming up off the ground and throwing himself across the fire at Lobos. He slammed his manacled wrists into Lobos's face. Straddling the man's body as it went down, he beat at him again. Over Lobos's yell, Hagar caught the scuffle of feet behind him. A blow on the head drove his face into Lobos's chest. He sprawled helplessly on the man beneath him. Lobos struggled out from under, scrambling to his feet. Hagar tried to rise to his hands and knees, but another savage blow put him flat again.

"That's enough, Nevada," shouted Lobos hoarsely.

Hagar rolled over spasmodically, throwing his arms up to guard his head. He could see the giant, yellow-

191

haired man bent over him, heavy face stamped with a brutal hatred.

"That's enough, I said!" screamed Lobos in a rage.

Nevada grunted as he struck again. Hagar caught the blow on his shoulder, crying out with the stunning pain. The gunshot drowned his voice. He heard the thud of a six-shooter dropped by his head. Nevada's tremendous body crashed down, knocking the breath from Hagar. He was rolled toward Lobos, and he lay helplessly beneath Nevada, staring at the tall man in the blue dragoon's coat. Still holding his smoking Colt, Lobos Delcazar moved toward Hagar. His face was livid with rage, and bleeding where Hagar had smashed him with the handcuffs.

He stooped to roll Nevada off the sheriff. Hagar felt his body grow rigid. He lay there, stunned and sickened, knowing whatever he did now was no good, and his eyes opened wide and clear as he stared up at Lobos, because that was the way he would take it whenever it came.

Lobos's body was trembling perceptibly, and his gusty breathing had a harsh, uncontrollable sound. His black eyes glittered, the pupils dilating and contracting, and his lips writhed across his white teeth without any sound. He held his Colt pointed at Hagar's head. Hagar could see his finger quivering on the trigger.

Suddenly, Lobos took a ragged breath and straightened with a jerk, turning away as if to find control, and his voice shook. "All right. All right, Hagar. If it was up to me, I'd kill you for that. But it isn't up to me. Maybe this way is better. Killing a man finishes it off so quick, anyhow. You'll pay, Hagar, more than you can imagine, you'll pay."

The men around the fire had all risen, and were just

192

settling back now, watching Lobos or Hagar. Lobos untied his gaudy neckerchief and stooped to the big Army canteen. He wet the silk cloth and began to wipe his bleeding face. Squatting there, still holding his gun in one hand, he looked up at Abilene.

"You tell Fayette, if he doesn't like what happened, he can send another one of his sheriffs out, and I'll do the same with him," said Lobos. "Tell him to send you, Abilene. Yeah. Tell Fayette to send you."

Abilene's opaque eyes were as impersonal as his toneless voice. "Never mind. We didn't figure on using Nevada. He was too dumb to make the kind of tin badge Fayette wants. You saved us a piece of business, that's all."

He turned and rounded up the Teacup riders who had posed as troopers, and they filtered silently out through the wagons toward the horses. Still dabbing at his face, Lobos took the boiling coffee off the rocks and began to pour it into the tin cups. Hagar rolled over on his belly, shaking his head dazedly. The men around the fire were all watching him now, faces unreadable. There wasn't a white man among them.

Lobos held out a cup of coffee. "Go ahead, Johnny. It's all over now. You'll need something. We've got a long trip ahead."

Hagar took the cup, holding it tentatively in his hand. Lobos unbuckled his own gun belt and turned to take Hagar's ivory-handled weapons off Nevada. He caressed one of the white butts.

"You know," he said. "I'm sort of glad it happened this way. I always thought these guns would look nice on me."

He laughed suddenly, and shoved the holsters down snug against his legs. Hagar stared at Nevada's body.

193

He turned away, sickened. Lobos jerked his head toward the dead man. Two of the Indians rose and dragged Nevada away.

"Go ahead," he said. "Drink it, Hagar. Make you feel better, eh? Everything's over now. Drink it."

Hagar took a sip, grimaced. "Tastes like alkali."

Lobos looked into the fire, a peculiar lack of focus to his eyes, and he grinned inanely. "*Sí*, it sometimes does. You will get used to it after a while."

Hagar took another drink. "What do you mean? What's your cut in this, Lobos? Did Fayette promise you a soft spot in his county? Or cash on the barrel head?"

Lobos looked at Hagar without seeming to see him. "Neither, Hagar. I do not care to have a job with Fayette's bunch when he climbs into Brewster County's saddle, because he won't sit there very long. And whatever we do is not for money."

"We?" said Hagar, and looked around at the silent group again. They were drinking coffee, too, watching him over the rims of their cups. He suddenly felt dizzy. Then his head seemed to expand like a balloon. The tin cup clinked against a rock as he dropped it.

"We?" he said again, and giggled drunkenly.

Lobos laughed, too. "Yes, we. Not these men, specifically, though they belong to us."

"Us?" said Hagar, wondering what the hell was wrong with him. "What kind of coffee was that, Lobos? Us?"

Lobos took several reddish beans from his pocket and popped one into his mouth, chewing it slowly. "It was partly coffee. *Sí*. Sometimes we take it like this"—he put another bean in his mouth—"the traditional way."

Hagar giggled foolishly, swaying forward suddenly.

194

"Whaddaya mean? Whaddaya talking about?"

"You will find out, *Señor* Hagar, and, when you do, believe me, you will wish you hadn't."

Ⓥ Ⓥ Ⓥ Ⓥ Ⓥ

She was an old woman with a furrowed face the color of worn saddle leather, sitting cross-legged in the smoky wickiup somewhere north of Horsethief Crossing on the Pecos. She was a Comanche, with her stringy, gray hair braided over her right shoulder and falling down in front of her greasy, buckskin shift. She was Waco Warren's mother.

"So they killed my son," she said dully, and her utter grief shone in her eyes. "I know Ramón Delcazar. I didn't think he was the kind to shoot his friends in the back. But they are rising again, and how can we know who are our enemies any more, and who are our friends?"

She rocked slowly back and forth over the fire, hugging skinny arms tight against her chest. Elgera Douglas sat across from the old woman. The shimmering beauty of her long, blonde hair was filmed with dust, and a burning, feverish look marked her face. Finally the hag spoke again.

"How did you escape from them, *muchachita?*"

Señorita Scorpion shrugged wearily, forced to admire the woman's effort at self-control. "The alley behind the Alpine Lodge runs between Second and First. The Alamo Saddlery fronts on Second, a storeroom behind that opens onto the alley. I hid in there till night. Fayette's men had all the streets out of town blocked and were stopping all the riders, coming or going. They couldn't guard every inch. I slipped by them on foot and

195

hiked to Marathon where I got this horse."

Little by little the Indian's grief began to seep through, and her voice shook now, though she tried to control it. "You found Hagar in Sanderson?"

Elgera shook her head. "They didn't take him there."

The first hoarse sob escaped the old woman. Then she began to hum under her breath, a monotonous, choked sound, with her seamed face appearing from the smoke as she swayed forward, and disappearing again as she swayed back. Her hollow intonation grew louder, and Elgera realized it was the death chant for Waco Warren.

"He was a good boy," muttered the old woman in a stifled, sing-song voice. "It didn't matter if he was a half-breed. John Warren was a good man, and Waco Warren is gone to our old gods. And Johnny Hagar is gone, too. First it was Chisos Owens. Now Johnny Hagar. You would follow them of your own free will?"

"They didn't take Hagar to Sanderson," said Elgera tensely. "Where did they take him? What are they doing to him? I've got to go after him. Maybe it's too late for Chisos. But Hagar...."

"You don't realize what you say." The old woman's voice was a hollow chant. "You don't realize what it means to go after them. They have many powers that you or I do not understand. They are all around us. We cannot say who belongs to them, and who doesn't. Chisos Owens has lost his soul to them. Johnny Hagar is now in their hands. You do not know what you are doing."

Elgera's voice sounded desperate. "I do. I can't sit by and see this happen to them. They're my friends."

"You will avenge my son's death?"

"If I can. How?"

"The only way you can help Hagar, the only way you can stop all this, is to reach the one who thinks he is the reincarnation of Montezuma, and kill him," the old woman said in a sudden burst of viciousness. Then she resumed her chanting. "That would avenge my son's death. But only those who pay homage to the gods of ancient Atzalan know where Montezuma reigns. I do not worship Quetzalcoatl, but I am an Indian, and know many things the white man does not know. I can tell you that somewhere in the Guadalupes the Montezumans are gathering."

"I didn't think even the Indians knew what was in those mountains," said Elgera.

The old woman nodded, swaying back and forth more swiftly. "The Guadalupes are inaccessible in many places, and my people have never penetrated them. But the Montezumans are gathering. From as far south as Mexico City come Quills, and from the Sierra Madres come Yaquis, and from Chihuahua and Durango come Mexicans who claim to be descended from the ancient Aztecs. Each month on the first night of the full moon, the new ones gather at the deserted Apache Mine south of Pecos, and one of Montezuma's *techutlis* comes to get them."

"*Techutlis?*"

"The *techutlis* are a knightly order of the Aztecs," muttered the hag. "This *techutli* leads the newcomers westward from the Apache Mine, traveling only at night, and no white man knows of their coming or going. But the Comanches do, and the Apaches. Yet, even my people have only been able to trail them as far as the outer slopes of the Guadalupes. Those warriors who followed them in, never came back. Do you still wish to go, *muchachita?*"

"I told you," said Elgera grimly.

Waco Warren's mother began to nod her head in a
197

sharper rhythm now, and tears were streaming from her eyes, and it cost her more of an effort to go on talking. "Very well. In two days the moon will be full again. A new group will be meeting at the mine, and the *techutlis* will come for them. You will be one of their number. *Pues*, the Montezumans know you are looking for them. Your blonde hair would mark you as quickly as the gold color of your palomino marks it as your horse. You will not go as Elgera Douglas."

Elgera felt her breathing become heavier, and she licked nervous lips, watching the old woman sway toward her through the smoke, and sway away from her, and unconsciously she began to sway slightly, too, and the smoke rose up to envelope her, thick and choking and black, and funereal in its portent.

V

This portal's guard is Tlaloc
The God of Evil and Sin.
Death is the key to its lock.
Doomed are who enter herein.

THE TWO MEN SAT HUNCHED OVER IN THEIR SADDLES. Elder Fayette's heavy mackinaw was torn and burned down one side, and the granite planes of his face were covered with dark smudges, and there was a livid scar across one weathered cheek that might have been made by a bullet. His big-knuckled hands were gripped tightly on the saddle horn. The hard line of his mouth was twisted with the rage that shook him whenever he thought of what had happened.

"I might've known this is what I'd get, doing business with a loco Indian like that," he muttered through locked teeth. "All he helped me get Chisos and Hagar for was so I'd get those guns for him. It isn't just *guáchupines* he wants to burn…it's every white man in Texas, with me in the same warsack as the rest!"

Abilene was rolling a cigarette. "Five thousand cows. That's a lot of beef to mill in the river till they drown. Nobody else but Chisos Owens could've gotten through our boys to do it. I guess Montezuma knew what he was doing when he hitched Chisos to his team instead of killing him."

Elder Fayette's voice trembled slightly. "Maybe he thinks I won't come after him. Maybe he thinks wiping out my spread finished me like it did the others. I won't be finished till I find him. I swear to God, Abilene, I'll find him and tear his heart out with my bare hands."

He stopped, breathing heavily. The round glow of Abilene's cigarette bobbed in the darkness. Fayette looked downslope in the direction Abilene had indicated. The first of the cavalcade was hardly visible, winding down the bottom of the narrow cañon, mere shadows against the darker rise of the opposite ridge. Fayette kept his voice down with an effort.

"For once, Ortega was telling the truth. The Apache Mine on the first night of the full moon. This cañon on the third. That's about right for the distance, if they don't do any daytime riding."

"That isn't like Ortega, the truth," said Abilene. "Maybe he'd just as soon have you out of the way as Montezuma."

"And maybe I'll kill him, too, when I find him," grunted Fayette. "You coming?"

Abilene flipped his wheat straw away. "As long as you pay me on the first of every month, I'll follow any trail you put your horse to."

Fayette took a heavy breath and turned his Choppo horse down through the timber toward the cavalcade. Near the edge of the trees, Abilene gigged his mount up suddenly and grabbed Fayette's arm. They halted and waited there in a thick stand of somber aspen, while a pair of ghost-like riders padded through the timber just below them, some distance up from the main party in the bottom of the cañon. Fayette held his mare there for an interval, and another pair of flankers rode by. Then he nodded, sidling down the slope toward the tail of the cavalcade. He and Abilene had almost reached it when, above them, they heard the faint sound of a third pair of outriders passing through the timber they had left.

One of the last riders in the main line turned toward them as they trotted in. All Fayette could see was the dim flash of eyes from beneath a *rebozo* that served as both hood and veil. They might have been dark eyes, but the night gave them a strange, bluish gleam. A woman?

"You shouldn't fall behind like that, *señores*," said someone from farther ahead. "The *techutlis* will kill you if you lag."

"*Sí*," muttered Fayette, and saw the woman turn away.

Ⓥ Ⓥ Ⓥ Ⓥ Ⓥ

Dawn lit the morning sky from the east, and ground fog wreathed up around Fayette's legs, chilling him. He could see how high they really were now. The terrain dropped away behind him in a dim, dawn glow for what must have been a hundred miles. Out of the bluish-gray fog rose the peaks they had passed, and beyond that a vast expanse of salt flats he knew to exist somewhere

200

south of the Guadalupes.

Fayette glanced sharply to his right. A pair of riders who had been flanking the cavalcade all night sat over there, dim, haunting shapes on vague shadow horses. There was another pair on the other side. And two more were closing in silently from behind.

An indurate look crossed Fayette's dusty, smudged face, and he hunched bulky shoulders down into his mackinaw and gave his Choppo the boot, following the others down the slope ahead.

Nothing would stop him from reaching Montezuma. It was what he had come here to do. He would do it. In his utterly single-purposed mind it was as simple as that. And the rage that had been building in him ever since his spread had been burned was a hot, writhing, living thing that swept all doubt or questioning from his thoughts, leaving only the savage, driving desire to get his hands on the Indian.

They turned into a valley that soon became a narrow cañon, and then a knife-blade cut, with walls so steep that the pinkish, morning light faded into a darkness as cold as the night they had left behind. Finally the cavalcade was halted, and the riders began to dismount. Fayette saw that a file of Montezuma's *techutlis* had been waiting for them in the cut here, tall, hawk-beaked men with exotic plumed headdresses, gleaming bronze bodies, naked but for the gilt-edged loin cloth Fayette had heard Ortega call a *maxtli*. Striking a discordant note in their barbaric appearance was the bandoleer of cartridges each man wore slung over his shoulder, and the bright, new Henry repeater crooked in his arm. Sight of that brought a thin rage into Fayette's red-rimmed eyes.

They began gathering up the horses, and leading them

201

toward another cañon that opened into this one from the side, and Fayette was turned away when the *techutli* came to take the reins of his jaded Choppo. Past the dismounted crowd, Fayette had seen what he first took to be the box end of the cañon. Now he realized that huge square blocks of granite had been set into the knife-blade cut, forming a wall some fifty feet high that closed the cañon off completely. One of the blocks had been swung out at the base of the wall, leaving a dark tunnel that must lead on through it, but Fayette couldn't see the other side.

The woman in the *rebozo* turned to him, and there was something about the lithe movement of her body that he seemed to remember. She was tall, even in flat-heeled, rawhide *huiraches*, and a lock of thick, black hair curled from beneath her shawl. She wore a split, buckskin skirt, dirty and greasy now, belted around her slim waist by a string of hammered silver bosses.

Fayette bent forward. "Don't we know each other?"

"I am Lola Salazar," she said. "I danced in the Alamo Saloon at San Antone."

"I've been there," he said. "I don't remember you."

"I remember you," she said, and nodded her head toward the rock wall. "That is Tlaloc's Door. They will inspect each one of us as we go through. They'll see you're an *Americano, señor.*"

"Will they?" he said, and reached up for her *rebozo,* saying: "Lola Salazar?"

She struck his hand down, whirled, and ran toward the crowd. A pair of armed *techutlis* were standing by the door, stopping each man or woman as they passed through. Fayette took a step after the girl, then shrugged, turning to Abilene. The lean, impersonal man nodded, taking a drag on his wheat straw.

202

"You know what to do when we reach the door?" said Fayette.

"Go through it," said Abilene. "You take care of the two boys there. I'll cover your tail. We'll make it."

Four *techutlis* were coming up behind Abilene, and one of them looked intently at Fayette's face, and began to come forward faster. There were only three of the crowd left to go through the door. One was passed by the guards there, then the next. The girl was last. She said something in Spanish. The guard nodded. She disappeared into the dark tunnel.

"*Un momento, señores,*" the man behind Abilene said. "*¿Eres Americanos?*"

"*¿Americanos?*" said the guard at the door, and whirled around.

Fayette took three leaps to him and smashed him back against the wall, wrenching the Henry from his surprised grasp. The second *techutli* there spun around and pulled his rifle into his belly for a snap shot. Fayette whirled, swinging his weapon around in a vicious arc that caught the man in the face. The *techutli*'s Henry exploded into the air as he crashed back into the rocks and slumped to the ground.

Fayette tried to whirl around again to the man he had taken the rifle from, and dodge at the same time. But the Indian was already on him, grappling for the gun. Abilene's Beale-Remington boomed, and someone screamed, and it boomed again. Then another *techutli* threw himself on Fayette, and the big man went down beneath the two struggling Indians, still holding the rifle in both hands and jerking it back and forth savagely.

A rawhide *huirache* slammed him in the face. Spitting blood, he butted his head upward and caught a man in the belly, carrying him back to the wall. He let go the rifle and got his hands in the *techutli*'s long, black hair and beat his head against the stones once. He dropped the dead weight of the man and whirled.

The other Indian had gotten the rifle. He had it above his head, and even as Fayette came around, he saw that whatever he did would be futile, and that kind of a blow would finish it.

With the rifle coming down, the *techutli* suddenly gave a spasmodic grunt. Instead of putting his full weight into the blow, the Indian let go the rifle and fell forward against Fayette. The Henry bounced off Fayette's shoulder. He stepped back and let the man fall to the ground on his face.

The girl still stood in the bent-over position she had reached after striking the man. The rifle she had scooped off the ground was held in both hands, still a little off the ground. She dropped it, and straightened. Abilene jumped over one of the men he had shot behind her, holding his smoking Beale-Remington in one hand, and his cigarette in the other. Farther back, more *techutlis* were returning from the cañon to which they had taken the horses.

"You came back, to do that?" asked Fayette, looking at the girl with his surprise still in his face, and then glancing at the man lying at his feet.

"Do you know what it means to be captured by them?" she panted. "I couldn't let that happen even to you...Elder Fayette!"

She turned and ran into the tunnel. Fayette's mouth opened slightly, then he turned and followed her. Abilene came behind him, and the black shadows swallowed them greedily.

VI

Dance upon my coffin, hombres
Naught but death can be my goal.
Make the darkness ring with tombes
The red peyote has my soul.

SOMETIMES HE HAD A DIM MEMORY OF ANOTHER LIFE, far away from this one, and sometimes it seemed to him that he had been known by another name. They called him Quauhtl now, which meant Eagle, and was a good name, they said, for the war lord of Atzalan. Often, he would sit cross-legged like this on the first terrace of the House of the Sun, trying to remember that other life, that other name.

He was a big man, Quauhtl, with shoulders that revealed their singular size even under the mantle of brilliant, egret feathers he wore. His heavily muscled torso had a ruddy look, as if freshly exposed to the sun, and his square, solid flanks were covered meagerly by a *maxtli* fringed with fur.

From where he sat on this giant pyramid, he could look across the broad valley to where the mountains rose in purple haze many miles away. He could follow with his eye the winding Road of Death that led to the narrow cañon in those mountains that contained Tlaloc's Door, the only entrance or exit from this City of the Sun People. Absently, he took a reddish bean from a pouch at his waist and popped it skillfully into his mouth, chewing it slowly. His eyes seemed hard to focus, and he smiled inanely. It always affected him that way. Peyote. His religion, now. The beans were mild compared with the ritual performed every month, five days after the first full moon, in the sacred fire chamber where the eternal blaze was kept aglow for Montezuma, and for the gods of Atzalan. There, for five days and five nights, with the *tombes* beating out their monotonous rhythm and the fires burning red, the *techutlis* made peyote anew. For many days after that Quauhtl lived in a wild haze. He could recall only vaguely the rides to the outer world where he fought the *guáchupines*, pillaging and burning and looting. Then, in about three weeks, the effects of peyote began to wear off, and instead of remembering battles and war, he would begin to recall that other life, and that other name. But before anything became clear, he was taken to the fire chamber again and treated once more to peyote.

All around him were gigantic pyramids such as the House of the Sun. Most of them had been built by people from Atzalan many centuries before, and were in ruins. Only recently had *Tlatoani* Montezuma set out to rebuild them. Every month a new party of workers arrived, and new warriors, and new slaves, and just this morning another group of them had come marching down the Road of Death from Tlaloc's Door.

They were in the courtyard below Quauhtl now, and soon, he knew, they would begin their revelry, as they always did the night after their arrival. They had to be inculcated into peyote, too, for it was their religion. They would do it in the courtyards, however, for only the knightly order of the *techutlis* were ever allowed in the sacred kivas. He was a *techutli*; he was a great warrior, so they told him. He sighed heavily, popping another bean into his mouth. He didn't know. Sometimes he could remember being a warrior. Sometimes he couldn't remember anything. Just now, he couldn't think.

Quauhtl felt the first throbbing of the *tombe*. He could see one of the ceremonial drummers beating his huge skin drum on the first terrace of the House of the Moon across the courtyard. Another *tombe* took up the rhythm, slowly at first, an interval of perhaps half a minute between each echoing thump.

The gaudy, feathered mantle swirled around Quauhtl's great frame as he rose and moved toward the steps leading from the House of the Sun down to the courtyard. His heavy Bisley .44 sagged against his bare leg, and he shifted the cartridge belt with a hairy hand. Already fires had been lighted in the braziers. He stopped by one, finding the huge Guadalajara jars of mescal, pouring a drink into a smaller, clay *olla*. He drank deeply, leaving only a few drops to toss over his shoulder for the God of Revelry.

"Tezteotl," he muttered, "may you be drunk forever," and then laughed thickly and turned to watch the dancers.

The *tombes* were beating faster now, and more drums had joined in, and the high notes of a flute added their eerie call, rising and falling on the last, red light of a dying afternoon. Some of the men and women kicked off their *huiraches* and began the *Matachine*, the dance of Malinche, their bare feet slapping against the checkered, marble floor in time with the *tombes*. Quauhtl saw one swarthy half-breed in rawhide *chivarras* pulling a woman into the dance. She was trying to break free from his greasy hands, looking around her wildly.

"*¡Pelada!*" the man shouted at her, tearing off her *rebozo*.

Her hair had been piled up beneath the shawl, and it fell in a blue-black cascade about the shoulders of her

207

silk blouse. Quauhtl felt his huge, rope-scarred fists close slowly. *Where had he seen that girl before?* She was no *charra* girl, brought in to marry one of the slaves. The half-breed stood there a moment, holding the *rebozo* in one hand, staring stupidly at the woman. Perhaps he had never seen one so beautiful before. Her rich lips curled around something she spat at him. The half-breed flushed, then made a lunge at her.

"Dios," he shouted, *"que una bella...!"*

She whirled from him, trying to run, but the crowd got in her way. The half-breed caught her arm, pulling her toward him. The others were laughing and calling to them now, and the woman looked around like some wild animal caught in a trap. There was something about the flushed look of her face, the stormy flash of her eyes that drew Quauhtl irresistibly. He started shoving his way through the crowd, grabbing a man's shoulder to thrust him aside.

"¡Bribón!" the Indian yelled, turning to grab at a Bowie in his belt. Then he saw who it was, and stumbled backward. "Quauhtl," he muttered. *"Techutli* Quauhtl...!"

Quauhtl shoved on, hardly hearing it. The half-breed had the struggling girl in his arms and was laughing drunkenly, trying to kiss her as he jerked her out onto the dance floor. Quauhtl reached out a heavy hand and caught the half-breed's arm, squeezing as he pulled.

The man's face twisted, and he jerked around, releasing the girl as he tried to pull free. Quauhtl spun him on around almost indifferently, and then gave him a shove. The half-breed stumbled backward, tripped, fell.

"¡Borrachón!" he said hoarsely, grabbing for his gun as he rolled over and started to get up. *"¡Cabrón!"*

Then he stopped cursing, and stopped trying to get

up. His mouth stayed open a little, and a fascinated look came into his eyes as he stared at Quauhtl. There was an ineffable menace to the big man, standing there with his great shoulders thrust forward slightly, settling his weight a little into his square hips. His craggy face didn't hold much expression, and his dull eyes hardly seemed to be looking at the half-breed. The wailing flute had died, and the drums were slowing down. The half-breed licked his lips, and began moving away in a crawl, and then stopped again.

"*Dios,*" he almost whispered. "You want her? Go ahead, take her. Go ahead."

Quauhtl waited a moment longer. Then he grinned inanely, and turned his back on the man. The flute rose shrilly, and the drums thundered into life again. The half-breed scrambled to his feet and disappeared into the crowd, casting a last, pale look over his shoulder. Quauhtl caught at the woman, not surprised that she didn't resist this time. He was their war lord, wasn't he?

He began to spin her, slapping his feet against the floor in the traditional steps of the *Matachine* that they had taught him. The sweat broke out on his forehead, and the peyote heated his blood, and he threw his head back and roared, spinning faster and faster. The girl tossed her head wildly, a strange look on her face. She seemed to abandon herself to the mad beat of the drums, whirling with him till her skirt whipped up about her bare legs, her hair swirling in a perfumed curtain about his face. The other dancers began to pull away from them, watching.

"*¿Quién es?*" shouted someone.

"She is Lola Salazar," answered a man. "She was a dancer in San Antone, she said. *Por Dios*, I believe it."

"No," shrilled a woman from farther away. "She is no

Lola Salazar. You wanted Malinche? There she is. The daughter of Montezuma. The bride of Cortés. Come back to rule beside our *Tlatoani*."

"Malinche," howled a Yaqui, and the others took it up in a crazy chant that kept time to the *tombes*. "Malinche...Malinche...Malinche...."

Quauhtl saw the look in her eyes, then, and realized she had been watching him all the time that way, and now, as if she had waited for the swelling roar of the sound to drown out what she said, he saw her red lips part in a word, and didn't know whether he actually heard it, or read it in the shape of her mouth.

"Chisos," she almost sobbed. "Chisos...."

"What?" he shouted. "Chisos? I am Quauhtl."

"Don't you know me, Chisos?" she panted, whirling in close to him. "Elgera. Don't you remember? What have they done to Hagar? Please, Chisos...."

The echoing crash of a great cymbal drowned her voice. Quauhtl spun to a stop with his feathered cloak settling about his bare legs, and the intense silence hurt his eardrums. The flute had stopped; the drums had stopped; everything had stopped. He was still holding the slim, lithe woman when the voice came from above. It wasn't a loud voice. It was sibilant and cultivated. Quauhtl saw the flush drain from the woman's face, leaving it suddenly pale.

"The Lord Montezuma would see this woman, Quauhtl. Bring her to the House of the Sun at once. It is his command!"

Elgera Douglas followed Chisos Owens through the silent crowd of men and women, feeling their eyes on her all the way. She had lost Fayette at Tlaloc's Door. They had gone through it and gained the inside before they had seen more *techutlis* coming toward them on the

Road of Death, drawn by the gunfire. Abilene and Fayette had disappeared into the timber on the slopes inside the door, but Elgera had caught up with the rest of the newcomers who had already gotten through, and lost herself among them. Waco Warren's mother had dyed Elgera's hair and brows black, and given her the clothes, and she was tanned deeply by the sun, and up to now had passed for the dancer from San Antone.

Chisos guided her up the stairway with a heavy hand on her elbow, and kept looking at her in a strange, puzzled way, his eyes clouded and dull. Behind, the *tombes* had begun to beat again, and the flute wailed. On the first level of the terraced pyramid stood a large screen of parrot feathers, hiding a statue from the profane eyes of the commoners below. The idol was carved from shining, black obsidian, representing a man, ears bright with earrings of gold and silver, lips painted with gilt. Upon its head was a golden miter, and in its right hand a sickle, and over the shoulders was thrown a magnificent, white robe.

"You like the *itzli, señorita?*" said a soft voice from behind them. "It is a statue of Quetzalcoatl, the Serpent God."

She turned slowly, hiding her surprise well enough. It was the same voice that had ordered her brought to the House of the Sun, and she had recognized it below, and she recognized it now. There was something puzzled in Luis Ortega's dark, vulpine face as he bent forward to study her.

"Lola Salazar? Is that what they said your name was? Have we met?"

"I danced in San Antone," said Elgera huskily.

He tilted his head toward the stairs, ascending to the second terrace, and allowed Chisos to lead the way.

211

"Ah, *sí*, San Antone. I have been there. *Pues*, no, *señorita*, the *techutli* who brought you newcomers here has already told *Tlatoani* Montezuma of your singular beauty. And now the people have begun to think you are Malinche. It has been written in *TONALAMENTE*, the BOOK OF FATE, that she should be reincarnated along with Montezuma. And if our lord thinks you are Malinche, you will be empress of all Texas, *señorita*."

They passed a pair of wooden-faced guards at the third terrace. Ortega caught Elgera's elbow, slowing her so that Chisos pulled ahead of them on the next stairway up. Elgera shook Ortega's hand off.

"You mean Montezuma wants me to…?"

Ortega nodded his head vigorously. "*Sí, sí*, he has been waiting for Malinche's return. And, as I say, if he thinks you are Malinche, you will marry him and rule with him. *Así*, you will need someone to help you along here, someone to smooth the bumps that will inevitably arise among such strange people. I know their ways, their rituals, their gods. A personal advisor, shall we say? *Sí*, a personal advisor."

"What do you get out of it?"

He raised his eyebrows in that hurt look. "Ah, *señorita*, not what I get out of it, but rather what you get…."

"I know you, Ortega."

"*Dios*," he said, and then chuckled. "It would seem my reputation has spread further than I thought. All right, *señorita*. Montezuma means to wipe the white man from Texas. He is loco, but that is beside the point. As empress, you will have access to…ah…certain things that would benefit me to some extent."

She couldn't help smiling faintly. "Anything that could be converted into cash, you mean."

He grinned slyly. "You *do* know me, don't you?"

"And you'd rather Montezuma wasn't aware of this little arrangement," she said.

"*Señorita*," he chuckled, "how well we understand one another."

At each of the seven terraces there was another pair of guards, all with Henry repeaters, not seeming to be aware of the girl as she passed. With the *tombes* pulsing behind them, they reached the top. In the center of the final level was a building built of the same blocks of porphyry that formed the pyramid and covered with a polished coat of lime that shone weirdly in the red, afternoon sunlight. Ortega muttered something to the guard at the entrance. The tremendous, oak doors stood open, with curtains shutting off the entrance, embroidered heavily with silver and gold. They clanged metallically as the guard pulled them aside.

Ortega and Elgera walked down a huge, colonnaded hall with fires burning in stone braziers along the walls faced with gleaming alabaster. Their footsteps echoed dismally on the smooth floors, coated with ochre and polished till they shone dully. The girl was ushered through a portico decorated with grotesque carvings of serpents, and into a great audience chamber. She stopped short, with her first look at Montezuma.

He sat on a dais across the floor of checkered black and white marble. His majestic head was crowned by a *copilli*, a golden miter that rose to a point above his forehead and fell down behind his neck. There were three other corridors leading from the room, one on either side of the high-backed throne, and one directly behind it.

Ortega led *Señorita* Scorpion across the great hall. Her glance was fixed on Montezuma's darkly ascetic

213

face, and there was something about the peculiar lack of focus in his eyes that reminded her of Lobos Delcazar.

"This is the woman?" said Montezuma, and the hollow rumble of his voice startled Elgera. "Did you do business with her, Ortega?"

Luis Ortega's lithe body seemed to stiffen. "*¿Qué?*"

"Like you tried to do business with Elgera Douglas?" said Montezuma. "Ramón Delcazar has come from Alpine. He tells me it was you who helped the blonde girl escape from the sheriff's office there."

Ortega's voice was suddenly obsequious. "Ah, *Tlatoani* Montezuma, only to better serve your interests. I was leading her to you."

"Better to serve *your* interests, you mean," said Montezuma. "If you had left her alone to be taken along with John Hagar, she would have been handed over to Lobos Delcazar, and would have been in my hands now. You have been talking with a forked tongue long enough, Luis Ortega. I am glad to see you brought me this woman promptly. You have, at least, carried out your last duty without a mishap."

Ortega's eyes darted around the room in a sudden, fearful way. "My…last duty, *Tlatoani?*"

Montezuma waved his hand imperiously. A pair of stalwart guards stepped from the squad standing to one side of the throne, moving with a swift, measured tread toward Ortega. He took a step backward.

"No," he almost whispered, and then his voice began to rise. "*Tlatoani* Montezuma, I swear I am your slave. My life is yours. I would never do anything against your interests. *No, no, no…!*"

The last was a scream, and he turned and darted toward the curtained doorway of the corridor to the right of the throne. Two guards appeared through the hangings. Ortega whirled back. The other pair of guards came up from behind him. He struck at one with his cane, stumbled backward, then they had him, wrenching his arms behind his back.

"No!" he screamed. "*Señorita*, don't let them do this to me. They will sacrifice me to Quetzalcoatl. No. *Tlatoani. Señorita.* Empress Malinche...!"

Writhing and screaming, the two husky *techutlis* carried him through the door at the rear of the throne. Montezuma waited till his howls had died away down the corridor. Then he bent forward, and his eyes were suddenly glittering intensely at Elgera, and she felt herself swept with a strange dizziness.

"Malinche," he intoned, and there was a fanatical sincerity in his voice. "They were right. You are Malinche. We shall wed before Quetzalcoatl and rule all of Texas. The white man shall burn with the *guáchupines*, for they are all tyrants, and my people shall have the land that belonged to their ancestors."

The sound hadn't been audible at first, above the throbbing background of *tombes*. But now Elgera saw Montezuma's great head tilt upward, as if he were listening. She heard the gunshots, too.

From the corridor leading off to the right, a guard burst through the curtains and dropped them from behind him with a clang. He stumbled toward the throne, holding bloody hands across his belly.

"*Tlatoani* Montezuma," he gasped, and fell to his knees. "*Esta que borrachón*, Elder Fayette. *Esta* Fayette!"

He fell over on his face, and didn't say anything else, and wouldn't be saying anything else again, ever. Elgera saw the faint rise of Montezuma's great, bronze chest beneath his feathered mantle. It was the only sign he gave. He raised his hand, about to say something. Before he could speak, a guard ran into the chamber from the corridor that led out to the front of the pyramid.

"*Esta* Abilene," he shouted. "*El Americano*...."

Another volley of shots behind cut off the rest. Someone yelled outside. The *tombes* had ceased now.

"Quauhtl," said Montezuma composedly. Chisos Owens bowed, called something to the guards by the throne as he whirled, and ran toward the corridor from which the second guard had come, pulling the Bisley he wore. Four of the *techutlis* followed him from the squad by the dais, and Elgera heard the echo of their feet down the corridor, and then a sporadic series of shots. She looked around swiftly.

"You are afraid, *señorita?*" said Montezuma. "They will never reach me. I am invincible. I am immortal."

"Are you?" said Elder Fayette, stepping through the doorway to the right of the throne.

There were only two guards left by the throne. They turned, jerking Henrys around. The sound of Fayette's six-gun rocked the room. The first guard went down without firing. The second got a bullet out, but it went into the floor as he fell forward on his face. The hammer snapped on Fayette's gun as he pulled the trigger a third time. He tossed the weapon aside, still coming forward, stepping across the body of the guard who had first come from that doorway. He didn't seem to see Elgera. His burning eyes were fixed on Montezuma. From outside there was another rattle of shots.

"That's Abilene," said Fayette through his teeth. "He came up one stairway. I took the other. I guess he won't get by Chisos, will he? That's why we split up. I knew one of us would have to meet Chisos, and I knew that one wouldn't get through. The other one reached you, though, didn't he, Montezuma?"

Montezuma rose, nostrils flaring like some wild stallion in a rage. Yet he seemed held there for that moment by the sight of that big, inexorable man, coming steadily toward him in a heavy, unhurried walk. Elgera could understand that. Few others would have gotten this far. Perhaps only one other. The one Fayette had recognized for being that kind. Chisos Owens.

Fayette took a step across the first guard he had shot and stumbled, and Elgera realized he was wounded. But his voice was steady, and he kept going toward Montezuma.

"Did you think you could play the game both ways to the middle like Ortega?" he said heavily. "Let me get those guns for you and then wipe out my spread? Did you think that would finish me like it did the others? I won't be finished till I get you, Montezuma. I don't care much what happens after that. Nobody's crossed me yet and stayed around to tell about it. You won't be the first. I've come to get you."

Montezuma leaned forward, all his fanaticism suddenly bursting through his austerity with a hissing venom. "And did you think I wouldn't wipe you out with all the other *guáchupines* in Texas. Oppressors. Tyrants. You are one of them, Fayette. You can't harm me."

Fayette staggered and began to move forward faster, his voice gasping. "Go ahead, pull that hide-out. Remember what I told you? You haven't got enough lead in that cutter to stop me before I get you. Go ahead...."

His words were cut off by the blast of the first shot. Fayette grunted sickly, bent over, and stepped across the body of the second *techutli* he had killed. The next shot

217

thundered. Elgera saw Fayette jerk, and bend farther forward with his hands outstretched now in a blind, groping way. As the third shot filled the room, Elgera ran to the side of the throne, reaching for something beneath her shirt.

Montezuma bent forward for the last shot. His face twisted as he squeezed the trigger on his Krider Derringer. It took Fayette square. With a terrible, animal scream of pain, Fayette threw himself forward, his indomitable will carrying his heavy body two more stumbling paces to crash into Montezuma.

For a moment they struggled there, Fayette's head buried in Montezuma's chest, blocky hands clawing the feathered robe off. Montezuma took a step back and almost fell off the raised dais, trying to pull free. Fayette smashed him in the face. Montezuma took another step, striving desperately to tear the relentless man off. Then the Indian quit struggling and looked down at the head buried against his chest, and a strange look crossed his dark face. He reached up and pried Fayette's hand from around his neck as if he were releasing himself from something vile. The marks of the fingers showed white on his bronze skin. He pried Fayette's other hand off the smooth muscle of his shoulder. He took another step back, and let the dead man fall to the floor.

Chisos Owens came through the curtain of the front hall. "We got Abilene. Fayette...."

He stopped as he saw Fayette, and his eyes raised to Montezuma, and they widened as they saw *Señorita Scorpion*.

"This is a nopal thorn I have pressed against your back," the girl told Montezuma. "It's been soaked a year in the venom of a hundred diamondbacks. An old woman down by the Pecos gave it to me. She didn't

218

think you were immortal. Make the wrong move, and we'll find out."

While he had been struggling with Fayette, Elgera had gotten around behind Montezuma. She stood with one hand caught in the golden belt around his muscular middle, the other pressing the sharp point of the nopal thorn into his flesh. She felt the slow stiffening of his tremendous body.

"Tlazteotl," he hissed.

"What's that?" she said.

"Tlazteotl," Chisos Owens answered. "Queen of witches!"

VII

The BOOK OF FATE *was begun*
In the sacred Temple of War.
It ends in the House of the Sun.
Read TONALAMENTE no more.

SMALL FIRES BURNED IN STONE BRAZIERS ALONG THE corridor, and their sibilant hiss haunted the ghostly passage, and the gleaming walls seemed to eddy and writhe with a thousand flickering serpents of garish, red-shadowed light thrown upon them by the flames. Chisos Owens led, glancing back over his shoulder with that confused look on his face. He was completely under Montezuma's domination, and he knew a wrong move from him would mean his lord's death. Elgera still walked behind the Indian, one hand in his belt, the other pressing the poison thorn against his back.

It was the same corridor into which Ortega had been taken by the two guards, and its gradual decline was leading them down into the bowels of the pyramid.

219

Elgera spoke thinly.

"This had better take us to Hagar."

"We are going to the sacred fire chamber," said Montezuma, having recovered some of his composure again. "The kiva. These temples were erected many centuries ago by a branch of the Aztecs who migrated this far north. I was born of Yaqui parents in the Sierra Madres and discovered these ruins when I was a young man. I knew then that it didn't matter who my parents had been. In *TONALAMENTE*, it is decreed that Montezuma should be reincarnated and find his old gods in the ancient city north of Tenochtitlán, which you know as Mexico. You cannot desecrate those gods, *señorita*. You are a fool to try."

The corridor opened abruptly into a square room with a statue of Quetzalcoatl in the center. Lashed to the sacrificial altar of jasper at the idol's feet was Luis Ortega, writhing and panting, his face bathed in sweat. There was a guard on either side of him, and an old, bearded *nualli* in a long, black robe.

"*Tlatoani* Montezuma," quavered the ancient medicine man, bowing low, and then he seemed to see the strained expression on Montezuma's face, and how close Elgera stood to the Indian. A guard made a motion with his rifle.

"Tell them how it is," snapped Elgera. "Tell them to drop their hardware and go ahead of us."

Montezuma obeyed, and the guards slowly let their Henrys clatter to the floor, watching Montezuma with puzzled eyes. Ortega's babbling voice rose shrilly.

"*Señorita, en el nombre de Dios*, free me. They are going to sacrifice me to the Serpent God. They are going to cut my heart out with a *macapan*."

For a moment she was moved to pity. Then she

remembered what Ortega was, and she realized, if she let go of Montezuma to cut the Spaniard loose, it would be her last mistake. Her face hardened. She shoved Montezuma on, the guards and the old man preceding them into the corridor on the other side.

"*Madre de Dios*," screamed Ortega, writhing on the altar. "*Señorita*. Cut me loose. *Señorita*. *Dios*, *Dios…!*"

His scream broke into a crazed sobbing, and then even that faded and died behind them, and the only sound was the serpentine hiss and snap of the small fires lighting the way. Finally, from ahead, Elgera heard the first, dim, monotonous chanting.

"They are inculcating the unbeliever, Hagar, into peyote," said Montezuma hollowly. "In two days he will no longer doubt our gods. He will be a *techutli* as great as Quauhtl, and with two men like that I can rule the world if I choose."

They twisted and turned through the maze of corridors that honeycombed the great pyramid, the strange chanting becoming louder. Then, from ahead, Elgera saw the outline of yellow light around a curtained doorway. The guards before the portal bowed to Montezuma till their parrot plumes scraped the ochred floor.

"Tell them to go inside ahead of you," said Elgera. "And no slips."

She felt the magnificent muscles of his back tense against her knuckles as he took a breath before he spoke. The guards bowed again, sweeping aside the curtain. Chisos followed them in, then the bearded *nualli*. Elgera shoved Montezuma after them.

The first man she saw was Johnny Hagar, the manacles on his wrists and ankles attached to chains socketed in the floor, spread-eagling him on the cold

221

cement. His only garment was the gilt-edged *maxtli*, clinging wet with perspiration to his flat belly and lean shanks. His dark eyes had a strange glaze, but there was recognition in them as he jerked his head to one side and saw her.

"Elgera!" he gasped.

"Oh," said one of the men who had been bending over him, and straightened. "Elgera."

"Don't do it, Lobos," snapped the girl. "You'll be killing Montezuma."

Lobos Delcazar stopped his dark fingers before they touched the ivory butts of Johnny Hagar's Peacemakers. The ceremonial drummers at one side of the room sat with their hands suspended over the skin *tombes*. Montezuma drew himself up, and his hands were around in front of him. Elgera tightened her grip on his golden belt.

"Unlock Hagar, Lobos," she said. "The rest of you move over to the wall. You, too, Chisos."

"Chisos?" said the big man. "I am Quauhtl."

The guards moved slowly to the wall, smoke from the blazing fires shredding across in front of them and hiding their tense faces for a moment. Lobos unlocked the manacles, and Hagar had trouble rising. He put his hand to his head and shook it dazedly. He almost fell when he reached out to unbuckle the cartridge belts of his Peacemakers from around Lobos's red sash. Elgera sensed the movement of Montezuma's hands, hidden from her in front of his body.

"What are you doing?" she snapped. "Stop it."

The first shouts came from outside, and the sound of running feet. She had expected pursuit as soon as someone found their emperor gone from the audience chamber and all those dead guards there. She couldn't help the turn of her head toward the sound.

Montezuma took that moment to lunge away from her. She yanked backward on his belt, throwing her whole weight against it. She crashed on back to the wall, belt flapping free in her hands. The sudden release caused Montezuma to stagger forward and almost go on his face. He had unbuckled the belt.

One of the guards yelled and knocked the fire out of the brazier, throwing the small kiva into semi-darkness. A *tombe* thumped hollowly as one of the drummers upset it, scrambling erect. Elgera had made Chisos give her his Bisley upstairs. She wrenched the .44 from her waistband, struggling away from the wall.

"Get out the door," shouted Hagar.

His guns boomed, and someone screamed. The body must have fallen into the other brazier, for there was a hissing sound, and the room was plunged into intense darkness. The Peacemakers boomed again, and a man went through the door, taking the curtain with him, and fell in the corridor outside.

A man crashed into Elgera, and she struck viciously. He grunted and went down. Hagar's guns drowned the other sounds after that, racketing hideously. Then she was caught by the elbow, and the sheriff's voice was harsh in her ear.

"Out the door, I told you."

"Think I'd leave you," she cried, and was carried across the body in the doorway by Hagar's rush. He yanked her down the corridor in the opposite direction from which she had come, for there were other guards running toward them down there. A man ran through the doorway, shouting. It was Montezuma. Hagar pulled her around a corner, and they were plunged into the darkness of an unlit corridor.

"Chisos," she panted. "We can't leave him."

223

"What could you do with him?" asked Hagar, running beside her. "He's filled with peyote. It's sort of a dope, like marijuana. Regular religion with the Indians for centuries. Takes about five days to get you completely. I've only had two days of it, but I'm in a daze already. Crazy with it. Feel like I'm drunk or swimming or something."

"How did they get you to take it in the first place? How did they get Chisos to take it?"

"Ramón Delcazar spent the night on Chisos's spread," said Hagar. "Must've mixed peyote beans in with his coffee, like they did with me. Can't tell the difference. I thought I was drinking coffee till it was too late. Devotees of the stuff eat the beans raw, like Lobos. In that fire chamber they force it down you in liquid form. Can't keep your mouth closed, tied down like that. They hold your nose so you have to drink it or choke to death."

"Isn't there any hope?" she said.

"For Chisos?" he panted. "Yeah. If we could get to him, there would be. The effect of the beans eaten raw is milder and lasts only a few hours. But these *nualli* mix something they call *teopatl* in with the liquid peyote, made from the roots of *vinigrilla* or something. Takes a man's soul, Elgera. Robs him of any will of his own. Makes him forget everything. It lasts about a month. At the end of that time they have to take him back to the kiva and dope him up again for five days. Chisos has been out about a month, from what Lobos told me. He must be about ready to come out of the haze. If we could only get him to recognize us, to remember who he really is...."

They must have been running through a section of the pyramid not yet rebuilt by Montezuma's slaves. The

224

corridor was littered with rubble, and Elgera kept stumbling in the utter darkness. From behind, the shouts and other sounds of pursuit drowned her gasp as she tripped over a rock and fell flat. She could hear Hagar, running on ahead. Then he stopped, and his voice sounded muffled.

"Elgera?"

"Here," she said, standing up and groping her way down the wall. She reached a corner. *Was that why his voice had sounded muffled?* Light glowed dimly behind her as the first man appeared, carrying a torch. Behind him were others, stumbling and tripping across the débris.

"Elgera," called Hagar sharply.

It seemed to come from ahead. She fumbled around the corner, and it was dark again, and she ran forward, feeling her way. She was quite far down this corridor when she saw the man with the torch pass its end and go on down the other corridor, and the others followed him. The silence that fell after they went by struck at her ominously. She drew a sharp breath to call.

"Hagar?"

There was no answer. She went back the way she had come, and turned out into the other corridor in the pitch blackness. Driven by a growing panic that she couldn't down, she began to run, and the sound of her footsteps rolled ahead of her and came back multiplied, and engulfed her with a thousand sibilant echoes, like the hollow shackles of some malignant giant.

She ran blindly through a maze of corridors, stumbling, falling, hesitant to call Hagar now for fear the others would hear her, Bisley clutched in a palm sticky with cold sweat. Then she began to see faint light from ahead, and finally burst through one of the silver-embroidered curtains into a square room where a man lay bound on a block of jasper in front of the idol of Quetzalcoatl.

"*Señorita*," moaned Luis Ortega weakly. "Please. I beg of you. Mercy. Cut me loose."

She sagged against the wall, brushing damp hair back off her forehead, unable to believe she had found her way back here. Then, still gasping from the run, she tore the *macapan* out of the idol's hand and sawed the rawhide lashings binding Ortega. He rolled off and lay on the floor a moment, panting. His gold-handled cane and blue cape were beside the statue. He got to his hands and knees and crawled to them, mumbling; then he rose and turned toward Elgera, eyes furtive.

"I know who you are now," he panted. "*Sí. Señorita* Douglas. Montezuma didn't realize what he was doing when he crossed your trail, did he? *Pues*, neither did I. But it was I who helped you. Remember? *Sí*, twice I helped you. I will help you again, *señorita*, and this time I won't ask a *peso* for my services. You can have them *gratis*."

He began to rub his forefinger with his thumb, and came on toward her, his voice growing stronger, more oily. She took a step backward, watching his face.

"There are secret doors leading out onto each terrace," he said. "*Sí*, we will not have to go back through the throne room. I think we're about finished here anyway, eh? It was a loco idea of Montezuma's. I don't think he could have ruled *Tejas*, even with Chisos Owens. There will be other empires to rule. We could do a lot together, you and I...."

She took another step back, and tripped on the altar. While she was off balance like that, she saw him whip the blade from his cane, and lunge.

226

"*¡Degüello!*" He screamed Santa Ana's cry of no quarter.

She threw herself backward over the altar. Ortega's blade flashed through the soft collar of her shirt. She twisted as she fell, catching the sword for that moment. As she struggled to rise, Ortega lunged away, trying to tear his steel free. She gained her hands and knees and threw herself at him from there. Her weight carried him back against the far wall. She heard the blade tear from her shirt.

"*Bruja*," gasped Ortega, whipping the sword free. "Witch."

She caught the blade in her bare hands, twisting it sideways away from her as he struck. It went past her body, and he tried to pull it back again. Steel sliced through her fingers with searing pain, covering them with blood. Ortega's whiplash body was like a writhing snake beneath her.

She rose on one knee and came down with her other in his belly. He gasped and collapsed back against the stone, face twisted. She caught the sword again. His grip on it was relaxed for that moment, and she tore it free, twisting it to grasp the gold-encrusted hilt in a bloody fist. She was straddling him like that with the sword turned, when he gathered himself and lunged blindly up beneath her. She didn't even see the blade go in. She only heard him gasp.

"*Madre de Dios....*"

He sagged back against the lime-coated stones. She let go of the sword and rose, looking blankly down at the dead man. Suddenly she turned and picked up the gun she had dropped and ran across the room to the hall leading above. Secret doors? How could she find them? She burst through a curtained aperture into the next

227

corridor, running on an upward slant. Her movements were sluggish and painful. She was breathing in short, agonizing gasps. She stumbled through another curtained doorway and came abruptly to a halt, realizing too late that it had led her into the throne room.

Guards were running back and forth across the great hall, and two slaves were carrying one of the men Fayette had shot out the door on the other side. A squad of *techutlis* was drawn up in front of the dais, and half a dozen robed, old men were fluttering around Montezuma. He was giving an order to a runner and, from the height of his throne, was the first to see Elgera. He stood up suddenly, and the direction of his glance caused the others to look that way. Chisos Owens turned toward Elgera where he stood at one side of the dais.

"It is the woman, Quauhtl," thundered Montezuma. "Kill her!"

Ⓥ Ⓥ Ⓥ Ⓥ Ⓥ

Johnny Hagar's hands were bleeding from feeling his way along the jagged, broken surface of the walls. He didn't know how long ago he had lost Elgera. Now he was lost. He had reached a dead end. He stumbled over the rubble-strewn floor, trying to find the corner of the hall to get his bearings. His breathing sounded harsh in the eerie silence. His feet made small, scraping sounds across the stone.

Once he felt himself swaying and knew that it was the peyote in him, and another time he was startled by his own drunken giggle. Then his bloody fingers slipped into a deep crack above his head.

"*¿A cuanto se vende?*" said someone in Spanish, and it sounded as if it came from the wall itself.

Suddenly the stone heaved outward, throwing him backward, and the next voice burst on him loud and clear. "Shut your mouth, or I'll show you what it will get us. If we don't find them, Montezuma will have our heads."

The man stopped, and stood there in the opening left by the huge rock that had swung inward on a pivot. He was silhouetted by the smoky, red light of a torch held by a *techutli* behind him. Hagar had been smashed back against the opposite wall and was too dazed to go for his guns in that first moment when there might have been a chance, and now he didn't go for them, because he saw how it was.

"Hello, Ramón," he said, and took a step away from the wall to get his elbows free for when it came. "I guess having your spread wiped out didn't hit you as hard as it might. Or did you burn it yourself to make everything look right?"

Ramón Delcazar had changed his white pants and shirt for a feathered cloak, but he still packed his black-butted Forty-Fives belted around his gilt-edged *maxtli*, and he shoved the cloak back, and kept his hands far enough above his guns, because he saw how it was, too.

"*Sí*," he said, moving carefully in through the door. "I burned my spread. It would have looked funny if mine was spared when all the others were raided, wouldn't it?"

"Give me some elbow room, cousin," said Lobos Delcazar, and swaggered in behind Ramón. He, too, saw that whoever made the first move now would start the thing, and he kept the curl of his fingers off the gold-chased butt of the Colt he had strapped back on. "It looks like I'll get those Peacemakers, after all."

"We'll toss for them," said Ramón.

The *techutli* behind Lobos stuck his torch into a brazier on the wall. There were two others following him, carrying Henrys, but up to now the two cousins had filled the narrow doorway and blocked Hagar off from the guards, and the *techutlis* were waiting for them to start it.

The echoes of Ramón's words diminished down the corridor and died reluctantly, and then the only sound was the harsh scrape of feet across the stone and the almost inaudible sibilance of the men's breathing. The scrape of feet stopped, and it was only the breathing, and then Hagar took a last breath and held it, and Lobos did the same, the way an experienced gunman will when he senses the moment at hand. Ramón and the utter silence held them all there for that last instant with the red light flickering across their strained faces and catching the waiting glitter of their eyes.

"*¡Carape!*" shouted Lobos, and started it.

Hagar was still grinning when his guns bellowed. Lobos staggered backward, and his Colt went off at the roof, and the *techutlis* jumped away from his body as it fell in their midst. Ramón spun up against the wall with a scream, dropping one of his Forty-Fives, desperately trying to throw down with the other one to hit Hagar as his hammer dropped.

The *techutlis* burst through the door over Lobos's body, Henrys bellowing. With the first .56 slug knocking him backward, Hagar thumbed out two more shots. Ramón grunted, dropped his other gun, and doubled over. A guard stumbled and went to his knees, and then his face, and slid almost to Hagar's feet before he stopped.

"Come on, you damned *borrachónes*," brayed Hagar, laughing crazily. "Come on, come on, come on...."

Drunk on peyote, inflamed with the roar of battle, he swayed there in that last moment, screaming at them, Peacemakers filling the hall with an unearthly racket as they bucked up and down in his bloody hands. The last two *techutlis* threw themselves on him with demented howls, shooting their Henrys from the waist. Hagar thumbed his right-hand gun, and then his left, and saw one man jerk to both bullets. Then another Henry slug caught the sheriff, and the man he had shot came hurtling on into him, and Hagar crashed to the floor beneath the body.

He struck the stones with his right-hand gun pinned between his belly and the *techutli*'s. He tore his left-hand weapon free, firing at the last man from where he lay on his back beneath the dying *techutli*. It was all a haze, a twisted, screaming face, the stabbing flame of a levered Henry blinding him, the rocking bellow of his own Peacemaker deafening him, and the jarring pain of Henry lead tearing through the body above him and driving down into his own.

Ⓥ Ⓥ Ⓥ Ⓥ Ⓥ

"*Kill her!*" The order still rang in Chisos Owens's ears. He stood there, looking at the girl, aware that the throne room had become silent, that all the *techutlis* were waiting for him to carry out Montezuma's order. But there was something in the girl's eyes. She held out her hand.

"Chisos," she said faintly. "Chisos…."

"Quauhtl!" roared Montezuma. "I command you. Kill her!"

Chisos? She kept calling him that. He couldn't take his eyes away from hers. They were deep blue, and he seemed to be sinking into them, and suddenly he could remember the other name. *Chisos Owens.* With that single memory, others began to come, crowding in, flooding his brain. Names he had tried to recall without success, people he had remembered only as nebulous entities that would never quite come through the fog of peyote. *Alpine. Johnny Hagar. Ramón Delcazar. The Santiago. Señorita Scorpion. Yes, Elgera Douglas.* He had loved her. Why did this girl bring back those memories? And what was he doing here in this great hall, with all these strange men in feathered cloaks around him, and that wild-eyed loco standing on some kind of a throne? *Elgera Douglas?*

"Quauhtl," thundered Montezuma. "I command you…!"

With an animal roar of rage, Chisos Owens whirled and threw himself toward the throne. The surprised guards didn't try to stop him till he was almost there. He crashed through their ranks like a bull through bee brush.

Without stopping or slowing down or even seeming to see the men who had tried to get in his way, he caught the first one's rifle and, using it as a lever, spun him away into the others. He smashed through two more farther on, knocking them to either side. He caught a fourth with a backhand swing that sent him rolling across the floor.

Elgera Douglas? He had loved her. And this Montezuma had sent him out to kill her. He remembered it now.

"Quauhtl…!"

Chisos crashed into Montezuma before he had finished shouting, huge frame knocking the Indian off the throne. They struck the floor, rolling over and over like a pair of fighting cats. Montezuma got his hands and knees beneath him finally, and tried to rise.

Chisos slugged him behind the neck with a blow that would have killed another man. Montezuma quivered, set himself, and heaved upward. Chisos struck him again, riding his gigantic torso. Montezuma took that one, too, and kept on rising, the muscles in his legs standing out in great, trembling ridges. He shot one of his legs out suddenly, catching Chisos behind the knees.

Chisos staggered backward to keep from falling. He hung onto Montezuma, and the two of them went stumbling and lurching out through the doorway that led to the terrace, both trying vainly to keep erect. Chisos's feathered robe caught on the angle of the opening, and it was torn from his great shoulders. Then they went down again, and rolled on across the terrace, fighting, grunting, slugging. Chisos sensed they were coming to the edge, and sprawled out to stop their momentum.

There was a terrible, animal vitality in Montezuma's writhing, swelling, surging body. Chisos got one arm hooked around the Indian's neck and struck him again and again, and any one of those blows might have finished it, but Montezuma's huge frame shook to each one, and he grunted sickly while he grimly fought to rise again.

Suddenly he shifted his weight and caught Chisos's wrist. Levered away from the man, Chisos couldn't hang on with his other arm around Montezuma's neck. The Indian released the arm and jumped up and backward. Chisos rolled like a cat, and was on his feet when the Indian threw himself in again.

The two men met with a fleshy, slapping sound there on the very edge of the terrace, bathed in the blood-red light of the late-afternoon sun. Montezuma's magnificent torso was wet with perspiration, and the straining muscles writhed beneath the smooth, bronze skin like fat snakes. Raging with peyote, Chisos fought like some savage animal, snarling and roaring, great calves knotting and rippling as he braced his feet wide on the ochred stone. They were locked inextricably together on the edge of the terrace, and a single wrong move from either man would have sent them hurtling over the edge. It was a contest of sheer brute strength, with each man straining desperately to turn the other one outward and force him off. Finally, Montezuma brought his greater height and weight to bear, levering Chisos around with his back to the empty space that reeled beneath them. Chisos could hear the strange sigh that rose from the multitude of slaves and workers gathered in the courtyard below.

Slowly, inexorably, Montezuma was forcing him to yield, bending him outward, backward, downward. The Indian's right arm was locked around the small of Chisos's back, and his other hand was in Chisos's face, shoving relentlessly. Chisos had his forearm around Montezuma's neck, and he could feel the man's muscles swell and bulge, and his grip there was gradually slipping. His ribs began to make popping sounds. Stabbing pain shot through his chest. He was bent like a bow, and the only thing that held him from falling was his arm around Montezuma's neck. He could feel his wrist slipping across the slippery skin. Then, from far away, he heard the girl's call.

"Chisos! Chisos!"

He drew in a great, last, desperate breath. His lips flattened against his teeth stained black with cochineal. The muscles across his tremendous shoulders humped into a bulging, obstinate line. Montezuma gasped hot in his face, trying to force him on down. Face twisting with the effort, Chisos Owens began to straighten again.

Montezuma braced his feet anew and gripped Chisos tighter, trying to stop him. He threw his weight against Chisos. He strained to halt that huge, straightening frame. Chisos came on up.

In final desperation, Montezuma shifted his feet farther back for more leverage. With the Indian's right foot sliding back, Chisos surged on up and twisted sharply in Montezuma's grasp. He caught the Indian's arm and slipped under it, his chest slamming into Montezuma's hip. The Indian tried to throw his weight over on Chisos. It put him off balance. With his own legs in front of Montezuma and the bulk of his torso bent down to one side, Chisos heaved. The Indian screamed as he went up and out and down, down, down.

Chisos fell to his hands and knees to keep from following Montezuma. Gasping and quivering there, he saw what had held the *techutlis* in a little knot just outside the door. Hagar must have found his way up from below. He sat against the wall, holding both guns in his lap, his face set in a bloody, grinning mask. Still on his hands and knees, Chisos turned to look over the edge.

A guard on the next level had run to the sprawled body of Montezuma. Another came up, and they turned Montezuma over. One of them looked upward.

"*Es muerto*," he said. "He is dead."

Ⓥ Ⓥ Ⓥ Ⓥ Ⓥ

Supporting the wounded Hagar between them, Chisos and Elgera moved through the great, silent audience chamber, down the corridor, out onto the terrace, and

235

down the steps. Abilene had taken these front stairs up, while Fayette had taken the rear. On the stairs between the third and fourth levels, they passed Abilene. He lay across the body of a guard he had killed. His Beale-Remington was gripped in one supple hand. A cigarette was in the other.

At each following level on the way down, two guards lay dead where Abilene had passed, going up. Elgera and Chisos half carried Hagar through the silent, stunned crowd, still staring, wide-eyed, up to that ledge where Montezuma lay. The whole incredible edifice of the cult had been built on the premise that Montezuma himself was invincible and immortal. His death utterly smashed that edifice. As if they were ghosts, Elgera and the two men moved out of the city. Once in a while someone turned to look blankly at them, and his mouth moved in some soundless word, and he turned back to look at the House of the Sun.

Elgera was watching Chisos intently. He kept shaking his head, blinking his eyes.

"All those ranches I raided," he said, "all those people I fought. They were my friends. I tried to kill you. I burned your Santiago and ran off your herds. I...."

"No," she almost sobbed. "You didn't know what you were doing. You weren't responsible. Don't you think your friends will forgive you? I forgave you a long time ago."

"As for your real friends, Elgera's right" gasped Hagar, "they'll forgive anything you did, Chisos."

The Indian guards still accepted Chisos as Quauhtl, their war lord, and got three horses at his order. The three remained there a moment, looking back through Tlaloc's Door to the doomed city.

"With Montezuma dead, they'll all drift back to their
236

own tribes," said Chisos dully. "It's hard to think that's all finished. Seems like I never knew any other life."

They had to help Hagar onto his horse, but he was grinning, and he looked at Elgera when he spoke. "Yeah, that's finished. But there are other things. I'm going to buy me a new, white Stetson and a pair of Mexican spurs with wheels as big as the wheels on a Murphy wagon, and the first Saturday night after we get back, Elgera, you'll find me on your doorstep, a-courting"

Chisos looked up, and it was the first time since Elgera had found him here that *Señorita* Scorpion had seen him grin.

"You're wrong, Hagar," he said. "She'll find *us* on her doorstep, a-courting."

ABOUT THE AUTHOR

LES SAVAGE, JR. was an extremely gifted writer who was born in Alhambra, California, but grew up in Los Angeles. His first published story was "Bullets and Bullwhips" accepted by the prestigious Street & Smith's *Western Story*. Almost ninety more magazine stories, all set on the American frontier, followed, many of them published in Fiction House magazines such as *Frontier Stories* and *Lariat Story Magazine* where Savage became a superstar with his name on many covers. His first novel, **Treasure of the Brasada**, appeared in 1947, the first of twenty-four published novels to appear in the next decade. Due to his preference for historical accuracy, Savage often ran into problems with book editors in the 1950s who were concerned about marriages between his protagonists and women of different races—a commonplace on the real frontier but not in much Western fiction in that decade. As a result of the censorship imposed on many of his works, only now have they been fully restored by returning to the author's original manuscripts. **Table Rock** (1993), Savage's last book, was even suppressed by his agent in part because of its depiction of Chinese on the frontier. It was finally published as he wrote it by Walker and Company in the United States and Robert Hale, Ltd., in the United Kingdom.

Much as Stephen Crane before him, while he wrote the shadow of his imminent death grew longer and longer across his young life, and he knew that, if he was going to do it at all, he would have to do it quickly. He did it well, better than almost anyone who wrote

Western and frontier fiction, ever. Now that his novels and stories are being restored to what he had intended them to be, his achievement irradiated by his powerful and profoundly sensitive imagination will be with us always, as he had wanted it to be, as he had so rushed against time and mortality that it might be. Among his most recent publications are *Fire Dance At Spider Rock* (Five Star Westerns, 1995), *Medicine Wheel* (Five Star Westerns, 1996), *Copper Bluffs* (Circle Ⓥ Westerns, 1996), *The Legend of Señorita Scorpion* (Circle Ⓥ Westerns, 1996), and *Coffin Gap* (Five Star Westerns, 1997). *The Lash of Señorita Scorpion: A Western Trio* is his next Circle Ⓥ Western.

We hope that you enjoyed reading this
Sagebrush Large Print Western.
If you would like to read more Sagebrush titles,
ask your librarian or contact the Publishers:

United States and Canada

Thomas T. Beeler, *Publisher*
Post Office Box 659
Hampton Falls, New Hampshire 03844-0659
(800) 251-8726

United Kingdom, Eire, and
the Republic of South Africa

Isis Publishing Ltd
7 Centremead
Osney Mead
Oxford OX2 0ES England
(01865) 250333

Australia and New Zealand

Australian Large Print Audio & Video P/L
17 Mohr Street
Tullamarine, Victoria, 3043, Australia
1 800 335 364